THE RIBBON MAN

Lottie Bird

Thank you, Southend Inklings and all who have dutifully listened to my chapters.

SECRET

This child, whose memory cannot be borne,
This child, who from my soul cannot be torn,
This child, whose clipped hair lies next to my heart,
This child, whose ashes I hide in the dark

Prologue

High above, a thin stream of pale yellow light haemorrhaged through metal bars, settled against a fissured concrete wall and bled darkly along tributary cracks. Had the light been brighter, or stronger, done what light should do on a summer's evening, it would have shown that far below a young girl lay on a thin, grimy mattress, her wrists secured with plastic ties to the frame of a rough wooden pallet underneath; it would have shown that a second child was next to her, lashed in similar style; it would have lighted upon a pitted screed floor strewn with fresh cigarette butts and sharply crumpled beer cans and glanced off brown rats as they scurried amongst detritus. But it didn't, the hours had passed. Instead, the light shrank, backed away and then disappeared, swallowed up by an encroaching night.

She was cold. Not like in the winter, when it's exciting because Christmas is coming, but cold like in the spring, when summer's coming so you think it should be warm, but when instead it drizzles for days on end and you forget what summer is like, because the rain will go on forever. It was the sort of cold that made you want to miss school and stay at home with your little sister, watching films on the tele, eating popcorn and chocolate and drinking coke, wrapped up on the sofa, snuggly and safe under the blue blanket that smells of mum: nivea face cream and pantene shampoo. She twisted her head and strained to wipe her wet cheek on the mattress; mum said that she had a colourful imagination, but the fabric only smelt of dirt.

Something was crawling up her thigh, confidently, like it belonged there, like it knew she couldn't do anything and was going to do just as it pleased. Last weekend, they'd all gone to the beach at Southend-on-sea, a special treat day when mum and dad didn't have to work. A big, black, stubborn fly had landed on her back. She hated insects. She had jigged around and jumped up and down and then screamed for rescue, "Daddy, daddy, I need you." He'd waded out of the water and run across the sand, knocked the fly away and grabbed her tight, laughing. But there was no rescue here. She had shouted and yelled and screamed and prayed, yanked and pulled at her wrists until they were chaffed and cut and bleeding. Only echoes responded. At her knicker-line, the crawling paused, turned and continued onwards, towards her buttock.

She didn't know where they were, or how they'd got there, or how to escape. She only knew that she was the most scared she had ever been, so scared that her heart was jumping like it would burst out of her chest, so scared she'd wet herself. She knew that they were in terrible, real, never even imagined danger, the type of danger they warned you about at school, even before then, when you were little.

And that no-one tied up eleven-year-old girls if they didn't have evil intentions.

A hinge whined open. A door clanged shut. Two sets of heavy footsteps moved methodically closer.

Fingers stroked through her hair. A palm touched her spine.

She stopped breathing out.

Chapter 1

It was a chance contact, a lucky fist that erupted unannounced from the blurred melee of flailing limbs and butting heads. It landed squarely on Mack's left jaw. The pain spiralled through his ear and spiked at the top of his head, an assault that in the normal scheme of things would have the favour returned - in full. After another hard five minutes and a couple more chasing down the one who thought he'd get away, the miscreants were subdued, handcuffed and settled nicely into the back of a police van: not bad for two men and a dog, whose backup had conveniently arrived just as their detainees were being lined up neatly all in a row. Maybe Mack's DI would crack a grin. Then again, pigs might fly.

The moped gang had rampaged across Essex for several hours until being caught with spike strips, skidding into a grass verge, abandoning their bikes and fleeing. Like all police services, Essex had been hit by the swingeing cuts of the past decades: Mack hadn't known he was political until he joined the police. The operation had demanded a full complement of response cars, dog handlers and anyone else who was free, which had included newly promoted detective sergeants.

It was a tenacious German shepherd, racing ahead of his panting handler and Mack, who found the lads cowering between bushes and a broken fence in the back garden of a terrified old lady. Like Mack, the canine had taken a punch for his trouble; unlike Mack, he'd not been a good copper and restrained himself – the gobby git responsible had light teeth marks in his forearm. Good dog.

By three a.m. Mack was back at his desk and the detainees were booked into custody and snoring off their exciting evening. They were all minors, albeit violent, despotic minors, responsible for spreading mayhem across the sprawling county for several days prior to capture. An unlucky colleague from the next shift would have the task of interviewing them – the stress of a harassed parent or even more harassed Social Worker acting as the Appropriate Adult adding to the joy. Small mercies.

Paperwork added three hours to his twelve hour night shift and he arrived home at eleven a.m. His jaw was sore and throbbing, ditto head. And Mack was pretty certain he'd be waking up to a black eye, because at some point during the arrests, he had taken a thump to his nose. He swallowed painkillers and awoke mid-afternoon after a few hours of unsatisfactory sleep, deciding that a visit to the pub would speed his recovery.

He was already sprawled in an armchair, more than several eager sips into a frothy pint and making eye contact with the pretty, dark-haired girl opposite when he got the call saying he needed to cover – a colleague had called in sick. Their team was invariably short-staffed. Mack had forgotten he was rota back-up. The pub was loud and the police-issued phone recycled, by the time he heard the third call, his colleagues had squealed and called his manager, who was on the other end of the phone demanding to know where the hell Mack was: an urgent case had come in and a response car was free and on the way to collect him.

The flirting would have to wait. Mack's promotion was only a few months in and since then he'd managed to upset Detective Inspector Kennedy several times. Not a difficult task, not for Mack, anyway. In fact, it was generally considered to be his most accomplished skill; his team liked to regularly remind him of that notable achievement - yeah, thanks. He started a sprint home, his gut lurching: Kennedy's reprimands weren't to be sought and were usually conducted in public. The squad car pulled up outside his flat just before him.

He arrived at Chelmsford police station just as his sweat was drying. Some flirting with the two pretty PCs who had driven him secured a sniggering promise of silence in exchange for a bottle of wine each next time they were in the pub. The Inspector wasn't such a pushover;Mack had to hope the extra-strong mints lived up to their name. But Tim Kennedy was too busy, too stressed and too short-staffed to take time out to give yet another lambasting to his new sergeant. Mack knew he'd survived by the skin of his teeth. He pulled out his notebook and tried to look assiduous.

Kennedy called order and stood to the front of the briefing room. "Right, now that we're all here," he glanced at Mack, looked harder, shook his head slightly and turned back to the white board - clearly, the eye was a shiner, "I'll bring you up to speed. Three-eleven-yearold girls were attacked this evening at about six p.m. in a swing park on the Mead council estate in Bellington. One girl," he pointed with his biro to the board, "a Keeley Knatchbull, got away. The other two girls were abducted. Keeley said that she saw them being put into the back of a white van. She says there were two men, one fat and bald and the other one tall and skinny with dark, curly hair. The cameras picked up a white van that exited the Mead Estate sliproad at six ten p.m., travelled along the main arterial road, the A127, back to the Chelmsford turn-off and took the A13 road towards London. The number plates are covered and it's speeding, so it's obviously of interest. It's being tracked. We've got cars on the way to try to intercept it. Scene of Crime Officers and uniformed police are at the park and we've got officers starting a search all three girls' homes."

"What about door-to-door, Guv?"

"Yes, that's underway, DC Cooper. The swing park is on the edge of the Mead estate, right away from the blocks of flats, next to the road that becomes the sliproad to the A127, so chances are no-one would've seen much, but we might get lucky.

"So, the blokes just ran up to them, out of nowhere?"

"Yes, apparently. They charged them."

"How did Keeley get away, then?"

"She said that she was already away from the two other girls, who were on the swings, which are at the back of the park. Keeley had walked away a bit and was at the side of the park entrance, cos the others were being noisy and she had to call her mum and couldn't hear properly. The fat man swung at her, to grab her, but she pulled away and ran. That's as we understand it currently, but the exact sequence of events will need to be clarified in interview. Keeley ran past a woman and her children. The woman stopped her and asked what was wrong and then dialled 999."

"What about the girls' phones, Guv, do we know if the parents had activated the 'find my phone' app? Can they be traced?"

"Been checked. Keeley has it on her phone, but not the others. Ok, DCs Cooper and Bailey, go to the scene and get an update. Find out where we are with the searches and door-to-door.

Sergeant Sumerson, get around to the home of the girl who got away. Sort out the Achieving Best Evidence interview – make sure that the child's not too tired or stressed – we don't want evidence being thrown out of Court. Do a risk assessment and report back."

"Who's going to the homes of the girls who were taken, Guv?" Mack was rummaging in his jeans pocket for more painkillers – he'd planned to eat at the pub, but it was clear that food was off the menu for the evening. His head was threatening to erupt into a migraine, if he was going to be dealing with screaming mothers, he at least needed to prepare himself.

"I am, with Jenny," said Kennedy. Mack waggled his eyebrows at his colleague and grinned. She shook her head: Kennedy never could get his head around addressing women by their surname. "Right, we haven't got a minute to waste. Get to it!"

Mack tasked a colleague with tracking down an officer trained to interview children and to phone Social Services to alert them to the case. Then he found a police constable to drive him to Keeley's address - Kennedy's opinion of Mack was already in its coffin, any whiff of drink-driving would ring a death-knell.

Keeley Knatchbull and her family lived on the Mead estate in Bellington, originally a narrow slice of the small Essex town of Laindon that now sprawled out towards London into its own postcode. It was an area more than familiar to the local police, especially Mack for a reason he had yet to fathom, although his suspicion was it had something or maybe everything to do with his boss' disapproval of him. The social housing was a hotbed of criminality, disaffection and poverty. It had initially comprised three buildings containing twelve flats each, built on an old Essex farm after the war to house the blitzed-out homeless East End. The estate was enlarged in the late seventies with uglier, taller and flimsier tower blocks. A subsequently necessary school and then a small shopping area took up the bulk of the remaining land. Invariably, the flats' lifts weren't working and the stairwells stank of urine, usually there was drug paraphernalia dumped in dark corners for good measure. Mack had decent clothes on, wished he'd had the forethought to change at least his shoes - the last time he was on the Mead estate, he'd needed to freeze off three lots of chewing gum and disinfect the soles of his trainers after walking through lumpy and bloody vomit.

But the Knatcbbulls' home was on the third floor of one of the original blocks and was a surprise. It was airy and spacious. A small, square, tiled fireplace occupied the breadth of a neat chimney-breast in the sitting room and black-coated steel railings edged a balcony that overlooked what the council euphemistically called a field - in reality, a few square feet of sorry grass, separated from a service road by three large sycamore trees that were in full leaf. Keeley's dad was leaning over the balcony smoking a roll-up when Mack arrived. A PC was making tea. Mack caught his eye, raised his eyebrows and nodded at the kettle – he was parched. Mr. Knatchbull stepped back into the room, pulled together sliding glass doors and locked them behind him.

"About bloody time, too. We've been told we couldn't do anything 'til CID got here. I take it that's you, is it?" The man was tall and broad. He towered over Mack's six feet by a good few inches. His mouth was drawn tight over stained teeth. Mack saw Knatchbull give him the once-over, take in the clothes and shoes, knew he would be working extra-hard to get anywhere here.

He showed his warrant card. "We're sorry to have kept you waiting, Mr. Knatchbull. As you can imagine, there's always a lot to be done behind the scenes on cases like these." He saw Knatchbull draw breath and beat him to it. "But we're ready to move on, Sir." Mack gave his best professional smile. "Do you mind if I sit down?" Knatchbull nodded and Mack sank into an armchair. The PC came in and handed out the teas. "So, Mr. Knatchbull, where's Keeley? And your wife?"

"They're in the loo, Keeley didn't want to go by herself, she was still feeling scared, so her mum's gone with her. Me other girl's with a neighbour."

"Ok and how old is she and what's her name?"

"Claire and she's nine. Look, we've been through this already. Can't we have a bit of peace?"

"Sorry, Mr. Knatchbull, I know you've had a terrible shock and it's tedious to keep being asked the same thing, but I do need to go over it again. Please could I have your account first and then we'll talk about interviewing Keeley. So, start from the beginning. What time was it when you were you alerted to a problem?"

"'Bout ten past, quarter past six. A woman knocked on the door with Keeley. She was in a right state..."

"Who, Keeley or the woman?"

Knatchbull stared at him. "Don't be a tosser! Keeley, of course. I know the woman, vaguely. Most people know each other in these older blocks. She lives in the next one along."

Mack turned to the PC. "Have we got all her details?" He nodded wordlessly. "Ok, please carry on, Mr. Knatchbull."

"When I opened the door, Keeley ran into the hall. Her mum was in the bedroom and she rushed straight into her, screaming and crying. The woman told me that she'd found Keeley down near the swing park, crying and in a state, screeching's the word she used. Keeley told her that two men had tried to take her, that she'd got away, but that they'd taken her two friends. The woman had already called 999. I heard the police sirens right then, even before the woman had finished speaking. Don't know why it's taken so long for you plain-clothed lot to get around to it."

"Was Keeley hurt at all?"

"Nah, I think they made a lunge for her, tried to grab her by her top. But there were three girls and only two blokes, so they were always gonna struggle, weren't they?"

"Right, thanks Mr. Knatchbull. Has Keeley been asked to change her clothes?"

"The other lot's beat you to it. The clothes she was wearing have already been taken."

"Ok. I know that Keeley gave an initial description of what the men looked like to the PCs who first attended. Did the men sound familiar to you at all?"

Knatchbull glared. "Course they bloody didn't. What's wrong with you? What, you think I hang around with child-snatchers?"

"No, no of course not. I just wondered if maybe they sounded like someone who lives on the estate, or who's been seen lurking, a stranger, anyone suspicious."

"Oh, well, no. Otherwise I'd have said, wouldn't I?"

"Ok. We're going to need to interview Keeley formally, Mr. Knatchbull. Has that been explained to you?"

Knatchbull frowned, heavy black brows morphing into a grey-speckled caterpillar. "What do you mean? She's said every-thing she knows already."

"Because she's a minor, we have to interview her in a special way and it'll be by a trained officer. It's called an Achieving Best Evidence interview, ABE for short. It'll be video-recorded. Then if Keeley needs to go to Court to give evidence we'll have that re-cording ready - sometimes the Judge will let the Prosecution use the video, rather than exposing the child to any defendants. It's standard practice, really."

"No, I don't like the sound of that. She's been through enough, said what she knows and I don't want you lot going over it all again and upsetting her."

"I know. It is a lot for a child, Mr. Knatchbull, but we do need to get it done. As I said, the police officer who does the interview is specially trained." He paused, his DI would have some choice words if Mack didn't nail the situation and get Keeley down to the station. ("You're a copper, Sergeant, use your professional authority.") He took a breath, "Of course, you're worried, we completely understand that. You or Keeley's mum will be there the whole time. We can have a Social Worker there, too, if you like."

"I said no, didn't I? She's my daughter! I decide what happens. What part of that don't you understand?"

Knatchbull's decibels throbbed across Mack's forehead; he tried not to wince – ibuprofen was no match for a throbbing jaw, black eye and accumulated hunger fed by beer. "Mr. Knatchbull, we need your permission to interview your daughter. However, as much as we sympathise with your concern, you must understand that we need to get as much information from Keeley, as soon as possible in a way that complies with the criminal justice system. You understand that, don't you? All her information will be vital to finding those two other girls. And we need the information now. Right now." What was it with the man: his daughter had been almost abducted, her two little friends were missing... "Thing is, Mr. Knatchbull, you don't want my Inspector to think that you're perverting the course of justice, wondering if you've something to hide."

The other man had pulled up a hard-backed chair to sit down in front of Mack. It screeched back. "You bleedin' pervert." Stale smoke piggybacked the other man's plosives and dissipated somewhere not far above Mack's nose; he caught the tail of garlic as it drifted down. He remembered that his baton was at home, he'd forgotten to collect it when he ran back from the pub - something else that would upset Kennedy if he got to hear of it. Knatchbull was tall and strong, some might have described him as having muscles on his spit. Just as the other man's face was looming close enough for Mack to count the veins in his eyes, the door to the room opened and a woman came in followed by a swollen eyed and puffy-faced, dark haired child wearing blue tracksuit bottoms and a short sleeved, smiley cat t-shirt.

In the end, it was Keeley who persuaded her dad to let Mack take her down to the station. He admired her. She was a plucky little thing, sure of herself, standing up to a bloke who to Mack seemed to be a thug by any other name. "But Dad, I want to help the police find Samantha and Emma."

"I've said no and that's it. You've been through enough. Me and your mum want you to go to bed and get a good night's sleep. Maybe we can think about it again in the morning, when you're feeling a bit better."

"It could be too late then, dad, the police need to know all about it now," she turned to Mack, "Don't you?" She peered at him through bloodshot eyes, pleading for an ally, smearing snot with the cat's tail.

"We certainly do, Keeley. The sooner we can get all your information and what you remember, the sooner it can help us try to find your friends." Mack kept his eyes firmly on Keeley's face; Knatchbull had perfected the art of the unblinking stare, probably from a young age - toddlerhood most likely.

"You see, dad, oh please let me go. I promise I'll go straight to bed when I get in." In his peripheral vision, Mack caught Knatchbull exchanging a glance with his wife, heard the rattle of a smoker's sharp intake of breath.

"All right then, Keeley, your mum'll go with you." He turned to Mack, "But I don't want her getting upset, otherwise I'll have more than something to say about it. Do you hear me, Sergeant?"

"Absolutely. Mrs. Knatchbull, if you and Keeley could get a jacket and we'll drive you to the police station."

"What station are you taking them to?"

"Chelmsford. We'll bring them back as soon as the interview's finished." Mack opened the front door for Mrs. Knatchbull, noticing the latch, deadlock, chain and two heavy duty bolts. He wondered who her husband had been upsetting, didn't find the prospect particularly surprising and filed the thought for later.

11

Chapter 2

Clarence Hope left her Bellington Social Services office exhausted and in need of a substantial glass of dry white wine. She
had spent the last hour of her day seeing a seven-year-old boy,
who was refusing to talk to anyone after being removed from an
abusive home. He'd decided to trust her in the last ten minutes
of their session; they'd over-run, the foster father was short on
time and the day had ended without her having had a chance
to talk to her supervisor and get some perspective. She was the
Local Authority's only Social Worker cum Child Psychotherapist
and there were huge demands on her time.

She drove her red Mercedes convertible through country lanes
dusty with late summer and arrived at her home on the edge
of an Essex village half an hour later, crunching slowly into the
gravel drive. A solitary, small, terracotta brick cottage was ha-
loed by a low and smouldering sun. On a high side wall sprawled
two ginger cats, head to head, fat furry flanks to the heat, green
eyes following her progress to the house.

Springing into life as she walked to the front door, the animals
wound themselves around her legs, purrs vibrating the length of
their bodies. Clarence bent down and ran her hands along their
torsos, revelling in their sensuous warmth and the wet touch of
their noses pressing into her palms. Both cats were beautifully
hot and reminded her, unbidden, of her last Mediterranean holiday, taking her back, dragging her down, her response still as
raw and harsh as ever. Blinking away the memory, she straightened up, opened the front door and nearly tripped over the cats
as they rushed through her legs into the cottage.

Leaving her bag on the hall table, Clarence followed her pets
into the white-tiled scullery at the side of the kitchen, where
the cats were already stationed next to their bowls on the floor,
mewing loudly. "That's all I am to you two", she muttered as she
undid the pouches and emptied the food, "One big feeding station." The cats pounced.

She took a bottle of chardonnay out of the fridge. Once a glass was decently half-full, Clarence opened the doors from the dining-room and went into the garden. West-facing, the space was hot and hazy. Heat radiated from enclosing walls. A small lawn sprawled into deep borders brimming with dark shrubs and bright petals – wild flowers sown carelessly. Perfume filled the air. Insects hovered and darted.

She sat down next to a weather-stripped, wooden garden table. The wine was sharp and cold. She held the glass against her forehead after the first few sips.

Seven years to get over a relationship, apparently, and she was only two years, four months and twelve days in. Every reminder hurt. But she didn't need reminders. Dreams still full of him, waking with a dead weight in the middle of her chest, taking one or two seconds to remember why. Tears coming on birthdays, Christmas, New Year's Eve. The smell of his after-shave on another man, aching with desire every time she saw a couple laughing together. She wondered how other people married just a few years after a relationship break-up. Seven years, she thought again. I'll be forty-six years old – he will have been forty-seven. We would have been seven years into our marriage after our perfect, Italian honeymoon.

She stood up to go to make some supper, trying to physically shake off the melancholia and leave behind the pain if just for a few seconds. Yep, she thought, trying to lighten her own mood, widowhood definitely sucks.

Chapter 3

Mack's ideas didn't always hit the spot where his superior was concerned. In fact, he could only remember it having happened once, a suggestion to raid a home in an ongoing drugs investigation when he'd still been a DC. His civvy mate had given him the tip-off, not that the Inspector needed to know that. His boss thought Mack's success was the one indication that he might – possibly, maybe - have a miniscule capacity for detective work. And it wasn't for Mack to disabuse a DI - never went down well. But the new case smelt of more trouble than the trouble it already was; missing children were bad enough and it was clear that Mr. Knatchbull was only going to add to the burden. Yeah, Mack thought, let's take a punt. He dialled Kennedy's number. "Guv, I wondered whether it would be a good idea to get Clarence Hope involved in this? You remember we used her to consult on the Peters case, Christmas before last?" It had been Mack's first serious child abuse case. The memory still made his throat tighten.

"Hold on, Sergeant." At the other end of the line, Kennedy shouted. The microphone on Mack's phone screeched, and the thumping in his temples jumped to order. Kennedy came back. "Why do we need her to consult?"

"Guv, this kid is really, really distressed. And the father's hostile, he's potentially going to be disruptive. I think we could do with an experienced Social Worker to help out, you know, someone who knows what's what, not just whoever's on duty."

"Yeah, ok, makes sense. That's fine by me. Try to get hold of her, then. But don't let her rack up loads of hours."

The little girl's face had been white and pinched, her breathing so shallow she was turning blue. In the end she'd survived – physically, anyway. It had been Clarence who worked tirelessly to gain the child's trust. He still had her number on his phone. He pulled it up, suddenly unsure and not too keen to think about why.

Before that case, before being first on the scene, before being at the hospital and seeing the finger bruises on the pale skin of thin arms - before his baptism of rape - they'd always been kids, insignificant, largely irrelevant specks of humanity; afterwards, they were children, vulnerable beings to be protected at all costs (well, except maybe moped despots – he rubbed his jaw) and the bastards who harmed them to be hunted down and locked up at all costs. And they had hunted down the bastard. Another first for Mack: twelve years for destroying a little girl's mind, body and life. He'd known thieves get longer. And the bastard would be out in six. The recollection nudged somewhere ajar at the back of his mind, a whisper escaping on a sigh. He turned away, to the pleasing, blonde curly head that housed the phenomenal brain belonging to Clarence. He guessed that she was in demand. His thumb hovered over the keypad. He dialled the duty social work number.

The Social Worker was snowed under, but called Clarence for him, who agreed to consult on the case and to represent Social Services at the police station that night for the ABE interview. She would be there within the hour.

Keeley was calm by the time Mack had settled her in the interview suite at Chelmsford station. He introduced her and Mrs. Knatchbull to the ABE-trained officer, Mandy. Then he and Mandy formulated their interview plan. By the time Clarence arrived, they were ready to start. He met her at the front desk and led her through code-locked doors to the interview suite.

"Thanks for coming, Clarence. Have you been updated?"

"I got the call from the duty Social Worker, all I know is what she told me, which is that there was an attempted abduction of three girls this evening, that one girl got away, that's who's being interviewed, now."

"Yep, that's it in a nutshell. It happened in the swing park of the Mead estate in Bellington – so two girls are missing."

"Any progress?"

"None. We're examining CCTV footage, but we've not made any headway. The girl who's here is called Keeley Knatchbull.

She's eleven years old. Lives at home with mum, dad and little sister and has just left the Mead Primary school, due to go up to senior school in September."

"Are the other girls, the ones who were taken, the same age?"

He nodded. "They're all friends. They were mucking around on the swings when the blokes pounced on them. Keeley managed to get away."

Clarence stared. "That's bold. They took them in broad daylight, out of the blue?"

Mack nodded, "Apparently."

"Any other attempts?"

"No. Let's hope it stays like that."

"Have forensics been done?"

"Yeah. Keeley said that she thinks they didn't touch her, just made a swipe at her top. We've obviously taken her clothes anyway and done a fingernail scrape to be on the safe side."

"Ok, so how are we going to do this. Do you want me to observe? Have you asked mum what she thinks? Or Keeley?" A loose curl escaped from a hair-clip and dangled over one eye, Clarence pushed it out of the way. "Do you want me in the room?" Her question tipped him out of work mode. He refocused.

"I talked it through with Keeley on the way here. I know that this should be done on camera, too, but we're obviously up against it, time-wise. Mandy and I think that Mrs. Knatchbull should stay in the room with Keeley; she was really distressed earlier, but she's calmer now. Mum isn't implicated in any way, or a witness, so there's no reason for her not to be present for the interview. We've got an equipment operator in there, too. So, we thought maybe you could act as the second interviewer, but outside the room. What do you think?"

Clarence nodded. "That's fine by me. Four adults in there would be too many. How does Keeley feel about being interviewed?"

"She's ok about it. Really wanted to come, that wasn't a problem for her, she's desperate to help find her friends." He glanced at his watch. The DI would be expecting results. "Shall we crack on, then?"

Mandy had used the time waiting for Clarence to start to build rapport with Keeley. Once the equipment was running, Mandy moved through the preliminaries of confirming the date and time of the interview and then asked Keeley if she knew the difference between a truth and a lie. "If Sam was playing football and kicked the ball into his neighbour's garden and broke a window and then told his mum that his friend, David, had kicked the ball, would Sam be telling the truth?" asked Mandy. Keeley had more than a good grip on reality. Mandy moved on. "Ok, Keeley, I don't know very much about why you're here tonight. Would you like to tell me why you think you're here?"

Keeley took a deep breath. "Cos I need to tell the police what happened to my friends. Well, they're actually my best friends. They're called Emma and Samantha. And they're the same age as me. We're eleven. Two men took them and put them in a van. They tried to take me, too. And the police need to find them. They need to look for them really fast. Really, really fast." She exhaled. "That's what I wanted to say."

"Can you tell me some more about what happened, Keeley?"

"We were in the swing park – the one near the flats, the flats where I live, on the Mead estate. Samantha and Emma were playing on the swings. Suddenly, two men came in and they ran up to them and took them. They were fast. I didn't even see them come through the gate, only when they were going up to the others." She sniffed.

"You're saying that two men came into the swing park and took Samantha and Emma..."

Keeley nodded, took the tissue proffered by her mum. "They tried to take me too, on the way out, but I ran away. I could hear Samantha screaming, really loud, and shouting, 'Put me down, put me down' and a lady stopped me and asked what was wrong and I told her and she called the police. I told the first policeman who came, but then I had to come here so that I could say it again to be recorded for the Judge."

"So, Samantha was screaming and telling the man to put her down. Is there anything else you can tell me about what happened?"

"When I heard Samantha screaming, I turned around to see if they'd got away, but they hadn't and the men were putting them into a van. A white one." She pulled out several more tissues from the box.

"Could you explain to me how the men were doing that, Keeley?"

"What do you mean?"

"Well, I wonder whether they were putting them into the doors at the front door of the van, for example."

She shook her head vigorously. "No. It was in the back doors. I think they must've been open already, cos Emma was already inside when I looked. She was lying on the floor, the floor of the van I mean, but Samantha was trying to fight them, she was trying to pull the man's hands off her – he was holding her under her arms and across her chest – like this." Keeley jumped up, tucked her elbows under her arms and clasped her hands in front of her chest. "So she was against his tummy."

Mandy nodded, "Yes, I see."

"And she was banging her head back on him, back on his chest." Her pony-tail jerked. "And then the other man was grabbing her legs and Samantha was trying to kick him, but then he got hold of her ankles to keep them still. She tried really hard to get away. That's all I saw, cos I was running. I wanted to go back and help, but I didn't know how to."

"Thank you very much for telling me all of that Keeley. You've done really well. Would you like a break now? A drink, or do you need to go to the toilet?"

Keeley slumped into her seat. "No, no I'm fine thank you. I just want the police to find my friends."

"I know you do, Keeley and all of this is helping the police to do that, ok? You are doing very well, really well."

Keeley nodded, "Ok."

"I'm going to need to ask you some questions about what

you've said, Keeley. It's so that I can make sure that I understand everything that happened today as well as I can. Do you understand?"

She nodded, "Yes. I have to help my friends."

"I'd like to hear about your whole day, Keeley, right from the beginning, what you did first of all, after you got up."

"Well, it's school holidays, so I went to the school holiday club and then I was allowed out with Emma and Samantha."

"That sounds great. Did Samantha and Emma go to the school holiday club, too?"

"We all go. It's on Mondays, Wednesdays and Fridays. Our mums said we could go to the shops in Laindon afterwards to buy a milkshake, as long as we took our phones."

"Oh, that sounds nice. What flavour did you have, Keeley?"

"We all had chocolate."

"Yummy, my favourite, too and what time did you do that?"

"About half past two."

"How did you get to the shops, Keeley?"

"We got the number two bus – it's only about ten minutes, just four stops."

"And was the bus busy?"

"I can't remember. We all sat down, so I think there can't have been that many people on there, sometimes on a Saturday you have to stand."

Mrs. Knatchbull interjected. "They have a packed lunch to take to the holiday club. That starts at ten a.m. and finishes at two p.m. She left home to meet the others at nine forty-five a.m. I knew exactly where Keeley was, all the time."

"That's great. I'm sure you did. Thanks for clarifying that, Mrs. Knatchbull. I do need Keeley to answer now."

"What did you do after you'd had your milkshakes, Keeley?"

"Looked around some shops."

"Can you remember which ones?"

"New Look, we tried on some clothes."

"And how long were you in New Look for?"

"Dunno, about half an hour. Then we went to the bookshop. I

want a cat and mum said that if I learn about how to look after it, she'll think about if I'm allowed one."

"Oh, that'll be nice to have a pet cat, won't it? So, you went to look for a book about cats – can you just say yes for me as well as nodding, Keeley?"

"Yes. I got a big book, one with photos. Will this help to find Emma and Samantha?"

"You're doing really, really well, Keeley. Yes, all of this will help the police with looking for them."

"Are they looking for them, now? Right now?"

"Yes, they are, right at this minute, the police are working very hard trying to find them. Shall we talk some more about the shops?"

"What, they're driving around in police cars? How do they know where to look?"

"They'll be using lots of different ways of trying to find Emma and Samantha, Keeley. For example, looking at CCTV. You know the cameras that follow traffic?"

Keeley nodded. "To look for the van?"

"That's right."

"Ok." She sucked in a breath. "We didn't go to any more shops after the bookshop."

"Can you remember the name of the book shop, Keeley?"

"The one next to Marks and Spencer."

Mrs. Knatchbull leant forward. "Waterstones, she's got the receipt if you want it."

"That's great, Mrs. Knatchbull, because it will have the time on it. Thanks."

"You bought a book about cats. What happened then?"

"We got the bus back to the estate and went to the swing park."

"Did you go anywhere else after you got off the bus and before you went to the swing park?" Keeley shook her head, remembered the instruction.

"No."

"So, you came out of the town centre, caught the bus and went back to the estate and then straight to the swing park. Have I got that right?"

"Yes."

"Did you talk to anyone, or did anyone talk to you while you were on the bus, or when you got off and were going to the swing park?"

"No. Oh, wait, we saw our friend from school near to the flats, but we didn't talk to her, just waved."

"Ok, we're going to need her name, Keeley, and her address, so that we can talk to her and see if she remembers the time she saw you. Can you tell me that now?" Keeley nodded, provided the details.

"And what did you do when you got to the swing park?"

"I texted mum and asked what time I needed to be home for tea. She said half past four." Keeley glanced sideways at her mother. "Really, I already knew it was tea then, cos mum told me earlier, before holiday club. She said not to be late, but I was late, cos Samantha wanted to play on the swings and she didn't have to be home 'til seven o'clock. But my mum always makes me go home early, much earlier than my friends."

"You were in the park. Emma and Samantha were on the swings, which are at the back of the park and the men came into the park and went straight up to Samantha and Emma. Did they pull them off the swings?"

"Yes, they just picked them straight up off the swings and on the way back they tried to get me, too."

"They tried to get hold of you on their way back out of the park?"

"Yes."

"Did they already have Samantha and Emma when they tried to take you, Keeley?"

"Yes, Samantha was already screaming."

"And how did they try to take you Keeley. So, I wonder if the man tried to get hold of your hand?"

"No, he pulled me by my top. I had a white shirt on. It's quite big. He tried to get it at the back. I don't know how he was going to carry me, cos he was already carrying Samantha, I think he was going to put me under his other arm, or maybe drag me to the van."

"Do you know if he actually got hold of the shirt?"

"I don't know. If he did, it was only a bit."

"And you ran away. Which way did you run?"

"Back to the flats, that's when the lady stopped me."

"Whereabouts were you when the lady stopped you, Keeley?"

"Round the corner. You come out of the swing park, go up a road and then turn the corner to get to the flats." Her face crumpled. "It's all my fault, if I'd gone home when mum said and if I'd made Emma and Samantha go home, none of this would've happened." Keeley had pulled her mum's arm around and under her chin, resting her face into the crook of the elbow. She held on tight. Mack watched a spreading stain of tears darken Mrs. Knatchbull's white sleeve.

Keeping hold of her daughter, Mrs. Knatchbull stood up. "That's it now. She's had enough. We're going home." She gathered her belongings with her free hand.

Mack felt his heart jump. He spoke into Mandy's earpiece, "Mandy, try and get her to stay, just long enough for us to get any more details of what happened when the men arrived." He turned to Clarence, "Do you think you could say anything to persuade them to stay?"

"It's not a good idea to interview a child under pressure, Mack, you know that. She's had a horrible day, she's exhausted. You know it could be used by any defence counsel, why not see if you can get her back and resume tomorrow?"

Mack was watching Mrs. Knatchbull through the observation window and on the computer monitor. She was trying to prise Keeley's face from out of her shoulder to get her jacket on. "No, the father isn't going to agree to a second interview, Clarence - it was hard enough getting agreement for her to come tonight. We need that information. I know it's not nice for her, but I bet it's worse for Emma and Samantha right now."

Clarence paused for a second, then nodded. "Yeah, ok, all

right, I'll give it one shot." She left her seat and went into the interview room, closed the door softly and sat down in the chair next to Keeley. "Hi Keeley, hello Mrs. Knatchbull. My name is Clarence. I'm a Social Worker. I know you must both be absolutely exhausted. I wonder if I could sit with you for a very short time?"

Just do your thing, Clarence, I really need this to work. Mack watched her twiddle briefly with an earring, remembered that she had that habit.

"Keeley, this police lady, Mandy, just needs to talk to you for a few more minutes. Do you think you could be very brave and manage that? I know you're really, really upset. You've had a nasty, horrible day. Could you be brave for just another five minutes? I'll stay here, too." Clarence looked at Mrs. Knatchbull. "I know it's distressing for you too, Mrs. Knatchbull. This will be over very soon."

Mrs. Knatchbull narrowed her eyes and looked at Clarence. "I don't hold much truck with Social Workers," she looked at the camera, finally nodded and sat down again, keeping a tight arm around her child.

Mandy resumed the interview. "Ok, Keeley, is there anything else that you tell me about what happened at the swing park?"

Keeley sniffed hard. "We were smelling some new perfume that Emma had."

"Where did she get the perfume from, do you know?"

"No, it was just in her bag. Maybe she bought it with her pocket money. I kept telling Emma and Samantha that we had to go home. I was already late and my mum kept texting and calling me, even more than she normally does! We didn't even *hear* them. They went up to Emma and Samantha and pulled them off the swings and then picked them up. It was the fat one who tried to get me."

"And this happened at the time you were calling your mum back?"

"Yes, but she hadn't picked up the phone yet."

"Ok. We'll be able to see the time that you dialled the number.

You're saying that they picked up Samantha and Emma first and then the fat man tried to grab you?"

Keeley nodded. "Yes."

"And that's when you ran out of the park?"

"I ran out of the park, back towards the flats."

"So, you came out of the park and turned left, ran up the road and turned again, towards the flats?"

Keeley paused, then nodded. "Yes."

"Where was the van parked?"

"On the other side of the road, opposite the gate to the park, the way that leads to the main road."

"Thank you, Keeley. I just need to ask you a couple more questions. When they were in the park, did you hear the men say anything? To you, or to each other?"

"I don't think so, but Samantha started screaming."

"And have you seen the men before? Together or by themselves?"

Keeley shook her head. "No, I'd remember, especially the fat one."

"And can you remember anything else that happened when you were running out of the park, Keeley?"

"Just that they put them in the van. And I think Emma would've started crying when she was in the van, while they were trying to get Samantha in. Emma's a bit of a cry-baby. She cries more than me and Samantha. She'll be crying all the time now that some bad men have got her. And Samantha was shouting 'let me go, put me down, put me down, stop it, *stop* it. She was screaming and screaming, 'no, no. Let me go'. Her eyes were closed tight, like she didn't want to see. Screwed up." Keeley squeezed together puffy eyelids. "She was really scared. She tried to make him put her down. She was trying to kick the man on his legs," she bent down and tapped her shins, "This part, but he was fat. He had a massive tummy, it came over his jeans and Samantha and Emma are only eleven-years-old, like me. We're only schoolgirls. They couldn't fight them." She dug knuckles into her eye sockets and rubbed hard. "Do you think the men are hurting them; you know, like, doing bad things to them? Cos that's why they've taken them, isn't it? They teach us about it in safeguarding time at school."

"We're going to try to find them as soon as possible, Keeley. You said earlier that the van was white. Do you still think that?"

Keeley nodded. Her mouth was edged in white gunk. Mack found himself rubbing his own bottom lip. "At school, the teachers say that we have to be careful. But we *were* careful. We *always* try to be safe, like everyone tells us. They tell you all the time, 'specially if you're a girl. My mum and dad say it every time I go out and that I must keep my phone on. We didn't do anything wrong. Did we?"

"No Keeley, you didn't do anything wrong at all. Not you, or Emma, or Samantha. And you have been really, really brave. The only people who have done something wrong are those men. Ok?"

She nodded. "Ok," tears spilt down her cheeks. "Please find my friends, please, please, please help them. I don't want them to get hurt."

Clarence looked at Mack through the observation window: time to stop; they'd pushed it too far already.

Mrs. Knatchbull leant forward, grabbed tissues from the box in front of her, brushed wet hair out of her daughter's eyes and held the tissue to her nose, "Blow." She turned to Mandy. "Right, that really is it. This is over." She stood up, pulling Keeley with her, "She's had enough."

"Just one final question, Mrs. Knatchbull. "Keeley, can you re-member what the men were wearing?"

Mrs. Knatchbull was walking her daughter towards the door. "No. No more questions. We're done. Can someone take us home, please, or do I need to call my husband?"

Mack arranged for a squad car to transport and jotted down a reminder to himself about making sure Keeley's phone and bookshop receipt had been collected. He phoned the DI, who agreed that the interview should be ended. Kennedy wanted Mack's view about whether it was it safe for Keeley to be at home, whether a safe house was needed. "I can't see it, Sir. The family have said they don't recognise the men from the sounds of it. Mr. Knatchbull seems more than capable of looking after himself to me. And you can't get into the flats without being let in downstairs. I looked at the front door to the flat before I left earlier; it's got bolts and a deadlock, an excess level of security, actually, no-one could get in."

Chapter 4

Reggie Bull was pissed off. "We know you're not happy, boss." Not happy? Not fucking happy? That had to be the understatement of this not-fucking-happy year. Talk about balls up. As usual, he'd planned to the last detail. None of this could be laid at Reggie's door. And the irony of it was that he'd only done it for a mate, for old times. Now they had a squealing kid, a dead kid, and a missing kid about whom more questions than necessary were going to be asked.

His blacked-out SUV glided smoothly along the dark dual carriage way and took the exit to Chelmsford. He glanced at the back seat - she was still unconscious. His tic was starting. He tried to get his anger under control. Why the idiots hadn't just waited and stuck to the plan, he had no idea, apart from the obvious: they were bleeding thick. He knew he should have stopped using them a long time ago; given the choice, he would never have started, but it was hard to get the hired help these days.

At some point in the near future, Tony would need to be dealt with, got rid. The second flunkey, Michael, was more compliant, did as he was told, as long as he got to dabble with the goodies afterwards. But Tony, different kettle of fish: too cocky, too fat and conspicuous and too fond of thinking for himself. Yeah. Decision made. Before the end of the month, Tony would be feeding the fish, the worms or the local Chinese takeaway customers, for all Reggie cared. But not before he'd cleaned up the mess he made.

One thought led to another. Reggie wished, now, that he hadn't left it to Tony to dispose of the dead girl, but his fury had had the better of him – a perennial problem. Had he been thinking more clearly, he would have had Tony deal with the remaining child, too, put a clean lid on the whole operation.

Reggie had planned to perfection. As usual. The girls were identified. The letters written. Sure, there would have been a whole heap of angst, police searches, TV appeals, all the usual malarkey. But the girls would never be found. The searches would go on for years and eventually, they would become another runaway or missing statistic. Worked every time and he'd been doing it for long enough to know. It was harder nowadays with CCTV, social media, all the inconvenient, modern interference, but it was still doable – unless, of course, you relied on idiots.

He'd walked into the bunker to a strong tang of fresh urine: bad sign; it was always going to go downhill after that. He had caught Tony with the body slung over his shoulder, no doubt hoping to get away before Reggie arrived. Tony was whining out some excuse about her trying to escape, that he tried to get her under control and eventually gave her a thump that turned out to be too hard, "It was a mistake, boss, honest." Mistake his arse. Tony was too fond of acting first and thinking later. The other girl had been awake, face smeared in snot and drenched and stinking in her own piss, wrists bleeding and choking down hysterical sobs that would soon morph inexorably into uncontrolled screaming – Reggie knew the pattern, he'd been doing it long enough. It was a mess. Clearly, neither child had been given enough fentanyl to knock them out for even a few hours. Bloody useless twats. Luckily, Reggie kept emergency chloroform in his car – archaic but effective and quick, especially on children. And the place was filthy, Tony never kept it clean. There was rat shit everywhere. One of the little runts had strayed too close and Reggie had kicked it into the corner; the squeal and subsequent thud of flesh against concrete was satisfying. Reggie hated the dirty rodents - he'd had to squirt his shoe with his portable disinfectant there and then. And fuck knew how much DNA was lurking amongst all the droppings; still, wasn't like the cops were ever going to find it.

He needed to pee. Getting old was crap. He pondered whether it would be safe to stop the car and take a slash at the roadside, but there were big houses with security cameras along that stretch and if Plod came sniffing, he didn't want anything caught on anyone's CCTV. He didn't even have a bottle to use. And there was no way he was going to let his old-man bladder ruin the decent and expensive trousers he was wearing. No, he'd have to hold it and take the pain.

He slowed down and reversed the car into a long driveway in a leafy Essex suburb near Chelmsford. High hedges shielded the large, detached house from its distant neighbour. He stumbled out of the car, fiddled with his fly and emptied his bladder into the shrubs next to the front door; he'd held it for so long, it took a couple of seconds for the muscle to relax enough. Normally, he was fussy about smells and bodily fluids - dirt by any other name. But age was bringing a new perspective to his hygiene.

He let out his breath, zipped up, heard the pleasing, reassuring bolt of the deadlocks responding to his front door key and went back to the car. Emma was still motionless. He wrapped her in the waterproof sheeting that protected his car seats – crucial - lifted her gently and carried her into the house. He was always careful with the children, force of habit. His clients had been wealthy, powerful men, some of them didn't like to see damage or bruising, they liked to pretend that the transaction was con-sensual, civilized. Reggie laughed as he carried the child up the stairs. What a joke: even he knew that none of this was *civilised*.

Chapter 5

The headache from the punch to his jaw was fading, but tiredness had taken up the baton, idling along at handover, having a discussion about which part of his brain to attack next. Mack had needed to write up his reports before leaving work and hit the pillow at three a.m. The DI had called a briefing for eight. Mack arrived at the station with a minute to spare. Everyone else was seated. The Superintendent was there. There were photos of all three girls on the magnetic whiteboard, their names, dates of birth and physical description underneath. Tim Kennedy had the floor.

"Right, I'm the Senior Investigating Officer for this case. Here's what we know so far: we've been able to track the girls' trip through Laindon High Street, to the various shops and out again. There's no-one following them, nothing suspicious to see. We've checked the CCTV on the buses they took and spoken to the drivers; there's nothing of note. There's no CCTV that covers the road that leads to the Mead estate from the bus stop. There's no CCTV covering the swing park or the side road and based on what Keeley has said, we think that the abductors' van or car was parked there, facing the arterial road, the A127, ready to go, back doors open. The cameras picked up a white van that exited the Mead sliproad onto the arterial road, at six ten p.m., then it took the A13 towards London. The number-plates were covered. It travelled up the A13 and then took a left to go down a road that leads to an old farm – that road only services the farmland, just before the Purfleet exit. There are no cameras that could follow it beyond that point.

The 999 call came through at six twelve p.m., just after the van joined the 127, we should've been able to find it, but by the time we'd checked the cameras, the vehicle had already joined the A13; when the response cars got there, it had disappeared. It was clocked going at 90mph. We've had units and dogs out all night searching the whole area, but there's no sight of the van, or the girls. There's an old, abandoned farmhouse and a couple of farm buildings – all deserted. They've been searched, as have the girls' homes; nothing of note has been found.

So, the plan for today is this this: CCTV to continue to be checked. I want every available camera accessed and gone through with a fine toothcomb. Again. Door to door is to continue. I want a second search of the victims' homes and of the farmland in daylight. We don't yet know if this was an opportunistic attack, or whether it was planned. For all we know, Emma and Samantha could have been the targets and Keeley got in the way, or vice versa, or all three could've been targets. It was an audacious abduction, still daylight. Having said that, the swing park is nicely tucked away, shielded with hedging and out of sight of the flats. Ideal really for snatching kids, just thoughtless 1970s town planning.

We've kept the news quiet until now, until we knew what we were dealing with, but there's to be a press conference later this morning and it'll be going out on the news bulletins.

Ok, that's it." Kennedy look around the room, "These girls must be found today. Now! Get to it."

Gathering his papers, Kennedy called out to Mack. "A word please, Sergeant Sumerson." Mack followed Kennedy into his office. The DI was upset again. He looked unblinkingly at Mack over metal-framed glasses slipped low on his nose.

"Sir?"

"I want some more progress today with Keeley, Mack. Have you arranged for a second interview? Is Mandy around to do it?"

"I didn't ask the parents for an interview today. It was hard enough to get them to agree to one last night. Clarence suggested afterwards that Keeley draw a picture of the two men. I was going to see if Clarence and I could go back to the family home today to pick them up."

"Well, it would be better if she could describe them in interview," snapped Kennedy. "Wouldn't it? In fact, it would have been better if you and Mandy had thought to start the ABE interview with that last night."

Another balls-up: a major one; Mack couldn't disagree, he didn't have a leg to stand on. He had realised himself afterwards, when Mandy was asking a sobbing Keeley about what the abductors were wearing. "Yes, I agree, Guv, but like I said, Keeley was very upset, tired..."

Kennedy cut him off. "Sergeant, just ask them. If they say no, get the efit officer to their house and see if Keeley can describe the men to him in some more detail. See if she recognises any mugshots. We can do better than a child's drawings in this day and age." He stared at Mack and shook his head. "Police work is about process and procedure as much as chasing down crooks, Sergeant. More so! As you well know! Or should do." He tutted. "You're lucky I haven't got the time to think about that level of incompetence at this moment: you and Mandy. But you're the sergeant!" Kennedy sat down at his desk. He took off his glasses and rubbed his face. "Oh, just get on with it, Mack. Take Clarence with you to see the family. She might be better at getting them onside. If we're paying for her, we may as well get our money's worth. And if the parents won't agree to any of that, ask Clarence if we have grounds for any type of Court order compelling them to agree and let me know immediately."

The Inspector was in no mood to be challenged. Mack jiggled with some change in his pocket, the coins tepid from the heat and considered his options. There was no way that Knatchbull was going to let his daughter be interviewed again. Kennedy looked at him.

"Mack, you're a copper. And get your hand out of your pocket, man. You're a detective sergeant in the crime division of a large county police force. I have absolutely no idea how, but you are. You need to learn to use your professional authority to get the job done. We've got two missing eleven-year-old girls. They've already been gone for too long. Keeley is our only witness. Think about that." Kennedy replaced his spectacles, paused and took a deep breath. "Mack, I have to find them. There is no other option; there is no-one else who saw what happened. Only Keeley. You must make this work. Is that understood?"

"Yes, Guv." At least Kennedy hadn't been overheard by half the room.

He phoned Clarence on the way to the car. She'd checked with her supervisor, who had formally agreed for her to consult on the case. Thursdays were her office day, she had no meetings or clients booked, she could meet Mack outside the Knatchbulls' in an hour. She wondered if Kennedy had realised that Social Services would be charging the police for her time. Oh yeah. Kennedy knew.

Mack got himself a strong coffee and a bacon sandwich from the local take-away cafe and drove to the Mead estate, parking in one of the two emergency services bays. It was a sweltering, end-August day. He looked at the dashboard: 32 degrees. There was barely any breeze. He had all the car windows down, letting what air there was blow through the vehicle. He saw Clarence drive into the car park through his rear-view mirror. He positioned his arms by his sides and his hands in his lap; he hadn't had time for a shower before work, only achieving a quick spray of deodorant - any malodorous hints would be magnified in the heat.

Clarence backed her red convertible into one of the visitor parking bays and centred it in one smooth manoeuvre. The electric roof meandered its way over her bright, blonde head and clunked into place: good idea, Mack had seen more than one car trashed on the estate. An obviously feminine convertible would be a loudspeaker to any despotic teenager with a bit of time on his hands (and he reckoned there might be a few of those on the Mead). She crossed the carpark and opened his car door. Tanned legs folded themselves into his passenger seat, a swishy skirt settled to just cover shapely knees. She looked cool, calm, collected and controlled; in fact, when he thought about it, he'd never seen her looking anything else. Her perfume reached him. He hoped the favour wasn't mutual. He tightened his armpits against his body and relayed Kennedy's displeasure regarding the first interview and expectations about a second.

"Well, we are up against it, I agree with you, if the mother's reaction last night is anything to go by, the likelihood of them agreeing to a further interview is virtually zilch, especially given how distressed Keeley was when the interview finished," mused Clarence. "From what you've said, Mr. Knatchbull doesn't like the police and Mrs. Knatchbull made it more than clear that she hasn't got time for Social Workers."

"Kennedy suggested going down the Court route if the Knatchbulls really won't play ball."

"No, that's a bad idea. We need to avoid that. It wouldn't help her after all she's been through already."

"Yeah, well, you gonna tell Kennedy that?"

"If I need to." She glanced at him. "Easier for me – he's not my boss. I know the police have got an urgent agenda, Mack, but we can't justify traumatising Keeley further to accommodate it. Can't happen. I can't see what Court order we could ask for anyway and the Court would have to consider Keeley's welfare. There'll be a different way. I wonder if we're better off just turning up with the efit guy, what's his official title?"

"Facial identification officer"

"That's it, and the mugshots, take the choice away. I know it's a bit unorthodox, but if the Knatchbulls are resistant, it could be worth the risk. It might be our one chance and it needs to be done asap, anyway. Also, I was thinking that I could offer to see Keeley for some supportive counselling, that might mollify them a bit and she probably need it, anyway. Anyone would, after what she's been through."

Mack was sure Keeley did need counselling. He wasn't sure it would mollify Mr. Knatchbull. He phoned the efit officer. He was free and had been told to give the case priority; he was in Chelmsford and would meet them at the family home in about forty minutes. Clarence offered to go up to the flat first, to try to smooth the way: it was already eleven a.m., with a bit of luck, Mr. Knatchbull would be at work. But Mack couldn't begin to imagine Kennedy's ire if Knatchbull lost it with Clarence, or maybe he could: no, they'd go up together. This time he had his baton.

It was Mrs. Knatchbull who answered the intercom and

buzzed them up. She was waiting for them on the landing outside the flat, stiff and straight, arms folded across her chest. "My husband's not here, which makes this your lucky day. I know you people have got to do your job, so I'm letting you in. But I'm going to be clear with you. We don't like police and we don't like Social Services and you don't need to mind why. So, get this over with and then I want you to go away and leave us alone. Is that clear?" She pushed open the flat door. "Now, I'm guessing you want Keeley to look at some photos or something? So, you'd better come in." She turned back to them, "I don't want her getting upset."

The flat was clean and organised. Keeley and her sister were watching daytime children's TV. "Claire, go to your room, these people need to speak to Keeley."

"But mum, I was watching the film." Mrs. Knatchbull picked up a laptop from a side table and handed it to her younger daughter, her voice softened. "Go on, now, you can watch it on this, all comfy on your bed. Take a biscuit from the tin."

Mrs. Knatchbull turned off the television. Mack waited until Clarence had settled herself next to Keeley on the couch and took the opportunity to look around a bit more. Like the front door, the living-room window and sliding balcony doors were fitted with high-grade security: excessive for a third-floor flat. He glanced through an open door into the kitchen. Even on such a hot day, only the small window in front of the sink was open and then on the first notch. He wondered if the flat had air conditioning, he'd have expected it to be sweltering with all the closed glass. He decided to do some exploring.

"Er, Mrs. Knatchbull, sorry to be a nuisance, but could I use your loo?"

She looked at him. "What are you, a child? Couldn't you have gone before you came out?"

"I know, sorry..."

"Go on, down the hall, second door on the left. Don't be disturbing, Claire, mind."

He found the bathroom. The small, frosted window was

locked. He had a neat rummage under the towels and bedlinen in the airing-cupboard. There was nothing interesting to find. The bathroom cabinet held the usual paracetamol and outdated medicines. He lifted the lid off the cistern, peered inside, flushed the loo, washed his hands and wandered back to the living-room, on the way putting his head around the doors of the two unoccupied bedrooms to satisfy himself about those windows - he wasn't wrong. Clarence had prepared the way for the facial recognition officer, who rang the intercom just as Mack was about to upset Mrs. Knatchbull again by asking for a glass of water.

It was after two p.m. by the time Keeley had said all she had to say and looked through the images on a laptop. The facial recognition officer had used his best techniques, but Keeley's memory was confined to her first description of one of the men being short, fat and bald and the other being tall with curly, dark hair. She pointed out one man who she thought could be the tall abductor, but she was by no means certain.

Mrs. Knatchbull flatly declined the offer of counselling for Keeley. Clarence left her card anyway, stressing that ultimately it might be something Keeley needed. The three professionals left together.

The facial recognition officer wasn't without hope. "It's not uncommon for victims to recover some memories a while after the event. You should know that, Clarence. I think you might get something out of her yet, just make sure you keep in touch. Mind you, the mother's not exactly welcoming, is she?"

"Outright bloody hostile, more like." Mack's phone beeped: Kennedy wanted an update. "Ok, folks, the Inspector wants to know how it went, so I'd better give him a ring. Thanks for all your help."

Kennedy took Mack's update wordlessly; he had another job for him. Someone needed to speak to the school and get as much information about the girls as they could, see if there had been any men hanging around, etc. and get access to any CCTV footage. That should have been done first thing, but the DI hadn't had any officers to spare. Mack was in the area, he could go now. Mack wondered whether to point out the obvious - it was school holidays, but before his mouth moved into gear, his brain kicked in and he remembered that there was a school holiday club. The school was only around the corner from the Knatchbulls' flat, if he was lucky, he might catch someone there.

There was a small grey fiat in the school car park, Mack pulled up next to it and wandered towards the school building. A voice called across the tarmac. "Can I help you?"

A grey-haired, short man, Mack judged he was probably in his early fifties, neat in short-sleeved white shirt and dark linen trousers, was coming around the side of the building. Mack walked over and showed his warrant card. "Police, Detective Sergeant Mack Sumerson. And you are?"

"Mr. Bridge. I'm the headmaster here. I presume you want to talk about the missing girls?"

"Thanks. I'd appreciate your time."

"Come inside, then, it's too hot to talk out here." Mack followed the headmaster into the school, down a corridor that was breeze block offices on one side and glass on the other. Dust, disinfectant and library wafted across his nose: school smell – never changed. "I'm here sorting out some bits for the school holiday club. Now, what can we do to help? Obviously, the whole estate knows what's happened. I heard the press release on the today's lunchtime news, but the word was out last night. Already, I've had parents calling to say that they won't be sending their kids to the holiday club tomorrow. I was going to make contact with the police school liaison officer to ask advice about whether to still run the club. This is a very close school – the other pupils are devastated. Please, come and have a seat."

The office walls were brightly painted and several noticeboards were pinned with drawings and poems in children's handwriting. School photos adorned every surface and on the desk was a portrait of, Mack assumed, the headmaster's wife and two daughters. A kettle and tea-tray was laid out on top of a cupboard, along with a bottle of coke and a carton of orange juice, a packet of digestive biscuits was half-consumed, melted chocolate around the edge of the neatly folded-over packet.

"Tea, soft drink? I'm afraid we can't run to filter coffee here, but I expect you'd like something cold," he glanced at the coke, "Or at least luke-warm?"

"A coke would be great, thanks. So, Mr. Bridge, we'd like to get as broad a picture as possible of these three girls. It would be very helpful if you could fill us in on what you know of their background and home life. Also, whether you've had any suspicious individuals hanging around the school, anyone who's concerned you?"

"Well I can put your mind at rest about strangers, Sergeant. We've not had any reports of anyone lurking. This is a close, relatively small school, it really only serves the Mead estate. Obviously, we have a wider catchment area, but given its location, you know, off a sliproad and given how busy the A127 is, the population in the catchment area is pretty sparse, so I'm confident that any strangers hanging about would have been noticed."

"Do you have CCTV?"

"Yes, we do, it only covers the front gate, though. You've welcome to what we've got."

"Thanks, I'll take those details before I go. So, what can you tell me about Emma, Samantha and Keeley?"

"Samantha and Emma have been best friends right throughout the school, from year one. Keeley has always hung around with them, but Samantha and Emma are inseparable. Their parents socialise together. Keeley's parents, the Knatchbulls, tend to keep themselves to themselves. They're reasonable in their dealings with us, but not particularly friendly and I've not heard that they go to any social events, certainly not like Emma and Samantha's parents. All three girls have younger siblings at the school."

"And have you ever had any concerns for their welfare, Mr. Bridge?"

"Never Keeley's. A year or so ago, I mentioned to Emma and

Samantha's parents that I'd noticed the girls hanging around the estate on a couple of occasions when I'd left school late. I know that both sets of parents work. So whether that's got anything to do with it I don't know, can't see how, though, because I've never seen the younger siblings out, so someone must have them when the parents are at work."

"And what was the parents' response to your concerns?"

"Oh, they were blasé. Said that the girls had to be home by seven p.m. in the summer and earlier in the winter. I even ran it past duty Social Services, but they weren't interested, didn't think the parents were being unreasonable, didn't want to know, actually. The school nurse has never had any concerns. That's about all I can tell you, I'm afraid."

"How about their work. How do the girls do academically?"

"Keeley does rather well, actually, I've taken classes she's been in, pleasure to teach: engaged, articulate. She's a bright little thing - only missed passing her 11plus by a couple of marks. Emma and Samantha are average, not outstanding, but by no means unintelligent. They do distract each other, sometimes they've had to be separated by the teacher. But in the main, they're fine."

"Ok, thanks Mr. Bridge. I appreciate your time. Have you got a number that we can contact about accessing the CCTV?" Bridge fiddled around in his desk drawer and found a business card. "A private company manages it. You need to call them."

Mack gave Bridge his contact number and asked to be kept updated if the headmaster remembered anything else. Just to be polite, he asked a passing question. "Have you always worked in this area Mr. Bridge?"

"No, I was in Oxford and then Tower Hamlets before here. I trained at Oxford, but then I worked in the London East End for quite a few years. I moved to Hertfordshire when I got married – my wife is from St. Albans and we liked the idea of living there. She's a teacher, too. We managed to end up working at the same school, one very different from this one. A state school in a very wealthy area - private by any other name, really. It virtually ran itself. I got bored, as did my wife, so when this post came up, I thought it looked like a challenge and went for it, never regretted it. By then we had two children, so it made sense for my wife to be at home for a bit."

Mack nodded towards a photo on the desk. "Is that your family? Are your daughters at school locally?"

"No. No, they're not." Bridge frowned, "And that's not really anything to do with you, is it, Sergeant?" He stood up and opened the office door. "Anyhow, I must be getting on." He proffered a stiff hand. "Good-bye, you'll know the way out." The door closed in Mack's face.

He stood still for a few seconds, wondering what had just happened. Weird. It was another issue to park and re-visit when he had the time to think.

Chapter 6

Reggie Bull was seriously regretting coming out of his retirment. And all because he owed an old mate. The situation had gone bad from the start and it was set to get worse. The girl had woken up the morning after the night before and wouldn't be comforted or told. In the end, he'd dissolved another pill in orange juice, pinned down her chest with one hand and used his other to syringe the drink down her throat. He was pleased with himself for not reacting when she choked and spluttered, spraying liquid back onto his shirt.

Reggie had followed all his usual procedures, made sure that he had the necessary info; being prepared usually saved a lot of trouble - and he would know. He knew that both parents of both the children worked. This girl, Emma, had a mum who was a part-time cleaner and a dad who was a lorry-driver. He had gone through his usual spiel: wouldn't you like to help your mum earn some money and have some nice things, this is a way to do it, yada, yada, but the girl wasn't having any of it. Screaming and crying hysterically, she had wet the bed. He congratulated himself on at least having the forethought to use a waterproof mattress protector: fuck knew where it all came from; girls always tended to piss themselves more than boys, he'd never worked out why. She had bruises now, three livid blue finger marks in a row across one collar-bone, her pale skin had marked easily, more easily than he liked – the commercial aspect was always a consideration. But it had been the only way.

The police had been quick off the mark. The press release had gone out on the lunchtime news, not even twenty-four hours after the children had gone.

After that, no-one would take her off his hands. He had tried all his contacts. The man who'd asked for them in the first place was running scared - the girl was tainted goods. Reggie pondered getting rid of her and burying the body, but he was past getting his hands dirty like that – had never liked it in the first place – urine was bad enough, but the outcome of relaxed bowels was something else entirely. And his back was aching just from carrying her upstairs, it wouldn't take the digging, or any other type of disposal for that matter. He couldn't trust his two flunkeys with the job, that would just be another fuck-up. And he avoided the only other help available unless it was absolutely necessary.

He pondered keeping her for himself for a while, but it still left the problem of what to do after, and he was an old man with prostate trouble...still, she was a pretty little thing. Her skin was peachy-smooth, hair still a fine, wispy baby blonde. And she had eyes that were button-round and mid-blue, the type that really hit the spot for him, just touched something inside.

He got off the bed and trod softly across the room to the large cabinet that occupied most of the wall opposite. He liked to come to look most days. He caressed the edge of the mahogany with a thumb-tip, slowly opened the brass-handled glass doors and surveyed the contents: an obeisance to his ego. Yes, a blue one for her, it always perfectly complemented blonde hair and peachy skin: a navy blue one, velvet, with neatly snipped ends.

Chapter 7

Clarence had numerous reports to finish, but couldn't focus in the interminable heat of a summer that had come early, settled into itself and seemed determined to claim autumn: global warming writ large. Her office was located in a corner of brown, squat concrete on the edge of Bellington. It was a building poorly designed for its purpose of housing social services, cold in winter and hot in summer; there were few private offices and no child-friendly spaces, the walls were paper-thin. The one mitigation to the misery was a long and dense border of ancient oak trees that had survived 1970s town planning and sheltered the building's occupants from the excesses of noise and fumes of the main road. Clarence's second floor office window opened straight into the lower leaves.

There was a job that she'd meant to finish before meeting Mack that morning. She logged on, pulled up the Social Services database and typed 'Knatchbull' into the search engine. There was only one match. A Peter Knatchbull had at some point been known to Essex Social Services, having previously lived in Poplar, East London. There was no other information. Clarence guessed that a half-hearted attempt to upload paper files had been interrupted, or more likely, abandoned. She emailed the records clerk and asked for the old folder. There was nothing under the names of Keeley and her sister, Claire. And the Knatchbulls' address on the Mead Estate had no matches, which meant that the children hadn't ever come to the attention of the authorities: police, or social services. She made a note to remind herself to update Mack.

She had seen Mack's jaw clench and his shoulders stiffen when the call came through from his manager earlier. Clarence felt for him. Her trained eye saw a lurking anxiety that he tried to manage, probably some days better than others. DI Kennedy was a reasonable, fair man and always pleasant enough, but he had a bent towards authoritarianism that he didn't always keep in check and a tendency to bark out commands only a couple of decibels lower than shouting. He stood unusually straight, often with his hands behind his back. She wondered if he'd ever been in the military; he had the bearing of authority, the air of a sometime taskmaster. On the last case that she'd worked with them, Mack had still been a detective constable, the Inspector had asked a lot from him then, so would almost certainly be expecting more since Mack had passed his sergeant's exams. She thought that Mack was doing well with the missing girls case. He had correctly gauged the Knatcbhbulls' hostility and taken action accordingly. She couldn't see that there had been an alternative course of action. Privately, she thought Mack needed to stand up to Kennedy a bit more: Mack was a sergeant, needed to own his seat; she guessed that Kennedy would back down if presented with a fair perspective - he wasn't an ogre. She wondered about Mack's background, whether his dad was still around, what their relationship had been, she'd lay a bet on anything it was problematic.

She had a Court statement that needed to be submitted the following week; it needed a brutal edit. She woke up the computer, and pulled up the document, but her thoughts were still roving, swaying between whatever horror could be happening to the missing girls, and Keeley, who was surely experiencing such acute guilt and depth of loss.

Inevitably, loss ran through Clarence's work, from death, or children being removed from home, right down to the loss of hope. Before Ted, before her own bereavement, Clarence had had a professional response. After, she had a personal one and not always helpfully so. A knurled knot of pain sat permanently next to her heart. Keeley's trauma, the potential for something truly terrible to have happened to the other girls, the oppression of the interminable weather, the heat that seemed to wrap around and just keep squeezing, had engorged it, until it was a fist pummelling against her chest wall from the inside, dictating the rhythm of her heart.

She knew her friends and colleagues fretted for her: they

urged her into therapy, to accept, move on. Move on to what? To whom? How could her husband be replicated? Why did people even *say* that to someone grieving? She wondered if she'd ever said that to her clients before, resolved not to, never to; it was a crap, trite, insensitive thing to say.

A movement caught her eye. A soft soughing was beginning to tiptoe its way amongst the high leaves outside her window. She watched for some moments. It was just the wraith of a breeze, a distant harkening of the season to come, a disturbance trailing through the sultry stillness.

Chapter 8

Gemma had discovered the disused MoD beach some two years ago. A professional dog walker for ten years, she had seen the climate change rapidly, people were neurotic if they saw a woman walking several large dogs – isolated walking spots had become a professional necessity.

So, Friday early mornings in the summer were always beach walks. Her morning regulars, Bertie, a large lumbering bloodhound; border collie, Dixie; a yapping Yorkshire terrier inexplicably named Kitty and Bella, her own retriever, who'd come along for the ride, were already panting in the early-morning heat. Gemma drove down a narrow, unadopted track, parked the van as close as possible to the high fence that partitioned off the beach and she and the dogs squeezed through a wooden plank in the fence that she'd loosened when first exploring the area.

Gemma used steps to reach the beach, but the dogs scrambled down the steep bank, galloped across sand and splashed straight into the still water, barking and yelping with ecstasy, patiently waiting for her to divest of her shorts and t-shirt so that she, too, could swim, albeit in her underwear.

Bertie – large animal, heavy, felt the heat – was usually the first to start his swim, but today he lingered, wet only to his tummy, head turned away, towards the end of the beach. Some five hundred yards away from them was an old, wood and iron jetty, its walkway still sturdy, intact and out of waves' reach at even the highest tide. It was concreted deep and solid into sand and mud and stood as a relic of the area's army days, now marking the start of a public beach on the other side.

Gemma paid no particular attention; Bertie's bloodhound brain was constantly connecting with scents that were indiscernible to even canine noses and she was used to his distractions.

Treading water as dogs paddled around her, Gemma watched Bertie lumber back towards the shore where he paused for some seconds, hazel eyes closed to the brightness of the day, large nostrils contracting and expanding, sifting the air. He started a purposeful, steady walk towards the jetty, head down, nose close to the ground, jowls and long ears trailing and gathering up sand – the van floor would be carpeted later. When he'd gone three hundred yards or so, deaf to her calls, she decided to follow him, suspecting that he had caught the whiff of something dead to eat. The dog's stomach was a source of constant vigilance, ingestion of rank foodstuffs usually resulted in prolific diarrhoea - to be avoided at all costs, especially in such a heat. She waded towards the water's edge, squelching across spikey mud and stepping onto the hot, powdery sand.

She started to plod after Bertie, aware that she hadn't used sunscreen and cursing the inevitable burn to her fair skin. The other dogs had come out of the water and were trailing her. Bertie's walk had moved into a neat, symmetrical trot; he had raised his head and was staring hard at the jetty as he approached it. Gemma increased her pace.

Suddenly, she came to a shocked, stunned halt, goosebumps pimpling her skin. The bloodhound had slowed a few feet short of the jetty and raised his head, opening his throat to the sky. The howling was mournful and piteous, thrown from his lungs in desperate bursts each lasting several seconds. Its piercing rent the air - a barbarous dissonance on such a hot, hazy, high summer day.

The wailing carried on and on during the minute or so that it took Gemma to reach Bertie: running hard, feet hampered by stony sand and grasping seaweed, heart pumping. She drew close to him. The howling subsided into a wretched whimpering. His wet nose nudged her fingers as she edged past him. Gemma rested her hand briefly on his warm head, wiped sweat and gritty sand out of her eyes. She was acutely aware, now, of the downside of the beach's isolation and of her state of undress, of being a lone woman with four dogs to protect. The other dogs had stopped next to Bertie. Telling them all firmly to stay, she trod softly towards the darkness of the underbelly of the jetty and stepped slowly into its shadow. She stood perfectly still, searching, scouring the shade, the nooks and crannies of wood and iron, looking for anything suspicious – expecting it.

To her relief, there was nothing to be seen, only a rank, stomach-churning stench in the trapped, still air was noteworthy, she presumed that was what had drawn Bertie. When she thought about it, she'd noticed the smell when she parked the van earlier; the rising sun and swiftly gathering heat was making it speedily, nauseatingly, worse. Her heart began to slow. She had been hoping for just a large dead fish or sea-mammal, but had feared – God forbid – a lurking lech, a threat she couldn't counter, but there was nothing, only smooth and warm yellow sand, untouched by anything, sloping softly into the gentle, rhythmic lapping of the waves.

Still puzzled, she turned her head to see that Bertie had moved and was close behind her. His whimpering had stopped. His heavy, heated panting was rhythmically fanning the backs of her thighs with hot air, his broad nose was millimetres from her skin. His whole body was trembling. She could see the grey-flecked brown fur on his flank quivering. His large, majestic head was turned up.

The body was almost directly above Gemma's head. It had been crammed, face-down, between the roof and a supporting strut of about a foot wide and then shoved hard, violently, against the jetty's outer frame. The girl's head lolled forward, blonde hair dangling and straggly from splashed seawater, faded, blue eyes bulged and staring. From the other side of the strut, her feet dangled earthwards, pooled blood mottling and swelling the flesh. One foot was still wearing a sparkly, little-girl sandal, wedged on with bloating. Blood, uncleansed by sea-water, clung to the right cheek - having tricked out of the right ear, it left a murderous pointer of death. Gemma knew what she was seeing. The publicity had been more than thorough. Grabbing Bertie hard by his collar, she ran back down the sand to her mobile, away from the monstrous sight, knowing the dogs would follow.

Chapter 9

Mack got the call from Essex police control room at eight thirty a.m. on the Friday following the abduction. A frantic 999 call had been made by a distraught dogwalker on an old MoD beach in Shoeburyness. Kennedy had been informed and was en route. It was Mack's rest day on the rota, but as he was learning, there were no rest days in a missing child investigation.

Kennedy and SOCO were already present and dealing with the scene. Mack's arrival was greeted by ferocious barking coming from a rocking, white van, the air conditioning units on its roof rotating furiously; presumably, the dogwalker was still giving her statement. The beach itself was blocked off from public land by ten feet high fencing, but several of the panels had been neatly removed and laid flat on the grass to accommodate police activity, exposing a narrow flight of steep, worn stone steps. He parked his car on police taped-off wasteland that extended some yards back from the fence before scrub and trees took over, his stomach already protesting at the smell in the air. Once down on the low sand he was enveloped by a fetid, heavy miasma that snaked into his throat. Desperate not to be a cliché (Kennedy appeared to have a stomach of steel), he swallowed and clenched tight. He had had dead bodies before, but never a child.

Mack walked into the conversation between the DI and pathologist, whose face was seeping sweat. He ran a gloved finger around the neck of his bodysuit.

"So, our working hypothesis is that this is Samantha?"

"Yeah, I think so, Tim. I re-read the description of what Samantha had been wearing when she went missing and it matches; at the moment, we can only find one of her sandals, though. The other one may have fallen off before she got here, or maybe it fell off here and has been washed away by the tide."

"Was she killed here?"

"On the beach? Don't know at the moment, so much will have been washed away."

"Speaking of which," said Kennedy, eyeing the lapping water, "How long before the tide's back in?"

The pathologist was thorough, had checked that, too. "We're ok, it's on its way out now, it's high tide again at six thirty p.m., so we need to get the searches on the sand out of the way by fiveish, I would think."

"Ok. Presumably, whoever brought her here got onto the beach the same way as the dogwalker, through a gap in the fencing. Is this beach still used by the MoD?"

"From what I can gather, it's not used, but still owned by them, so blocked off from public use - hasn't been swept for ordnance."

"Well, from what the dogwalker said, she's been coming here a while, so obviously there's no monitoring, CCTV or otherwise, because she would've been stopped, so they can't be that worried about unexploded bombs. Cause of death?" The body was still in situ. The pathologist beckoned Tim over, Mack followed.

"See this blood, how it's come out of her ear? Blow to the head and I think her nose is broken, she's a little girl, it would only have taken one punch. Not saying that's what killed her, but it probably did, for it to cause that type of bleeding. Need to wait for the post-mortem, obviously."

"And how long do you think she's been here?"

"Well, body wouldn't take long to start to decompose in this level of heat, Tim. Must be well over thirty degrees on this beach. In fact," he walked over to his bag, pulled out a thermometer and squinted. "Yep, thirty-six degrees. That's climate change for you." He looked around. The beach was lower than the surrounding area, hemmed in by a wall that was a montage of crumbling render and yellow London brick. A functional metal handrail traced the length of the stone steps. "And this is a sun-trap – perfect spot for a beach – army knew what they were doing. Body might only have been here couple of days, I'd say."

"So, she was taken Wednesday afternoon, was she killed then, too?"

"Almost certainly. But you know how it goes, wait for the report."

Kennedy started barking out instructions.

"Sergeant Sumerson, I want you to go to see Keeley and her family to update them; don't let them hear about this on the news. Then speak to Mead Primary and make sure that the school holiday club gets cancelled. We're dealing with a murderer, the school needs to be careful." He turned to Dave Cooper, "Constable, you go with the family liaison worker and let Emma's parents know. They're only going to think the worst from now on."

The pathologist looked at Kennedy. "Who's got the job of going to see Samantha's parents, then?" Kennedy's throat spasmed.

"That'll be me. I'll take Jenny. Keep me updated as to when the post-mortem's going to start would you, Crabbe?"

The pathologist nodded. "Need to get a formal ID, as well, Tim. Let me know."

On his way to Keeley's family's flat, Mack phoned Bridge, curious about the response he would get after the man's odd behaviour at the end of their last meeting. But the headmaster could not have been more professional. "You understand, Mr. Bridge, we can't comment on the identity of the body, nor on the cause of death. But as a precaution, my Inspector would like the school holiday club closed from today. Please don't speculate with the children, or parents. You can just say that the police have said that the club needs to be closed until further notice. Is that ok?"

"Of course, Sergeant, I promise I won't mention it to anyone, but you do know that the news will get out quickly? It always does, here."

"Well, be that as it may, Headmaster, please don't let it come from you."

"You have my word. Let me know if there's anything the school can do to help."

He made a second call. "Thing is, Clarence, I could do with some support in telling them. I haven't got a family liaison officer and Keeley, probably her sister, too, is going to be really upset."

Clarence was already waiting in the car park when Mack arrived. Mr. Knatchbull answered the intercom. He was as hostile as Mack remembered and some; his heart sank, it was only ten thirty and he was beginning to feel that he might already have had enough for one day; his stomach lurched in agreement. "Mr. Knatchbull, we really need to speak to you and your family. It is very important."

"My wife told you before. We don't need no police or social services here."

Clarence bent into the intercom. "Mr. Knatchbull. We haven't met, but I visited with Sergeant Sumerson yesterday. You need to listen to him. We have something important that we need to speak to you about and we can't go until we've done that."

"Bloody hell," the cursing was cut short by the buzzer. The flat door was open, Knatchbull was waiting. He gave Clarence a cursory glance, scowled at Mack.

"What do you want now? I thought my wife made it clear that we didn't want to see you here again?"

"I'm afraid we have some bad news, Mr. Knatchbull. We wanted Keeley to hear it from us, before anything gets into the media. Can we come in?" The door was slammed shut behind them. Mack heard the chain slide across.

"Is Keeley at home?"

"She's in her room, her mum's took her shopping, they're trying on new clothes."

"Ok, well, we needed to let you know that, unfortunately, a child's body has been found. There's a possibility it may be Samantha."

"Well, I'm sorry to hear that. It's a tragedy when a young life is cut short. But what's that got to do with Keeley?" He looked harder at Clarence, "Are you this Social Worker who offered to give Keeley counselling?"

"Yes, I am."

"Well, she don't bleedin' need it!"

Clarence would handle Knatchbull. She just had the knack; Mack wished he could cultivate it, police training didn't seem to be as thorough as Social Workers' when it came to managing idiots.

"Mr. Knatchbull, when I saw Keeley yesterday, she was ever so scared about what could've happened to her friends. Her fear has now quite possibly been realised. She's going to be very upset, shocked and, I'd guess, feel very guilty." She nodded towards the sofa, "May I?" Knatchbull didn't move. Clarence moved to the living-room and sat down. "We would like to be the ones to tell her, or to be present when you do. She's going to have questions. We probably won't be able to answer them today, maybe not ever, but if she's not allowed to talk about how she's feeling, it's not going to help her to come to terms with it. The body hasn't been formally identified. And Emma is still missing. The police are going to need to keep speaking to your daughter." She paused, tightened the back of her earring, looked him straight in the eye. "I know that you know all this, Mr. Knatchbull, I know that you love your daughter very much and that you want to protect her, why not let us help to support all of you?"

Knatchbull deflated in front of them, as though his anger had travelled south to buckle his legs. He slumped downwards into the sagging armchair. It creaked under his weight. He rubbed a hand across his forehead. "Keeley hasn't stopped crying. That's why I'm not at work. Her mum took her out to buy her new uniform for big school, to distract her, give her something to think about, so I've to look after Claire. Normally, my parents-in-law have them, but they're on a day trip out with the bingo club, had it planned for ages. They offered not to go, but I said it was ok, work's been understanding, and they'd been looking forward to it, do 'em good to get away from it for a few hours. And it's all affected Claire. She knew Samantha and Emma, she wasn't friends with them like Keeley was, but still… What am I going to tell them?"

"Do you want us to do it, Mr. Knatchbull?" Mack knew an opportunity when he saw one. Knatchbull nodded, heaved himself out of the chair and called his wife and both daughters. Keeley looked straight at Mack as soon as she entered the room. "What's happened?"

He waited until they had all sat down. "I'm afraid we have some bad news, Keeley. The body of a girl has been found. We don't know who it is, but we need to consider that it could be Samantha. We wanted you to tell you before it's on the news."

He saw her pupils dilate, like she was watching the pain as it seeped into her and found a comfortable spot to bed down. He turned to Clarence. She was steadily holding Keeley's gaze. There it was again, the soft draught from the back of his mind, a breeze that held the threat of storm. He glanced at the locked windows. There was something going on with the Knatchbulls, he was sure of it: all the hostility, keeping the authorities at arms' length; the Knatchbulls were reasonably articulate people, Mack suspected Knatchbull wasn't quite as stupid as he presented, there was no obvious cause for the aggression - it all added up to something.

Claire had burst into tears and was sobbing against her mother's chest. But Keeley was stony quiet and perfectly still. Eventually, she turned slightly to Clarence. "Why did she die?"

"The police don't know for sure that it is Samantha, yet, Keeley. And they don't know how this person died. There has to be an examination to find that out."

"Is that an autopsy, like on tele?"

"Yes, that's right."

"But even if it isn't Samantha, it's still a girl who's about the same age as Samantha and me and Emma, otherwise you wouldn't think it might be Samantha. Is that right?"

Clarence looked at Mack. "Is it?"

"Yes, probably."

"Where was she?"

"I can't tell you that, Keeley," said Mack. "As soon as the police can give you more information, we will, I promise. But at the moment, I can't tell you anything else. But we wanted you to be prepared."

Once outside, Mack raised his observations about the Knatchbulls. "He's worried about something, Clarence, otherwise why have all those locks? It's been boiling hot, yet all the windows were closed and locked - heavy-duty locks, too. And on the third floor? He even put the chain on the door after we went in."

"Yes, now you mention it, I noticed that, but it wasn't hot inside, was it?"

"I reckon he's got air-conditioning built in."

"Well, you're going to have to speak to Kennedy about your concerns aren't you, Mack? Has Knatchbull got a criminal record of any kind? He's got one entry on our database, just says that he was at some point in Poplar, East London – if it's the same person. I've requested the paper file, cos there was nothing else on the electronic record."

"I don't know about the police database records, someone would have checked when the girls first went missing, but Kennedy didn't mention it to me, so I doubt it. I'm sure the parents know something, not saying they're implicated…"

"I'm not a police officer, Mack, but wouldn't you need evidence to bring him in for an interview? You can't just start questioning him, can you?"

"No, no, but I'm thinking that if Keeley were to start seeing you, we might get some leads from that."

"Hmm, well let's see if the body is Samantha."

"Let's face it, Clarence. It almost certainly is, poor kid."

She looked at him. "I know," she paused. "Listen, my strong suspicion is that Keeley will be coming to me. Emma's still missing, I bet Keeley feels really, really guilty – the one who got away - her parents won't be able to cope with all that. Keeley's a bright girl, sharp, articulate. She'll make good use of some counselling. When will you get the outcome of the autopsy?"

"Dunno, later today, probably."

"Ok, I'll let you know if there's anything significant on the paper files once I get them."

Mack found Kennedy back at Chelmsford police station and gave him an update. "Er, Guv, I've got a few suspicions about Mr. Knatchbull. I wondered if there's anything came up in his checks?"

Kennedy was responding to emails; he didn't look up. "Cooper did those. There was nothing as far as I know. Why? What's happened?"

"Nothing's happened. It's just that I thought he had quite a lot of window locks and really heavy-duty door security, made me wonder what he's worried about."

"Sergeant, they're in a flat on the Mead estate, it's hardly a crime if the man wants to keep his family safe, is it? Especially given what's just happened."

"Yes, Guv, but he's had those locks on before all of this. I noticed it when I first went round the other night, Wednesday."

Kennedy stopped typing, took off his glasses, placed them purposefully on the mousemat, sat back in his chair and folded his arms. "Has he said anything to you to indicate that he or his family are implicated in this crime?"

"Well, no, of course not. But..."

"Do you have any evidence that Knatchbull and, or, his family are implicated in this crime."

"No, not evidence, but there's something not right there, Guv."

"Have you read the report of the officers who searched the property on Wednesday, straight after the girls had been taken?"

"Yes, Guv."

"You understand that we work on the basis of identifying evidence, that we don't make decisions or take action based on our feelings? And you know that there is no evidence to rouse suspicions about the families currently?"

He sighed. It was a lost cause, another nail driven home. "Yes. Guv."

"Then just get on with your write-ups, because I still have a missing child I'm hoping to find whilst she's still alive!"

The open-plan office was half-empty. He found a free desk and logged on. He had an email from the forensics lab about Keeley's clothes; they had nothing significant to report. He spied Dave Cooper at the coffee machine and got up again.

"All right?"

"Can't complain. Kennedy's got me running around like a blue-arsed fly with this case, though. You?"

"Same. Dave, listen. I heard that you did the checks against the families' names. I wondered if anything came up against Knatchbull?"

"Yeah, it did. Long time ago, though, ten years I think, about that anyway. I told Kennedy."

"He's forgotten, then. What was it?"

"Actual Bodily Harm against another guy. He got off with a six-month suspended sentence."

"Who was the guy?"

"I think it was a family member. Yeah, it was – a cousin, I think. I remember that cos it's an unusual surname and they had the same one."

"Oh, ok, nothing since?"

"Nah, been a good little boy since. The criminal justice system worked its magic."

"Where was it heard, do you know?"

"Poplar. I printed it out, to give to Kennedy. I'll leave a copy on your desk if you like. Why? Got something against him with this kiddy case?"

"No, no, just curious."

"Oh, just so you know, Mack, I went to the address of the bloke identified as a possible by the other kid, the one you interviewed."

"Keeley?"

"Yeah. A Michael Wiltshire. He got a conviction for sexually abusing his own daughter, got seven years, served four, was released three years ago. We went to the last known address. The place was just an decrepit mobile home in Stambridge, at the edge of some farmland. Nothing doing, just old clothes and a rotting cat, been deserted for ages, no leads. Farmer had let him park there for a couple of hundred a year but hasn't seen him for months. We went to his old address, met his ex-wife, who understandably hadn't had anything to do with him since the Court case, but nothing doing, Mack, sorry."

"Ok. Dave. Appreciate. Fancy a pint later, when we're off shift?"

Cooper nodded, "Yeah, could do with one."

Mack texted Clarence to see if she'd found any more information about the Poplar link. He had no doubt that Kennedy had simply forgotten about Knatchbull's conviction with the stress of the case. Still, it meant that Mack hadn't been completely wide off the mark. He bought himself a machine coffee, spat it out, went back to his desk.

Chapter 10

Mack got home that night relatively early, if ten p.m.was early after an eight a.m. start and a day with no breaks. Kennedy had taken him to the post-mortem. Mack had a suspicion that his boss thought he needed to toughen up. Everything about post-mortems disagreed with Mack: Dr. Crabbe's jokey interactions, the way that shoes squeaked across a hygienic floor, the sterility of the equipment. And the room, the smell, the state-endorsed evisceration of something that had once been a human being, a person with hopes and feelings, who loved and who was possibly loved in return, seemed to him the most grotesque of violations and slashed open an emptiness of hope that seeped into the air and leeched onto him, taking days to die and drop off. Samantha's hadn't been Mack's first post-mortem and he always hoped that each one would be his last. Kennedy, on the other hand, seemed to find each organ, each observation, each conclusion, fascinating, noteworthy and instructive.

The cause of Samantha's death was established as a blow to the head that caused a brain bleed. The doctor concluded that she'd probably been killed elsewhere and then moved to the beach. There was no water in her lungs and he would have expected to see more sand on her body and in her clothing if she'd been murdered where found. She had otherwise been in good health with no previous injuries and medical records showed only the usual childhood ailments, certainly there were no signs of previous abuse. It seemed that she had been tied tight by the wrists, probably with plastic that had eaten into her soft flesh. The pathologist was waiting for the toxicology results to see if she had been drugged.

Her parents came to conduct the formal identification just as Mack was leaving. Kennedy got Jenny to deal with that. And to update the Knatchbulls afterwards. Mack was grateful for the Guv's trust in womanly tenderness; the mother's screaming almost shattered his eardrums and followed him through the exit to bounce around his car as he drove home. His car speakers couldn't drown it out.

Kennedy had given Mack the next day off in lieu of the rest day, on the proviso that he keep his phone on and be available if needed for the case.

Mack had been in the police service for seven years, a graduate entry after a Mechanical Engineering degree from Newcastle. He hadn't particularly wanted to be an engineer, mechanical or otherwise, but it had been a choice following good Maths and Physics 'A' levels. Likewise, he didn't particularly know what had made him apply to the police, apart from the fact that he had wanted a good, steady career, early retirement and reasonable pension. The fact that the police had accepted him had been another motivating factor and he hadn't quite thought through how difficult the job might end up being. He had applied to the Essex service because his mum lived in Chelmsford, but had settled and bought a one-bedroom flat in Writtle, away from the centre, far enough away to avoid obligation, near enough for emergencies.

He kicked off his shoes and turned on the television. The late news was full of the dead and missing children. The Superintendent was giving another statement on air, announcing that the body had been identified as Samantha's and reassuring that the police were doing all they could to find Emma.

Yep, good luck with convincing the public of all that, he thought. The investigation was only coming up with dead ends. He wondered how long it would be before the tabloid press roused the monster of discontent that slumbered with one eye open in the belly of the Mead estate: a march, a riot, any type of hysteria about paedophiles was more than police staffing could accommodate and the case didn't need the distraction. Kennedy had had the dogs out a third time, going further onto the deserted farmland into which the white van had disappeared, all CCTV had been checked, including that from outside the Mead Primary school, none of it had yielded any leads. The van hadn't been found.

It was Friday night. He wanted to go out, have a few beers, forget the squeaking shoes, the screaming, the blood and the details of stomach contents. He debated texting Cooper and meeting up for their pint, but he knew he wouldn't get away with it a second time - Kennedy had made it clear that he would expect an instant response if Mack were to be needed. His boss's expectations had risen since Mack's promotion to DS; Cooper was a DC, he could get away with more. Mack decided to get a late takeaway and think some more about the case.

He checked his phone, there was nothing from anyone. There was no update from Clarence. He wished he had the skills with people she had. He knew that he fumbled around and got on people's nerves and that he wasn't above guffawing at his own jokes. Afterwards, thinking back, it would make him cringe inside, but once in the moment, he couldn't stop, like some little bit of him was attached to strings and controlled periodically and on a whim by some kind of diabolical puppeteer.

Clarence, in stark contrast, seemed to him to never lose her temper, or get intimidated and she had control of every situation he had ever seen her in. She'd faced out Knatchbull that day – had even sat down right in front of him - leaving the man towering above her. Clarence was a tall woman and probably quite strong, but even so, a man like Knatchbull would floor her with a single punch. Mack knew she was widowed, had heard that the husband was a copper and met with an accident shortly after their wedding - bad luck by anyone's standard. Mack had never met him, but by all accounts he'd been a decent bloke. Maybe that was part of it, maybe Clarence just didn't give a shit after that experience, but he came back on that, his sense was that most of her actions were down to professional skill. He found himself remembering the way she tended to play with her earring when she was concentrating, fiddling around with the back of it, pulling the butterfly off and pushing it back on: off on, off on - fingers tangling with her blonde hair, how the curls sprang back when released.

He couldn't fathom it. He figured that Clarence must have

been at least ten, maybe twelve, years older than him - heading into middle-age, for sure. And although slender, shapely, she was almost as tall as him - normally, he fancied petite brunettes. Mack had breezed through his adult life with tall, brown-eyed, conventional good looks and a reasonable intellect; he had never struggled to get girls, told himself that any attraction to Clarence was just a fad that would pass. He thought about the girl from the pub a couple of nights ago, wondered if she was there often. Yeah, that was his type - dark, pretty, lively, a girl who probably didn't think too hard about too much and who liked a good time. He decided to go back as soon as he could, get Cooper in tow, act out the 'do you come here often' cliche and see if he could get a date.

He ate his Chinese take-away and called his mum – he knew she'd be waiting up. It was a Friday night habit that assuaged his guilt and allowed him to cry off Sunday lunch. He was in bed by midnight.

He stumbled upwards from a deep sleep at nine a.m. when his phone screeched. Bellington police station front desk had a member of the public there who wanted to talk to someone about the missing girl case. They'd phoned Kennedy, who had told them to give it to Mack. He mumbled something down the phone and went to have a cold shower. He drove to Bellington and was there within an hour.

Belinda Owl was forty-five years old, married with two teenage children and lived in Benfleet. She had some information that she thought might be useful to the police.

"So, Mrs. Owl, how can we help you?"

"It's the other way round, Sergeant. I thought I should let you know about an incident that happened to my friend and me when we were eleven, which was 1981. It may or may not have a bearing on your case, but I think you need to hear it."

Mack took a gulp of strong coffee, courtesy of the front desk officer – instant, not machine, even smaller mercies - and hoped he wasn't about to waste his time, thought he probably was. He picked up his pencil, looked at Mrs. Owl and she carried on.

"I live in Benfleet now, but I grew up in Dagenham. My friend and I had gone for a bike ride with a picnic during school holidays that summer, we strayed too far and ended up out towards Upminster, near West Horndon. A man tried to abduct my friend, she bit him and I whacked him with my bicycle pump, he dropped her and ran off."

"Really? In broad daylight?"

"Oh yes, absolutely."

"And was it reported to the police?"

"Of course. We were terrified. We were on the edge of a field that had a few horses in it, but there were houses at the other side, we cycled across the field and went to the nearest garden. The woman called the police."

"And was the perpetrator caught?"

"No, but I think there was another incident a few months later with another girl. Can't remember that clearly now, but I'm sure you could look that up, find the records."

"Did you have any reference numbers from the police? Or did you by any chance get the car registration number?"

"No, but I know the make of the car. Funnily enough, my dad had the same one, had bought it that summer, the first brand new car we had, that's why I remembered it, before that we'd had clapped out old bangers. Anyway, sorry, you don't want to hear all that. It was a black ford sierra. The police did take all the details."

"Ok, so tell me again, what did this man do?"

"We'd stopped at the edge of a field. It's still there. If you go on the London-bound train, on the C2C line, there's a large field towards Upminster. There are horses in it most days and there's a row of houses - bungalows, actually - that have gardens backing onto there. The other side of the field is where we'd stopped, next to a road, obviously it was much quieter back then. Anyway, we sitting leaning against the fence, facing the road – the field actually extends past the fence for some reason, so we were on the grass. Suddenly, this car almost swooped upon us, a man got out, he left the engine running. He walked straight up to

63

Susan and picked her up under his arm, as if she were a toddler, you know, how you'd hold a child having a tantrum, sideways, under the crook of your arm, so you don't get kicked?" Mack didn't, but nodded anyway. "Susan just started screaming and struggling, whether it was shock, fear or anger I don't know, I don't suppose she does, either, it was just instinct. I happened to have unhooked my pump..."

"Pump?"

"Bicycle pump. My tyres had gone a bit flat. I'd unhooked it ready to pump them up after our picnic. It took me a few seconds to act, I was so stunned, but then I threw it really hard at his head just as Susan bit him deep on the forearm. We were both shouting and screaming. He dropped Susan, literally dropped her, ran back to the car and sped off."

"And what happened then?"

"Well, as you can imagine, we were terrified that he would come back. We pushed our bikes through the fence and cycled across the field as fast as our legs could go, I can tell you. The fence wasn't that high, maybe five foot, just panels with gaps. He could easily have jumped it if he wanted to. The nearest back garden had children playing in it. We ran up asking for help and the mother called the police. That was it."

"So if you were having a picnic, this would have been about lunchtime?"

"Yes, about twelve thirty."

"And he was never caught? You weren't asked to give evidence, or ever go to Court?"

"No, nothing. We gave statements, which we signed in the presence of our parents. We never heard anything else. As I said, I'm sure that there was a similar attempt some months later, but I can't recall anything more about that. Surely, you'd have it all on record, though?"

"Where did you give the statements, Mrs. Owl? Which police station?"

"Upminster."

"And what makes you think this could be linked to the current case?"

"I've got no evidence that it is. But something stood out to me when I heard about what had happened to those girls. And that was the audaciousness of the attack: exactly the same, walking up to girls in broad daylight and just taking them. Not your average criminal activity is it?"

She had a point.

"And what did this man look like, can you remember?"

"Indelibly printed onto my mind, Sergeant." She eyed him, "He was tall, probably slightly shorter than you are, getting on for six foot, maybe just under, five eleven, say. And a similar build to you, lean, but you're broader. I suppose rangy would be a good word for him."

"Hair colour?"

"Dark brown."

"And age?"

"At the time, I'd have said quite old, but looking back, now, I'd say probably mid to late thirties."

"Ok, thanks Mrs. Owl, is there anything else you'd like to tell me?"

"No, I made sure that I'd remembered all the details for you before I came."

"Ok, can I take your maiden name and Susan's and the addresses in Dagenham, and your contact details, please."

"I've already left them with the front desk, as well as my current details."

"Very efficient, very many thanks for coming in. I really do appreciate it." He held out his hand.

Just as Mrs. Owl was leaving the room, she turned back. "I almost forgot, Sergeant, I've got the shoulder numbers of the constables who dealt with it. My dad took them, just so he knew who he was dealing with and I've kept them, couldn't say why." She handed Mack a piece of paper; it was scrappy and fading, but the names and shoulder numbers of two constables were still clearly visible.

Mack suspected that Kennedy would have no tolerance with

pursuing Mrs. Owl's story to see if there was a link to their current case. The DI would see it as another example of Mack's irrelevant tributary thinking, like Knatchbull's security issues. Mack himself was inclined to think it was probably a dead end, that the abductor would have manifested again a long time ago, but he agreed with Mrs. Owl about the MO; even though the cases were decades apart, both smacked of audacity, not unknown, but rare. And it was the same county. If the man who had attempted to abduct Mrs. Owl's friend had been in his late thirties, he could easily still be alive. Mack had nothing better to do, it was his day off - sniffing around in his own time could hardly be criticised.

Upminster police station had an old cupboard full of records that no-one had bothered to upload – always pending according to the duty sergeant. The records officer was strictly Monday to Friday. Mack was free to help himself.

It took the best part of the afternoon to locate the file. Mrs. Owl had been specific about the month and year, but there had been a lot going on at that time – summer, school holidays, tourists. He found it buried on a back shelf, out of chronological and alphabetical order: a file marked 'Attempted Abduction'.

He made himself comfortable against some unsteady, piled-high boxes. The paperwork was sparse. The girls' statements were there, signed by them and a parent, giving the same facts as provided by Mrs. Owl that morning. The write-up of the initial call-out recorded the name and address of the person who had called it in, presumably the mother of the children in the back garden to which the girls had fled, "Two girls claim a man tried to abduct one of them in Upminster on X Rd. Current location as above, girls reported to be safe. Urgent attendance requested" and the names and shoulder numbers of the two officers who had attended initially and then dealt with the case. Their reports said virtually the same as the girls' statements. He checked them against the details given by Mrs. Owl. They matched. There was no record of what action had been taken to find the perpetrator and being 1981 there had been no traffic cameras along the quiet stretch of road. The lack of recording didn't surprise him. He had come across paper records before that were limp at best. The case had remained unsolved.

He considered his options. The way he saw it, there were three: phone Kennedy to report and risk a third bollocking in as many days; drive out to Upminster to do a recce of the location of the alleged incident; or try to find information about the PCs who had dealt with the case, see if they were still around and get their views. He ruled out number one for the same reason he he hadn't called the DI earlier, then decided that looking at a field full of horses and a road wouldn't tell him anything much. And wasn't Kennedy always telling him to use his authority and initiative?

He wandered round the station, looking for someone who might be old enough to remember something. The young front desk officer suggested the custody sergeant, who had been at the station, like, forever, and was coming up for retirement.

Custody was dealing with the fall-out of Friday night's Upminster social scene and the subsequent Saturday arrests for domestic violence, child assault and general all-round nastiness. The cells were half-full and the gaoler was feeding and watering the unfortunates who for varying reasons hadn't got to the Saturday Court sittings. Mack had to wait for Custody Sergeant Jenkins to finish bailing a youth who had punched an officer after being apprehended for defaecating into his own hands and then smearing the nearest shop window: teenage despots, they were everywhere. The lad was marched off by a swearing father.

"Two months," muttered Sergeant Jenkins as he finished off his paperwork, "Two months and I'm out of here. I'm bloody counting down the days." Mack could see that he wasn't joking; there was a calendar pinned to the side of the counter, each passing day crossed out in triumphant red marker pen. "It used to be just the old boys who we'd bring in to sleep it off, let 'em out again in the morning. Now, we have fifteen year olds off their heads on crack and crapping in the street in broad daylight." He turned to face Mack fully. "Anyway, what can I do you for young man?"

It was Mack's lucky day. Sergeant Jenkins knew both the officers who had dealt with the abduction case, remembered it himself as it happened, just because of the shocking nature of the event. He had been a young and newish PC at the time, but could recall that the alleged perpetrator had never been caught. One of the officers, Inspector James Brown, had retired just over a year ago, had worked way longer than he needed to, which appeared to be beyond Jenkins' comprehension. The other man, a sergeant, had retired some time ago, apparently due to ill-health. Jenkins saw Brown socially, just at the odd police function and had his home number, would be happy to call him for Mack, see if Brown could see him. Yes, it was a weekend, but Brown would be fine with that.

The retired inspector lived in a modern, extended bungalow on the Essex side of Upminster. Venetian blinds blinked at half-mast onto a faux-grass lawn that was an unnaturally deep green and surrounded on three sides by dull yellow rose bushes, their petals drooping and tumbling over the wall to litter the pavement. Mack cupped one and bent his head low; there was no scent. The heart of the flower was riddled with blackfly. He looked at the rest of the plant, the stem was alive – a scurrying plague of mini-beasts was sprawling along, across and under every surface. The rose came apart in his hand.

Inside the house, the decor was all magnolia paint, flowery carpets and parker-knoll furniture. Brown led him into the lounge. A round, chrome drinks-trolley on wheels stood next to a sideboard. It was well-stocked: good whiskey, cheap wine – Mack could guess which tipple was for James. The immediate space in front of the large television was domineered by a khaki-leather reclining armchair and a partnering footstool that was placed inches from the plasma screen. Brown unstopped a cut-glass decanter, "Retirement pressie from a grateful employer, Mack." He poured honeyed liquid into a matching glass and proffered it. Mack shook his head.

James Brown was a balding, large man, tall and with a

belly that shelved outwards from his chest and hung over low-waisted trousers; Mack judged he had probably gone to fat after retiring. His wife was washing-up after the couple's daughter and her family had been for dinner.

"So, young man," Brown was full of congenial affability "I understand you want to know about that attempted abduction all those years ago, linked to that missing girl no doubt, eh? As it happens, it wasn't far from here – can show you if you like."

"Thanks, Sir, but I know where it took place. I'd just really appreciate your thinking about the situation, anything that might show whether there could be a link to the current case."

"Course, of course lad. Anything to help." Brown squashed his bulk into the recliner, raised his legs and pushed up with his heels. The chair lurched backwards. Mack had seen the brand advertised – the reclining action had a much smoother manoeuvre on television. Brown rested the glass on his chest, nodded at the matching sofa. Mack sat down. "So, lad, how's the case going?"

It occurred to Mack, belatedly, which would be too belatedly for Kennedy's liking - Mack's stomach turned to face south, knew the drill - that Brown was on Civvy Street and therefore not to be privy to case details. "Oh, er, you know, pretty much as on the news, Sir."

"Mack, this is off the record, so just call me James. I'm not on the job now, you know." He guffawed and patted his belly, "Enjoying my retirement, boy, living the good life on my hard-earnt pension." Yeah, Mack could see. Brown had veiny cheeks and a nose to rival Rudolph's, only less pretty. A nasty gnawing was eating into Mack's gut. He was beginning to think that he might be stepping into a mistake that was going to roar open and drop him into a pile of crap that would make Sergeant Jenkins' problem look like pigeon shit.

"Anyway, Mack, I remember the case very well. There was a second attempt at an abduction a few months later, further up the train line, in Barking. That girl had been a bit older, about fourteen, I think. She'd been coming home late one night from school, it was winter, so it was dark. The same car, a black sierra, had followed her and slowed down, the driver opened his door and called her over, saying he needed help with directions. As she approached, he'd lunged at her and tried to drag her into the car. But I think he'd under-estimated the distance, cos she was able to pull away and he didn't pursue her, just drove off."

"And what happened then, er, James?"

"She was a canny thing, got half the number plate; that, coupled with the type of car, led us to an ID." Mack felt his heart give a brief flutter, maybe his detective's instinct was kicking in – Kennedy would be ecstatic. "Oh yeah, any joy?"

"We tracked the car's owner via DVLA. It was registered to an address in the East End. It was an old townhouse, really old, from the early 1800s, probably Regency rather than Victorian. There was just a row of them, about seven, that had survived the Blitz, everything around them had been decimated, yet those houses didn't even get their windows blown out, still had all the original stained glass in their front doors – no idea how." Brown paused, scratched his chin. "Anyway, the house was inhabited by a woman and a small child. There was no man there and no car. She rented from the council. She was a widow, her husband had died the year before from cancer. We even searched the house, there was no sign of a man there. She suggested - and we had no evidence to the contrary - that someone had falsely registered their car against her address."

"And did her story check out?"

"Oh yes, we could confirm the husband had died. And don't forget this was all before the days of mass traffic CCTV, so we couldn't trace the car. We linked it to the other case, the Upminster incident, but it never went any further."

"And there were no more incidents?"

"None, we assumed that he'd been spooked by his failed attempts and gave up."

"Really, you think someone who was bold enough to try that twice would just stop?"

"How long you been a copper, Mack?"

"Seven years."

"When you've been around human nature for long enough," Brown guffawed again, his belly rolls rippling with the effort, glass precarious. "You learn how fickle it is. Maybe the bloke had mental health issues and got better, maybe he died, maybe he moved countries. Sometimes, criminals just stop, you know. Anyway, we never heard any more of him. I very much doubt that he's linked to your case."

Mack stood up and held out his hand. Brown heaved himself up. The chair stayed in position, vanquished. "Thank you, Sir, I really appreciate your time and your thoughts about this. I don't suppose you'd know where the file for the Barking case is?"

"Like a dog with a bone, eh Mack?" Brown laughed, "Barking station, I suppose."

"And the name of the man to whom the car was registered? Just for my own curiosity, Sir."

"Surname was Ball, I think the first name was something like Reginald, can't quite remember, but an old-fashioned name, anyway. It's all in the records."

Brown showed Mack to the door. "Honestly, Mack, there's no link to your case here, move on, you'll be wasting your time. The house isn't there any more, by the way."

Mack didn't follow, "Sorry, Sir, what house?"

"Keep up, lad. The house in Poplar, it's all flats now. Council achieved what the Hun couldn't. Haha. Just saying, in case you fancied wasting some more of your time. Take it from an old copper who knows a thing or two."

Chapter 12

The dead child was all over the news. He should never have trusted Tony; how many times had he said that to himself in the last twenty-four hours? Whoever thought it was a good idea to hide a body on an MoD beach - *away* from the tide, *out* of its reach – and in the middle of blistering summer heat – needed to have his nut examined. There were brownfield sites, woodlands, even cemeteries that would have been better, but no, the wanker chose a beach, where the heat was going to speed up the stench and alert every fucker who passed. The news had said that the beach was no longer used by the military, but even so, for fucks sake. Reggie wondered who had found the body – who'd been noseying around in his business - but it wasn't like he had reliable staff to deal with the problem; that train of thought had to be abandoned. As did Tony, who had scarpered to the continent with some hussy he occasionally shacked up with. Reggie had contacts all over Europe; one phone call to a particularly vicious bastard had meant that Tony would soon be feeding the sharks, so who was having the last laugh, now, eh? Tosser.

Still, notwithstanding Tony's stupidity, Reggie was confident that there was nothing that could lead to his door; nonetheless, he planned to stay low for a while and there were a couple of loose ends that needed to be dealt with, mainly as a precaution, but there was one in particular that needed to be lasoo'd and reined in. The situation had focused his thinking and one could never be too careful. Reggie prided himself on his neatness and thoroughness, on making and cultivating the right contacts - legitimate businesses would call it networking. It was an approach that had given him a successful life with no interference from Plod. And now he was comfortably retired, surrounded by luxury. The latest job had been a rare lapse of judgement, but he was sure that the situation wasn't irredeemable with some proper planning. At least Michael could still be useful, and being dimmer, was more compliant.

Emma, on the other hand, was a less solvable problem. He'd let her fully wake up on Friday and she hadn't stopped crying, or puking, since. Throughout the day, she had periodically sobbed herself to sleep and woken again, interspersed with spasms of vomit, which at least was moving on to bile. The bed had been changed three times; that had made her cry, too, just being picked up and sat in a chair for fucks sake. At one point, he had been tempted to let her sleep in her own muck, but Reggie had always been a stickler for hygiene, wasn't about to let an eleven-year-old slip of a girl break his habits of a lifetime. That night, he carried her to the shower – more strain on his back – and scrubbed and washed the vomit out of her hair. He found some old baby shampoo in the bathroom cabinet, left over from when there were often children in the house. They all cried for the first few days, making their eyes more sore never helped - it wasn't a good look for the clients.

He'd been thinking about it constantly, but still had no idea about what to do with Emma. The ribbon that he'd tied in her hair was ruined, stained with bile, which had irritated him intensely and got his tic going, but he'd talked himself down, told himself that he had dozens more. It was a shame. The navy velvet had been *her* ribbon. He always knew right off, in his gut, almost in his soul, which ribbon was right for which little girl, after that, after his initial assessment, any other ribbon could never be quite right. And now that he was old, with prostate trouble, to be in even with a chance, he needed it to be *just* right, *just* perfect.

Yeah, getting old was a sod.

Chapter 13

Mack didn't want to call Kennedy. Every cell of common sense that he possessed was shouting that he needed to update the DI, that sooner or later, probably sooner, he would hear about Mack's little venture into autonomy and that it would be better heard from the miscreant himself. On the other hand, he knew that he would almost certainly be in for the biggest bollocking in the history of Essex police and possibly on his way to a disciplinary hearing. By Brown's own jovial admission, he was no longer on the job and even to Mack's apparently less than sharp thinking, Brown was an idiot. Why he didn't take his own advice, had a perennial tendency to do the opposite of sensible, was a constant mystery to Mack.

He was tempted to do some more follow up for himself, just to see if he could establish a definite link and then go to Kennedy. He went through the facts: decades old attempted abductions had a link to Poplar; a child with the surname of Knatchbull had narrowly escaped being abducted in the same manner; a Pete Knatchbull used to live in Poplar and was known to Social Services; it wasn't beyond the realm of possibility that the Pete Knatchbull known to Social Services was the same person as Keeley's dad, who had been back to Poplar some years previously to punch a cousin. When he thought about it, Mack knew that he wouldn't be able to do too much more investigating without Kennedy's authority or knowledge. At least it was a weekend, any lecture wouldn't be in front of the whole station. He came to a decision. Take it like a man, Mack. He picked up the phone.

Kennedy astonished him: maybe he had had a drink, maybe he had just had sex, maybe he had decided to retire; in any event, he listened calmly to everything and asked Mack to type up the report at home, print off two copies, then delete it and meet him in the morning. Told him to rest, but be on standby.

Mack texted Cooper: he was free, would be at the pub in an hour.

The Horse and Jockey was within walking distance and was Saturday-night-loud. He found Cooper at the bar about to order a couple of pints, but Mack was in a precarious position with Kennedy and was conscious that he might still be called upon - he stuck to orange juice and crisps. The pretty brunette was at a table with some friends. Mack grinned at her. She raised her eyebrows and smiled back. He and Cooper went outside away from the bustle. Mack filled Cooper in about his day, but stopped short at revealing his stupidity in visiting Brown - he needed to tell Kennedy first: maybe he was learning.

Mack pointed out the pretty brunette, but Cooper wasn't his usual lively self. He was quiet, drank his pint quickly and got up for a second after ten minutes.

"Sorry, Mack, I'm not up for much tonight, bad day."

"Why, what's happened?"

"I went home to see my parents. Did you know my older brother is disabled?"

"No, no I didn't. Disabled how?"

"Brain injury, happened when he was a kid. It's just upsetting, that's all. My parents provide his care, it exhausts them."

"Don't they get any help?"

"He is physically able, but he's not well enough to work. When it first happened, he used to get really aggressive, have terrible mood swings. But he's a lot better now. He has permanent memory problems, though, and gets agitated very quickly; some days they're walking on eggshells. It's exhausting to be around." He took a swig from his glass.

"And you're thinking who's gonna look after him when they've gone?"

Cooper looked at him. "Do you think that makes me selfish, a bad person?"

"No, I think it makes you normal, Dave. You're young, you don't want to look forward to a future of being a carer. I wouldn't, no-one would. It's understandable. Will the state put something in place for him? What about sheltered housing? A residential complex of some kind?"

Cooper sighed and nodded, "Yeah, I'm gonna have to raise it with my parents. They don't want to think about it, but I suppose they'll have to. It's not going to go away, is it?"

"No, course not. The sooner they get plans in place, the less they'll worry." He nodded at Cooper over his orange juice. "And the less you'll worry." There was a tap on Mack's shoulder. He turned around. The pretty brunette was there. "Oh, hi."

"Hi, I was wondering if you wanted to buy me another drink." She waggled the base of her empty glass at him.

Cooper grinned. "Don't mind me, Mack, I need an early night. There's bound to be some more blue-arsed fly running when we're back on shift." He drained his glass and left it on a table, grinning at Mack over his shoulder as he left.

Mack turned to her, "Sure," his endorphin levels sped up. "What'll you have?"

"Whatever you're having will be fine."

"Well, I'm on orange juice, so I'm guessing you won't want that." He eyed her glass, "Dry white?"

"Great, thanks."

He fell into bed after midnight. Alone. The girl, Susie, had been more than willing. But he was a copper, the MeToo movement had made its point, and Susie had had far too many. He left her number on his side table.

At ten a.m. on Sunday morning, Mack was having coffee in Kennedy's kitchen. He had taken the two copies of his report. He didn't completely escape. "Mack, you acted out of line yesterday. For a start, you didn't keep me informed; secondly, you went to see a member of the public, James Brown, and gave him sensitive information about a live case. He might be an ex-copper, but 'ex' is the operative word and there are other reasons, which I'll explain in a minute." Kennedy paused, took a deep breath. "However, I do think you could be on to something with this Poplar link, at the very least it's worth further exploration. And goodness knows, we need to go down every route we can to try to find Emma." He took a sip of coffee. "What I'm going to tell you, Mack, is strictly off the record. What I'm going to ask you to do is strictly off the record. And before you say anything, this is why." Kennedy's face spasmed, like someone with no choice about to dive into a sewer.

"James Brown is a nasty piece of work. There were rumours aplenty about him when he was still serving. Rumours that he was in with certain criminals, had a finger in a lot of pies. I nearly caught him, had evidence, a lot, but couldn't get it to go anywhere: needless to say, there's bad feeling, hatred really, between us. After that, he seemed to calm things down, whether that was because he became ultra-careful, or whether it was because he shut down his activities, I don't know. That's why this is off the record, because that bastard would try to sue me for slander if he knew that I was saying this and I wouldn't put other actions past him, either. That's what we're up against."

"What about the second officer in those cases, Gov?" Mack got out his notebook, "A DS Scott?"

"Scott's a good man. You can trust him. He tried to catch out Brown, too, and he helped me. He retired several years ago, got cancer. I've got his contact details. We catch up occasionally. I want you to go to see him. Talk to him about those attempted abductions, get his take, his thoughts. Then get some information about that Poplar address, go and take a look."

"Brown said that the Poplar house isn't there anymore."

"Did he," Kennedy narrowed his eyes, "Well, don't take that man's word for anything. Check it out yourself." The DI left the room briefly and came back with a battered, leather-bound address book. He copied out some details onto a sheet of paper and handed it to Mack. "Call Scott, see him as soon as he can manage it."

Mack stood up.

"Mack,"

"Gov?"

"Don't record any of this on the work computer, not 'til we know what we're dealing with. And don't store Scott's number on your phone. I know I probably sound neurotic, but I never knew how far Brown's tentacles had spread. I'm trusting you with this. Ok?"

As Mack was leaving, Kennedy called him back. "By the way, Mr. Knatchbull's called in. Spoke to control last night. Said you've been harassing him."

"Harrassing him? How?"

"He said there's been a car that's been parked up behind a field that his balcony looks out onto. Reckons you've been watching him."

"Me? Of course I haven't. Why would I?"

"I'm sure you haven't been, but obviously I needed to let you know. It's probably nothing."

Bloody hell, thought Mack, where would he get the time to be covertly spying on Knatchbull: in any event, given the man's temperament, there were probably a number of people whom he regularly pissed off.

Scott readily agreed to meet with Mack; he was better in the mornings, asked if Mack could get there for eight a.m.

Peter Scott lived in a one-storey, modern retirement complex in a quiet road in Benfleet, a small town a few miles to the east of Laindon. His flat was opposite a large, enclosed park, where dog-walkers were conscientiously clearing up after their pets' early-morning ablutions, depositing neatly tied green bags into red metal bins. Mack watched them while he waited for the bell to be answered; really, he thought, why would you. The door was opened by a pretty, dark-haired, young nurse, pretty enough for a second look. She smiled and let him in as she was leaving.

Scott called him into the sitting-room, where he sat surrounded by the apparatus of the sick: pill bottles were lined up on the table next to him and a yellow sharps bin stood in one corner. The bald head and lashless eyes immediately pointed to cancer. Scott saw him looking. "Don't worry, Sergeant, I'm not about to keel over. I had oesophageal cancer four years ago, that's why I retired; bastard's come back with a vengeance. But I've some time yet." He nodded at the chair opposite him. "Make yourself comfy, lad. Now, you're working for Tim Kennedy, aren't you? What can I do for you?"

Mack outlined the events of the past twenty-four hours: Mrs. Owl's attendance at the police station; her hypothesis about the link between the previous abductions and the current missing girls; what Brown had said, gave Reginald Bull's name and asked whether Scott could help.

"Tim Kennedy was always right about James Brown - he was on the make. He was a crook. I helped Tim in trying to gather the evidence against him, but it went belly-up and backfired massively. I expect he's told you?"

"He did mention it, Sir, yes."

"A lot of people guessed about Brown. But as far as I'm aware, Tim and I were the only ones who tried to do anything about it." Scott harrumphed deep in his throat. "I'm not proud to say that I got caught up with him, Brown, when I was younger, Sergeant. Occasionally, Brown offered the chance of a bit of extra dosh to other, select, officers: stupid officers, gullible ones, like me," he blinked. "It was never enough to make you rich, but it wasn't bad for a sideline. There was a small group of us, recruits just a few years below him. He was a sergeant in CID – fraud squad - and had a bit of swagger, access to stuff, contraband is the right word, I suppose. We were young and naive and looked up to him, wanted to be like that, get on quickly. We fell for it. After that he had us. Nothing serious, just a few illegal fags to sell to mates and bottles of booze, but it was enough. We realised soon enough that he intended to use it as blackmail for whenever it suited. We all talked for hours, weeks, about going to a superior, but we would have been sacked as well as him and by then we'd found out, the hard way, what we were up against. It wasn't just our jobs at stake. He was in with some nasty bastards: gunrunners – IRA that type of thing and," he paused, "More relevant as far as you're concerned – paedophiles."

Scott stopped, his face spasming. He leant back in his chair, heaving rasping breaths and indicated to the pills, "Get me some, yellow container, two." Mack grabbed the bottle and the glass of water, knocked out two pills and dropped them into Scott's hand. He waited whilst Scott swallowed.

"Are you ok, to carry on, Sir? I can come back later."

"No, no, this is important. And it might help you to find that missing girl. Brown covered for all of them." His breathing became more regular.

"The paedophiles?"

"Yes, all the crooks. He manipulated records using those of us in hoc to him if need be. I never went that far, resisted it point blank, but some of the others were too scared to refuse, cos he had them over a barrel. He was a villain through and through, hidden in plain sight. I've never found out how he got into it. Frankly, I don't care. Murderers, bank robbers, kiddy-fiddlers – he was in with the lot of them."

Mack watched the ashen face and laboured breathing of the man in front of him. He was surprised that his DI had been so controlled when Mack confessed: they were all in way above their pay grade.

"But, Sir, surely if there was a group of you, you could have got some help, gone to the chief super? Someone?"

"Mack, these were – are – men who would think nothing of threatening, hurting, killing your family; if you didn't have kids, it would be your old mum, or anyone you love. They are callous, murdering, ruthless bastards, people who think nothing of using young children for their own sexual needs. I think it's possible they murder them when they're done. I know that sounds excessive, over the top, sensationalist even and I have no proof. But I'm just saying. There was nowhere to go with it – I didn't know if other police officers were involved – for all I knew, the superintendent could have been part of it. See those photos over, there, Mack?" Scott nodded at the sideboard. There were photos of a wedding day, a dog, a baby. "That's my brother and his wife and their little family. Know what happened to them?" Scott's mouth twisted. "Car crash. They all died – even the bloody dog. Brakes failed – no-one ever got to the bottom of it - car had just been serviced. They were on their way up to Essex from Somerset to visit me. It was just after Tim Kennedy had tried to submit all his evidence, tried to get someone to listen. Brown knew that

I'd helped him. That was a message I was meant to hear loud and clear. It nearly killed my poor old mum at the time. Now she's dead and I'm on my way. There's none of us left."

Scott rubbed a roughened hand over where his eyebrows used to be, dry white flakes of skin drifted downwards and settled on his chest. He stood up and shuffled into the kitchen, Mack heard the rattle of more pills and the clink of crockery. Scott returned with a pot of tea and two cups.

"Now listen, I haven't got much time before these pills kick in - they send me to sleep. I need to tell you this. If you're going to use me for evidence and see if it can help to find this girl, you need to get a move on. You've got the Upminster file and you need to get the Barking one, quickly. I bet James told you about the house we visited after the first attempted abduction, didn't he? Said there was a young widow with a child? He will tell as much as is on the file, makes it credible."

"He said that the house was knocked down, to make way for flats."

"He's lying. It's still there. That house belonged to a family. An old East End family, surname of Bull."

"The same name as that suspect? But wasn't that name Ball?"

"No. Bull. That's Brown deflecting. But the woman living there when we visited wasn't called that. I can't remember what her name was, but I must've written it down in my notes. The Bull family had owned the house for years, since the 1800s, maybe since it was built, but sold it to the council after the war, needed the money, I suppose. They wangled it so that one of their members got a lifelong tenancy. It is true that there was a married couple and a child was there and that the husband died of cancer and I suppose it is possible that Bull wasn't living there and was just using that address for the car to avoid registering his address anywhere. What James Brown will never tell you, Mack - and this is information that he would guard by any means possible – remember that, remember what you're dealing with, never let down your guard - is that the house was used for child abuse, rape, exploitation. Call it what you like. Kiddies

81

were there and were used by men for their sexual needs: rich men; powerful men; politicians, surgeons, bankers – all of those bastards who had the power to ruin lives if they were found out. You know it went on – now it's in the news everywhere. Back then, no-one knew. If they did, they kept their mouths shut and looked the other way, for the sake of their families and their livelihoods."

"How do you know all this, how did you find out?"

"The young woman I met with Brown, on that day we went round to that house, chasing up the DVLA lead regarding Bull – I believe that she was, I suppose for the want of a better term, a breeding female. I have no doubt she was abused herself and that any kids were at risk of being used for the same purpose. I think she was impregnated time and time again – like a bitch on a puppy farm."

"What, she told you all this? That must've been risky for her?"

"I honestly think I just got lucky. No, she didn't tell me all of that, she told me bits, it's what I surmised based on what she said. I'd been watching the house for some time – all my off-duty hours – and there was this one time when I was pretty certain that she was all alone. I knew the patterns of the visitors, there was no-one due for a couple of hours. I went to the front door. She recognised me from my previous visit. She told me to go round to the back alley and she talked to me through the back garden wall - there was a gap in the brickwork."

"But what made you start watching the house in the first place?"

"When we first visited, I was struck by how unhappy she looked. Unhappy, really sad, and thin and pale. That's it. Made me suspicious." He smiled. "Tim Kennedy would call it having a copper's nose."

"And what happened after you'd managed to speak to her?"

"The next week, my family died. I'd written down everything, was hoping to submit it on the back of Tim Kennedy's evidence, get the woman and child out, but Tim had already been threatened with suspension; they treated him very badly, it made him ill. So, given that and what happened with my family, I'm ashamed to say, Mack, that I left it." He fumbled into his dressing-gown pocket, pulled out a handkerchief and wiped his eyes. "I honestly didn't know what else to do. If the police won't help you, who is there? It's haunted me ever since."

"Do you think Brown was responsible for those attempted abductions in the eighties?"

"Brown? Nah, he wouldn't have put himself at risk like that. And too fat - you've seen him!"

"I thought maybe he'd gone to fat after retiring."

"He's got bigger, but he was always a lazy bastard, liked the good life. The victims described the attacker as slender, no way it was Brown. No. Those attempts were this Reginald Bull, I'm sure of it. But Brown was in on it, make no mistake."

"What, you think Brown covered for Bull, fiddled the records?"

"I do. And that Bull never got fingered only because Brown and his mates helped him. I also think that they helped him probably set up a more sophisticated operation, pooled their resources. That young woman talked about someone who appeared to be the hub of the kiddie operation and it wasn't Brown. But she wouldn't confirm or deny anything about this Bull fella. Too scared. And I bet that this latest abduction and murder is Bull. I bet he's still alive, bastards like that live forever. You know what they say about psychopaths."

Scott sucked in air and then wheezed out and into a coughing fit that racked his throat for several seconds. "I'm ok, but I need a rest." He closed his eyes. "I get reflux cos they took out my oesophagus – nothing to keep the stomach acid down. It spills upwards, especially when I'm stressed." He paused and wiped his mouth with a handkerchief that came aware spattered with blood. "I've thought about this every day for years, it's tortured me, wondering what to do, what I could have done, hoping that Brown and his vile friends would be uncovered in this latest spate of disclosures that hit the news. I'm not a good man, Mack. I'm a coward; I knew about all that suffering and did nothing -

probably on my way to hell."

"Here," he reached for a pencil and pad that were next to the pills and wrote in spidery scrawl. "This is the address of the house. It's burnt into my memory. Go and update Kennedy. I've got evidence, but I need to rest now. Come back this afternoon, about four p.m., I'll need an afternoon nap - these pills hammer me - bring Kennedy. In the meantime, you need to get that file from Barking, in case it goes wandering, not saying it will, got no evidence to suggest that." A final exhortation, "And go and find that house. I've got the evidence that will get you a search warrant."

Chapter 14

Clarence wasn't surprised to get a call asking for help with Keeley. She was surprised that it was Keeley herself who phoned.

A little voice had whispered down the phone. "Hello, is that Clarence?"

She'd known instantly that it was a child, but couldn't place the name. "This is Keeley, I got your number from the card."

"Hello, Keeley, it's nice to hear from you. Is everything ok?"

"Yes, but I want to talk to you. Can I come and see you? You're the only one who understands properly."

"Ok, Keeley. Where are you now?"

"At home."

"And is your mum there?"

"Yes, but she doesn't think it will help me to talk to you,"

"Ok, Keeley, don't worry. Can you put your mum on the phone, please." She heard the phone pass hands and the gruff voice of Mrs. Knatchbull took over.

"This is Keeley's mum," she said unnecessarily, "It's true what she said, I don't think it will help her, to keep going over everything again. Better just to get on with things. I've made it clear before. I've no time for airy-fairy Social Working do-gooding."

"And I can see why you'd think that, that sometimes it's better to just carry on, Mrs. Knatchbull and in many circumstances that would be a good way of managing. How has Keeley been lately?"

"She's fine,"

"How's her sleeping?"

"Well, obviously, not like she used to, she's had a couple of disturbed nights, but I'd expect that. She'll get back to normal."

"Ok, any bedwetting?"

"No."

"And what about her eating? How has that been since Wednesday?"

"She's fine, I'm telling you." But Keeley wasn't fine; Clarence could hear her crying in the background, and a protesting voice. "I did wet the bed, mum, you know I did, twice."

"Mrs. Knatchbull, if Keeley wants to get some help with how she's feeling, don't you think she's old enough to have a say in whether that happens? She's a lovely girl, very bright. I think she would really like to spend a bit of time talking over things. What happened to her was truly terrible. It would be very surprising if she didn't need some help. Really." There was a pause before a reluctant reply.

"Oh, all right. But don't let on to her dad, he'll go mad. You can't see her here, I'll bring her to you. When?"

"How about tomorrow morning? You can bring her and stay, or go and have a cup of tea and come back and collect her. Would ten a.m. suit you?"

"Yeah, fine. Where?"

"The social services building. The address is on the card I left you. Just go to Reception and ask for me and I'll come straight away. It's not far from the Mead estate, about a ten minute walk." There wasn't a good-bye, the phone was abruptly disconnected.

Clarence went to find her supervisor and brought him up to speed. "Thing is, Warren, I'm not happy seeing that child without a witness. The parents are extremely hostile; Keeley is a very sweet, brave little girl, but I wouldn't trust the family to not manipulate her, or just fabricate allegations against me."

"Are the Knatchbulls implicated in the murder, or the missing child investigation?"

"Not as far as I know, but come on, it's a heavy case, nasty, all over the news, the whole country is talking about it. I'm really happy to see Keeley for supportive counselling, but there will have to be someone sitting in with me, just in the corner, unobtrusive. Keeley won't mind."

He signed. "I make you right. Probably be better it being another woman though, rather than me. Don't you think?"

Clarence nodded. "I do. How about the student, Donna? It'll be good experience for her and she knows when to stay quiet."

"Good idea, I'll speak to her practice teacher."

Clarence returned to her office and sat down to check her emails. There was a response from the records clerk regarding the request for the Knatchbull file: sorry, Clarence, the paper file is empty. It's bizarre. I can only assume that the sheets fell out somewhere in the exercise of putting everything on the database. There is an address on the front cover, though. I don't want to send that through the internal mail, as it's all we've got left! If you come to the office, I'll give it to you. You'll have to sign for it, though.

Chapter 15

His DI was surprised by Mack and his tenacity; he'd found a link that had bypassed everyone else on the investigation. Mack usually irritated the hell out of Kennedy, who thought him indecisive, lacking in motivation and more-than-occasionally stupid: if it had been up to Kennedy, the man wouldn't have been given the promotion. But he had to admit that Mack's work on the case had taken an unexpected turn that could be useful. And they needed something, because they had no other leads. He just wished it didn't have to involve a ghost from the not-so-distant-past.

Tim Kennedy didn't want to jump back into the quagmire that was James Brown's suspected criminal activity. The last time had nearly lost him his health, his marriage and his job - in that order. His marriage and job had survived, but it had left a legacy of stress that never completely disappeared and had to be managed with a military level of discipline. It wasn't helped by cuts to the budget and the consequent lack of PCs and senior detectives, all of which meant that the pressure on middle management was ever-increasing. He should have had a DCI managing the murder and missing child investigation, instead it was down to him, reporting directly to the Superintendent.

Kennedy had found out by dogged determination that James Brown was selling drugs. Kennedy had been a relatively new DC booking in a suspect for intent to supply at an East London nick. James Brown, a sergeant then, had wandered into custody and stood in the corner, nonchalantly watching. When Kennedy had returned a couple of hours later, ready to go for interview, his prisoner had had a bloodied nose and a black eye, been terrified and confessed straight off in interview - had even refused a brief. Kennedy was nonplussed; earlier, the bloke had been a loud-mouthed, cocky git, who denied everything.

None of the custody staff could offer an explanation for the prisoner's injuries and the custody sergeant had been in the gents with an upset stomach. No-one was prepared to take it further. Kennedy had raised it with his sergeant and was advised to chalk it up to experience and to keep a better eye on his prisoners in the future. When Kennedy had pointed out that he shouldn't need to keep an eye on prisoners in a police station, that there shouldn't be a safer place than a police cell, the sergeant laughed and said that Kennedy had a lot to learn.

Kennedy may have been a newish DC, but he wasn't a particularly young one: there and then, he notched up James Brown as worth keeping an eye on. Six months later, he watched as Brown sold a tidy quantity of white powder nestling nicely in a clear pouch to a scrawny young man in the toilet of a local pub. He had nicked them both. And then he'd called for back-up.

The young man had been charged with possession for personal use, by which Kennedy judged he must have had the constitution of three large men combined. James Brown had been given a slap on the wrist. The DCI who heard Kennedy's formal complaint told him how it went: police didn't dob in other police, and they definitely didn't arrest them; for sure, Brown had made a mistake, he was sorry, he had been read the riot act, he wouldn't do it again. Kennedy had to drop it.

But like the proverbial dog, Kennedy didn't drop it. He waited until he passed his sergeant exams and got a posting to Barking, where Brown had landed a cushty inspector role. Had he been asked at the time, Kennedy couldn't have said why he wanted to catch Brown, apart from the fact that he hated wankers who took advantage of their station in life and because he'd already had one career in which he had been obliged to look the other way - that had been for the greater good. Letting James Brown off the hook wasn't for the greater good, it was only for the good of James Brown and all the brown-nosing officers whom Kennedy was certain were living off Brown's trail of bullshit. And that really got his goat. Had she been asked, Kennedy knew that Clarence would say that he had displacement activity going on: that he had being unable to do anything about the bastards in his last career, so was doing something about them in this one - he freely admitted it. But to Kennedy's way of thinking, that didn't make it wrong, just gave it a helpful label.

Kennedy had watched James Brown for two years, amassed a dossier that would have given the Iraqi one a run for its money. And then he had submitted it.

And then his life had been blown apart. He was threatened with prosecution for unlawful surveillance, with disciplinary action for undertaking personal activity in work time and with libel for slander.

The anger had eaten him up for weeks, months even, verging on obsession. His wife had threatened to leave. In the end, he was signed off sick with stress.

In his more morose moments, he imagined the conversations that would have taken place about him:

Met corrupt senior officer: "Listen, mate, we've got an officer who needs a transfer. Good bloke, bit too keen, if you get my drift. Got any sergeant or inspector posts?"

Essex corrupt senior officer: "What, DI? Is he any good?"

"Oh, yeah, too good. Needs to be put where the sun isn't so bright."

"Ok, will he behave over here? Got a post going at Chelmsford. He can meet the transfer protocol."

And so, to his eternal shame, Kennedy returned to work after six months on an inspector's salary and to a different Service and a different police station.

So, yeah, the prospect of dipping his finger into James Brown's pies wasn't a pleasing one. But there was one difference, Kennedy reminded himself: now, Brown was ex-job. The old senior management were all retired, or even dead. There was a new chief superintendent, Kennedy was dealing with a high-profile case, his manager was prepared to throw all the last dredges of his sorry budget at the search for this girl and the solving of Samantha's murder. If James Brown was caught up in any of this latest case, even by one whisker on his good-living, smugly-retired, double-chinny-chin-chin, Kennedy would have him. This time for good.

Chapter 16

Mack sped over to Barking police station as soon as he had left Scott's, phoning Kennedy on the way and arranging to meet later. The station's records officer hadn't been able to see him initially, leaving Mack twitchy and bored. The machine coffee was as bad as at any other nick. Eventually, the officer dealt with Mack's request, only to tell him that he couldn't find the file, but was sure it was there somewhere, because he didn't recall it having been signed out. He took Mack's details and said he would be in touch.

The trip to Poplar had been more productive and Mack found the address easily enough. A row of old, London-brick, terraced townhouses sat aged and grand opposite a large, open park that was studded with ancient poplar and beech trees; according to Wikipedia, the borough's last namesake black poplar tree had disappeared in the 1980s. The area was surrounded by looming, grey tower blocks and was an oasis of elegance in a sea of concrete. Some of the houses in the little terrace had been treated with respectful and loving care: bottle-green front doors, new slate roofs, double-glazed sash windows. The house that Mack was interested in was still awaiting its return to glory.

The front door to number nine Poplar Square was an old wooden one that had cracked across the lock. Its blue paint was bubbled with age and weather. Brown had at least been telling the truth about one thing: the stained glass was still in place, remarkably uncracked; so were the original sash windows, but they were peeling gloss and, Mack guessed, leaking energy out and the rain in, the front garden was a dumping-ground of mud. It wasn't until after he had left that he realised none of the other houses in the terrace had a front garden; they all had steps down to basements.

The door was ajar. It creaked open and Mack wandered in onto a grey flagged floor and a heavy miasma of fry-ups tinged with an upper note of coffee and a bottom one of cigarettes. He found a young man in the front room lounging on an ikea sofa and watching football on a flat-screen television. Mack showed his warrant card and was told that the property was owned by a charity and was being used as accommodation for recovering drug and alcohol addicts. Mack took the charity details. "Ok, if I take a look around, mate? Just to get a feel of the place?"

"Sorry, probably not. The upstairs rooms are people's bedrooms. What's it all about, anyway? Why're you interested?"

"Oh, nothing to worry about. Just part of an ongoing enquiry. No probs, I'll contact the charity. Cheers."

As arranged, Mack met the Kennedy outside Scott's home at three thirty p.m. to update him before their visit. Kennedy had found a parking space directly in front of Scott's flat. Mack got into the passenger seat. It was as he was briefing Kennedy that his eye caught a movement in Scott's living-room window and he saw a figure outlined against the net curtains. He knew instantly it wasn't Scott, who had a shuffling movement; the nurse wasn't due back until seven p.m. – Mack had glanced at the visiting schedule pinned to Scott's wall - purely for professional reasons. He nodded over to the building. "Guv, there's someone in there."

"What?" Kennedy looked over to the window, leant down into the passenger footwell, grabbed his baton, jumped out of the car and sprinted over to Scott's front door. It was open. Mack followed Kennedy into the flat and closed the door silently behind him. In front of them was the bedroom. There were noises coming from the living room on their right; the door was open, sofa cushions littered the floor and an overturned cup dripped tea down the leg of a sidetable. A thin, tall man, his back to them, hair dark and curly, rifled through the drawers and cupboards of a sideboard. Kennedy cleared his throat.

The intruder spun round, pulling a knife from his jacket pocket. Mack reckoned it to be a four-inch blade, its tip and edge stained red.

"Take it easy," said Kennedy. "We're police officers. Drop your weapon. You can't get away - give it up and we can talk about what's been going on." More firmly, "Drop the knife." Behind his back, Mack extended the baton, acutely conscious that neither he nor Kennedy was wearing body-armour.

The intruder settled into his stance, knees slightly bent, body weight distributed, blue eyes focused.

The kitchen was behind the living room, the rooms linked via an opened door. An uneven patch of pale grey carpet was slowly absorbing wet blood. Mack and Kennedy watched Scott pigeon-step into the doorway from the side of the kitchen. He had a small saucepan in his hand. He half-raised it, aiming towards the dark curly head in front of him. The saucepan hit the doorframe, clanking on impact. The intruder twisted round towards the kitchen and Mack went after him, coshing him hard on his right arm and then behind his knees in two quick, successive moves. The knife clattered to the floor and Kennedy kicked it towards the window. Within seconds Mack had his knee in the small of the assailant's back and he was handcuffed. Mack turned him over, hauled him upright and then pushed him down to sit him against the wall next to the sideboard. Kennedy had run over to Scott, who was on his knees on the kitchen floor, clutching his flank.

Kennedy lifted the injured man and carried him to the sofa. He laid him down gently, keeping a hand under his head and stretching to retrieve one of the cushions from the floor. Mack ran into the kitchen, rifling, looking for tea-towels, anything, to stem the bleeding. He found some clean ones in a drawer and rushed them back to Kennedy, who pressed them over Scott's wound.

"Mack, call an ambulance," Mack dug into his pockets for his mobile. A hoarse whisper from the sofa stopped him. "No, no, it's too late. Look in the oven. Hurry."

Kennedy pressed harder on the wound, "You need an ambulance, mate. The rest can wait."

"No, no it can't, Tim. Please, please let me do this."

On the top shelf of the oven was a thick, buff, envelope file. Mack held it up, "This?"

"You need it. It will tell you everything. That's what he was after," Scott lifted a thin hand vaguely towards the direction of the intruder. "I'm sorry. I'm so sorry, so much suffering. I could have done more, should have stopped it." He coughed suddenly, spewing foamy blood that spilt down his chin and trickled onto Kennedy's arm. Scott's eyes locked onto Kennedy's. He heaved in air. "Pray for me, old friend." Mack watched as the weave of Kennedy's white shirt cuff was encircled by a jagged band of red.

Closing the dead man's eyes, Kennedy softly laid him flat on the sofa. He turned to Mack.

"Bag up the knife, Mack." Nodding at their prisoner, "Put that piece of filth in the back of my car."

"Gov, shouldn't I call it in? We need forensics. And the paramedics still might be able to do something for him."

"What? What the bloody hell are they going to do for a man who has advanced cancer and who's just been stabbed and bled to death in front of us, eh? Eh, Sergeant? Just do as I say."

"But, Sir..."

"Read my lips. Put that filth in the back of my car. You're not calling in anything. Find a number. Cancel the nurse. Lock up this place."

Mack's stomach went straight into shutdown, bypassed the shrivelling stage. He'd never known the his manager to flout protocol, not even protocol, the *law*. He gave serious consideration as to whether Kennedy had lost the plot and calling the station, or calling an ambulance anyway, or whether to just disobey the instruction. All of these thoughts and more raced through his mind, but behind them all, nudging and telling him to listen, was the instinct that he could more likely than not trust Kennedy and that, in any event, refusing to carry out the instruction of a senior officer was tantamount to career suicide.

So he bagged up the knife and went to put it in the glove compartment of his car, came back, hauled their prisoner off the floor and searched him, finding a retractable blade down one sock, and a cheap mobile phone in his jeans pocket, then walked him out to Kennedy's vehicle, put him into the back and secured the seatbelt. All the while he was remembering how Scott's arm-chair had been positioned for a good window view, fervently hoping that it wasn't a pattern re-created across all the flats, if so, his antics would almost certainly be being witnessed by several, nosey old people.

Kennedy was at the flat's front door, the folder under his arm. He'd found the keys and was deadlocking the property. "Right," he said, pocketing the keys, "Get in your car and follow me. And I mean this, Mack: do not answer your phone or make any calls. Are we clear?"

"Gov," Mack cleared his throat, got in his car and did as he was told.

Chapter 17

Mack followed Kennedy out of Benfleet and onto the main arterial road. They turned onto the coast road and followed the camber through the seaside resort of Southend and then headed inland again, passing through several small villages into an increasingly rural area. Forty-five minutes later, Kennedy turned into a deserted lane, driving slowly until he reached a small, green, metal booth on the left-hand side. Mack pulled over a few yards behind. Kennedy got out of the car and spoke to someone in the booth, showed his police warrant card and then pulled a second card out of his wallet. He walked back to Mack.

"Leave your car here, Mack, get into mine."

Mack's stomach was rhythmically spasming; soon he would need to find a toilet. His gut had never been reliable and was becoming steadily unmanageable. To label it an inconvenience would be an under-statement. He stayed still for a few moments, trying to work out how to get everything under control. "Guv, can you just tell me where we are? What is this place? We've got a murder suspect in our custody. We haven't even arrested him."

Kennedy hadn't calmed down. "Listen. I'm your superior officer and I expect you to do as I say. You know what we're up against. We just need to be someone completely away and safe. This is a military base."

"What do you mean, a military base? I've never heard of a military base out here."

"That's the point!" snapped Kennedy. " We'll get complete privacy here, even from the police. Get out of your vehicle and get into mine."

"Sir, I don't like this."

"Do it!" Mack did as he was told. Again.

Kennedy drove them through the checkpoint and over a bridge, crossing water and moving onto an island. The area was wild with rabbits, scrub and meandering creeks for one or two miles until buildings began to appear on the roadside: a church, some houses, and eventually a pub. Kennedy pulled into the deserted car park.

"Come on, leave him in the car."

"Shouldn't we unlock his cuffs? He's been in that position for a long time."

His DI looked at Mack as though he'd never seen him before. "Why are you worried? He's just murdered a man, an ex-copper, who was already dying of cancer. You gone soft, Mack?" Mack thought that, compared to Kennedy, he'd probably always been soft.

"I just think that we don't want to set ourselves up for a fall," understatement of the bloody year, "Sir. He might have done all that, but he still has rights."

"All right, well cuff him at the front, if you're worried." Their prisoner was silent throughout. Kennedy addressed him. "Don't even think about trying to get away. It really won't be worth it. We'll bring you some water in a minute."

Mack followed Kennedy into the empty pub. It was an old place, uncleansed by the smoking ban. Tar hung heavy in the air, mingled with the earthiness of wood and a tang of stale beer. High up, sunray filtered through wavey glass windows, catching up swirling grey dust on its journey downwards. Underfoot, wide oak boards were scattered with wood shavings. A tall, lithe man was re-stocking glasses behind a curved, mahogany bar, he glanced up at their entry.

"Tim Kennedy, if I'm a day," the barman extended his hand. "Long time, no see. What brings you to this God-forsaken place?" He glanced briefly at Mack.

Kennedy pulled the other man to one side and stayed talking for some minutes. He came back with a half pint for Mack and a bottle of water with a straw. "Take the water to the car, Mack. He can drink it with his cuffs on if he uses the straw. Then come back here, we need to go through Scott's file."

Kennedy was waiting at the table with his own half-pint when Mack returned. The file contents were spread in front of him. "Right, Mack, whatever this file tells us, we need to have in mind that our first priority has to be finding Emma. The rest can be dealt with later. If this doesn't give us a lead, we need to put it aside and come back to it once the current investigation is closed. Do you agree."

"Yes, Guv."

"Don't worry, Arse-Ache won't be left to rot in the car. There are cells here, he'll be all right, this used to be the Guard-House – accommodation's more than good enough for the likes of him. In fact, give me the keys to the cuffs, the barman will fetch him and sort him out with some food."

"What about Scott, Sir, we can't just leave him there; there'll be a smell soon." He thought back to the beach. "Especially in this heat. Someone will call the police."

"Scott'll be all right for one night, Mack. Stop fussing. All that's going on is that we need complete privacy to find out who's involved in this whole sorry mess. We don't know who's implicated, do we? Someone knew that you'd gone to Scott's today. Think about that. Who did you tell apart from me?"

"No-one, honestly." He paused. A nasty thought occurred to him. "If James Brown is dodgy, he might've guessed and told someone, might still be touch with this Bull fella, if Scott was right..." All of which would mean the whole sorry, murdering mess was because Mack had got it wrong. Again.

"Well, that's not outside the bounds of possibility, is it? So, it was either that, or you were being watched, or Scott was."

"And if James Brown definitely has contact with Bull and alerted him, Bull knew that Scott knew and wanted him dealt with."

"Exactly. Once we've worked out who knows what and gathered as much as we can from this info, we'll go to whoever the most appropriate senior officer is. That's why we're here; that's only why we're here. Nothing sinister is going to happen. Nothing's going to happen to our prisoner. Don't ask me about this location or my links; I can't tell you, never will. I can only ask that you trust me, Mack and keep the knowledge of this place to yourself." Kennedy took a gulp of beer. "I need to be clear that you're on board - if you're going to be an old woman about it all, you can go home now. Do we have an agreement?"

"Sure." Tired, on edge, feeling guilty and embarrassed at being spoken to like he was a child, Mack handed over the keys and Kennedy passed them to the barman.

Mack and Kennedy worked on the file into the night, interrupted only by a good meal of pie and chips. A few customers had arrived throughout the evening, sitting in the main on stools around the bar. No-one bothered them.

They planned their strategy the next morning. Scott had collected his evidence over a number of months, clearly at great risk to himself. His notes detailed the times and dates of the visits to the house by James Brown and another officer; Mack recognised the name – he was still serving. Scott had also recognised a criminal justice barrister as another visitor. There was a polaroid photo of Brown standing in front of the open front door of the house and Scott's own contemporaneous recordings of his attempts to bring James Brown's criminal connections to the attention of senior officers, their names and their responses, which were primarily ones of disdain and disbelief. He had also written up the conversation he had with the widow of the Poplar address, almost certainly the 'breeding woman' to whom he had referred in his meeting with Mack. Crucially, the woman's account of her life in the house talked about children being taken there and then going missing, her belief that they had been murdered and buried somewhere in the house's basement. Doubtless, they had enough evidence to search the property.

Kennedy looked hagged. His hands were clenched tight around a mug of scalding coffee, toast and eggs untouched. "I'm going to have to go to the Super, Mack, he's new to Essex, only been here a few months, might be ok."

"Where was he before?"

"Somewhere in Yorkshire, so unless the corruption has crossed several county lines..."

Mack had a suggestion. "Gov, how about, I mean – I know she's not police, but what about asking Clarence? She thinks clearly, has a good take on things. Might be useful to get her opinion on this?"

"Trouble is, Mack, we can't expose civilians to this level of risk – we probably expose her to too much as it is. We haven't got the time to go to see her, fill her in, let her mull it over and then decide. I do agree, she would be a really useful person to talk to." He grinned suddenly, "You've got a bit of a soft spot for her, haven't you?"

Mack brushed the heat off his cheek. "Course not. I just think that she could have a helpful perspective on it."

"Hmm, anyway, look, I'm going to phone the Superintendent. I don't know what else to do, who else there is." He paused. "We could be done for, really, Mack, we could. I'm sorry. I'm sorry if this ruins us both."

Mack half-raised a hand towards Kennedy's shoulder, then drew it back. "It's ok. We've done the only thing we could've."

"I'll just say it's about police corruption and say I have to see him today, asap. We'll drive back to Chelmsford. You book in the prisoner – say he's been arrested for suspected murder, get the knife logged. There'll be ferocious questions from the custody sergeant, about the time of arrest, where you've been, but don't say anything apart from the Super will be in contact with them. I hope. By the time that happens with any luck, we'll be on the move."

Kennedy went outside and phoned the Superintendent's PA.

Their suspect looked unblemished and fed and watered. They drove back to Mack's car. Another breach of protocol was troubling him. "Er, Gov,"

"Yes, Mack?"

"Gov, shouldn't we arrest him and read him his rights?"

Kennedy was fifteen minutes early for the meeting. He spent the time making a paper list of all the points. Without doubt, the hardest thing to explain would be his and Mack's foray into isolation with a murder suspect. And how he'd gone about it. In the end, it hadn't achieved much, but even after, he didn't regret it -

couldn't see what he could have done different. In any event, it was too late to rectify it. Kennedy didn't know how much back-story the Superintendent had, didn't know if he could trust the man. He had Scott's file with him and planned to tell no-one, not even his manager, that he had made a copy at home.

As it turned out, the Superintendent didn't know the back-story - not the corruption, nor Kennedy's personal one. He viewed the DI over his spectacle rims, "Military intelligence, didn't know that, Tim."

"Well, it is on a strictly need to know basis, obviously."

"So, why'd you leave?"

"Took a bullet, lost my spleen, got pensioned out."

"And wanted to keep busy, hence the police?"

"About the sum of it, Sir."

"But you must still have involvement, otherwise you wouldn't have access."

"I do consult, sometimes, just on the rare occasion. But as I said, Sir, it's strictly need to know."

The Superintendent cleared his throat, "Yes, well, I can see why you did what you did and chose to isolate yourself with this information, Tim, but I wish you hadn't and had spoken to me, there's going to be hell to pay with the CPS, the Con-stabulary and the Home Office if they hear about it, but given your reasons, we'll just have to hope for damage limitation." He leafed through Scott's file, his face tightening.

"First thing to say, Tim. I believe you about the previous stuff. You still got the evidence?"

"No, it was taken off me. They even went through my house."

"I'm sorry, Tim, sorry that you went through that. Your story's too detailed to be fantasy and this evidence from Scott, well, it's enough, isn't it?"

"I think so, Sir."

"So, let's plan. We have enough, I think, to justify pursuing this line of enquiry in the hope that it will lead to Emma. We need to pursue it, anyway, but not at the moment if it doesn't help the missing child situation. Do we have any other leads at this point?"

"None."

"Ok. So Keeley's dad has nebulous links to Poplar, it's possible that his daughter had been a target for the abductors, as well as Emma and Samantha. Similar audacious abductions from decades ago have links to Poplar, the same address. We have a named retired officer, James Brown, and one still-employed officer, who need to be brought in for questioning regarding their links to this house as contained in Scott's file and the allegations about what went on there."

"Do we need to see if there is any evidence at the house, first?"

"Ideally, yes, but we don't want to alert Brown and his pal, do we? We need to search their homes. I know it's a long shot, but given that, somehow, they were onto Sergeant Sumerson visiting Scott, because there's no way that was a coincidence, it's all going to have to happen at the same time. If we're wrong, then we're wrong. How long's the Chief Constable been in post, Tim, do you know? Would he have known about the past corruption?"

"Honestly, I don't know. Scott's been retired for several years, but that was due to ill-health. James Brown's only been drawing his pension for one, maybe two years, if that. I think that the Chief Constable was here before that. But Essex is a big county, I don't think we can assume that he did know."

"Ok, well leave that with me. Where's the murder suspect?"

"Custody."

"Ok, I'll sort them out, speak to them. Had you thought about what your prisoner's going to say about your little outing with him?"

"I thought maybe we could offer him a sweetener?"

"Hmm, well, it'll need to be a very big one. I need to think about talking to the Chief Constable. You need to organise search warrants, get some teams together for the Poplar house, James Brown and this other officer. What's his name?" He rifled through the file, "Yeah, Jenkins. Then update me. We'll decide when to act."

Kennedy's phone rang as he stood up. He listened and nodded a couple of times, glancing at the Superintendent. "Good work, Mack. Have you re-arrested him on suspicion of abduction? Are you going to go to interview now?" He paused, "Ok. Keep me updated." He turned, "Our murder suspect, we've got a match. Name of Michael Wiltshire. He got seven years for abusing his daughter, was inside for four, and prior to that had a couple of common assault convictions. It's the man Keeley identified as possibly being one of the abductors. We went out to his last known address, and others, but couldn't locate him. Mack's going to re-arrest him on suspicion of abduction and attempted abduction and go to interview as soon as the duty brief can get there." Kennedy wanted to punch the air: at last, a proper lead.

His jubilation was short-lived. Mack phoned him three hours later to say that Wiltshire had gone no comment for the whole interview.

Chapter 18

Mrs. Knatchbull and Keeley arrived on time for the appointment. They were waiting in Reception, Mrs. Knatchbull standing tall and stiff. Clarence had already prepared her room, briefed the student and seated her unobtrusively in a corner with a pad and pen, ready to make a note of anything significant.

"I hope you know what you're doing, Miss Hope."

"Mrs. It's Mrs. Hope." Clarence sounded gruff to her own ears.

"Oh, well, whatever. I don't want Keeley getting upset."

Clarence looked at Keeley's tired little face and the red-rimmed eyes that were grey underneath. "I think it's fair to say that Keeley's already upset, Mrs. Knatchbull. What we want to do is to help her to manage that better. Would you agree?"

Her mother stroked Keeley's cheek, "Yeah, I suppose." She drew her daughter's dark head close and planted a kiss on the crown, looked at Clarence, "How long?"

"Forty-five minutes."

"Ok." Mrs. Knatchbull stroked hair away from Keeley's face, turned, gave a final warning glare and left.

"Come on, Keeley, I'll show you my office. Would you like a drink?"

"Yes, please. What is there?"

"Well, I can offer fizzy water, orange squash, orange juice or milk – all with ice-cubes if you'd like."

"Orange juice with ice cubes, please." Clarence led the way to her office, where she had already had a tray laid out. "Chocolate biscuit?"

"Yes please. Can I have two?"

"Of course you can. You'll have to eat them quickly, though, otherwise they'll melt it in heat and make your hands all gooey, better have a tissue in case."

Keeley looked around Clarence's play-space in the corner of her office. "This is nice. Do lots of children come here?"

"Yes, quite a few."

"Can I sit anywhere?"

"Yes, anywhere you like." She watched as Keeley sat on the beanbag, stood up again and moved to a squishy armchair, "Here."

"Ok," Clarence sat down on the sofa. "Keeley, this lady is Donna, she's here because she's learning how to be a Social Worker, so she's watching what everyone does in this building. Is it ok for Donna to be here?"

Keeley looked at Donna. "Yes, it's ok. Clarence, what does a Social Worker do?"

"Well, we help people who might be having problems. We help them to find a way to make it a little bit better, or maybe a lot better."

"Do you help just children?"

"In this building, we just help children. But there are Social Workers who help adults, too."

"My mum and dad don't like Social Workers, or police."

"That's ok, we're still here to help you if you'd like us to, Keeley." Clarence paused, "So, when people come for help, to talk about what they'd like help with, it's usually for forty-five minutes at a time. That's why you've come today at ten a.m. and you mum's going to pick you up at quarter to eleven. Do you understand?"

Keeley gave a little grin. "I think forty-five minutes is quite a long time to talk for, but I can talk for a long time, or that's what my mum says."

"Mmm, yes, I'm quite good at talking, too. But today I'm going to be a little bit quiet, so that there's time for you to talk." Clarence sat back onto the sofa. "So, what made you want to come here today, Keeley?"

Keeley's words tumbled out. "Cos when you came to our flat, it was like you understood everything. My mum doesn't, nor does my dad, but my mum talks about it more. She says that I just have to get on with enjoying my school holiday, because when I go to senior school, I'll have loads of work and not much time to do anything else. But that just makes me cry again, cos

I should've been going on the bus with Samantha and Emma. And now Samantha's dead and Emma probably is, too." Clarence passed Keeley some tissues, waited whilst she mopped her face. "They were my two best friends."

"And you miss them very much."

"Yes, and now they're gone. Mum says that I've got to stop crying, but I can't." Clarence picked up a big, brown, stuffed bear with yellow ears that sat in the corner of the sofa. "Keeley, would you like to cuddle Bertie? I know you're going to senior school soon, but even much older children sometimes like to cuddle him when they're here." She leant over and gently sat Bertie next to Keeley, who picked him up and hugged him close. "It is very sad when someone we love dies or is missing. They're hard feelings to have."

"Yes. They're really horrid feelings. It's like they're all in my tummy. And my mum doesn't understand."

"I think perhaps your mum wants to take the feelings away for you, Keeley. Sometimes, grown-ups, parents, love their children so much, they want to take all the bad feelings away for them, to make them feel better. I wonder if that's what your mum and dad try to do."

"But they can't take them away, can they?"

"They can't take them away, but we can all help you so that the feelings hurt a little bit less. How do you think that could happen?"

"By not pretending that the feelings aren't there. When my mum tells me to stop crying, that's a way of trying to pretend, isn't it?"

"Yes, sometimes it is a way of trying to pretend. But sometimes, it is good to think about other things, too, Keeley, so that you're not sad and crying all the time."

"Yeah, but my mum wants me to think about the other things all the time and never about Samantha and Emma."

"Sounds like that makes you feel cross."

"Not much, but sometimes, yeah. I try and tell mum, but she doesn't listen."

"Maybe together you and I can think of some ways to help you say it so that your mum does listen, Keeley. Do you think that's a good idea?"

Keeley nodded vigorously, her head bouncing off Bertie, who was snuggled under her chin. "What could I say to her?"

"Well, let's pretend that your mum is here." Clarence stood up and went to the bookshelf, where a very large ragdoll with red plaited hair and wearing a green pinafore was perched on the top shelf. Clarence sat her down on the beanbag.

"Let's pretend this is your mum and that she's just asked you to stop crying."

"Mum doesn't ask me, she just tells me, 'Stop it!', like she's cross. And then I cry even more." She eyed the doll. "I don't think that my mum would like being a ragdoll."

"That's ok, because this is just pretend, so that you can practise what you could say to her in real life. What would you like to say to her?"

Keeley faced the beanbag. "I'd like to say, 'Mum, I feel sad, cos my best friends have gone'," she turned back to Clarence, "But she'll just say that it's no good to waste time being sad, that we have to get on with it."

"Ok, and what could you say to that? What would you like to say to that?"

"Ok...I think I'd say, 'I know it's not good to be sad all the time. But when something really bad happens, it's hard not to be sad sometimes.'"

"And I think that would be a good thing to say. How do you think your mum might answer?"

"I don't think she would mind that. My mum is nice, but she doesn't understand like you do."

"Sometimes Keeley, well, a lot of the time, grown-ups don't always get it right. In fact, grown-ups can get things badly wrong. And they're not as good as admitting it as children are. I think your mum is actually very worried about you and just wants to make you feel better. But her way of feeling better isn't your way, is it?" Keeley shook her head. "So it's good if you can help her to understand what you need to do to feel better. I wonder if you think you could say that to her."

"I think I would."

"Would you like me to help to explain it to her?"

"I'll try first. If it doesn't work, then can you try?"

"Yes, course I will."

"Clarence, do you think that the police will find Emma?"

"They are looking very hard, they're trying their best."

"You know the men who took them?"

"I know who you mean."

"I couldn't remember what they looked like when that man came and asked me. But last night I dreamed about them."

"About the two men? What happened in the dream, Keeley?"

"Just what happened in real life. But I could see what they looked like, a bit, only a little bit, though. I don't think I could tell that man, the one who came with the computer. If I dream about them again, should I draw them?"

"Would you like to draw them?"

"I think I'd like to draw them and then after that see the computer man. I'm going to make sure that I have my drawing-pad next to my bed, so that I can draw them when I wake up."

"That's a very good idea, Keeley. Would you like another drink?"

"Yes, please." Clarence got up and fetched another drink, pouring one for herself and Donna.

"It's going to be time for your mum to collect you soon, Keeley. Is there anything else you'd like to tell me before you go?"

"Can I come back?"

"Of course you can, we'll talk to your mum about it when she arrives. So, what are you going to do for the rest of today?"

"Mum's taking me and Claire for a burger and then to the cinema."

"Ooh, very nice. Do you and Claire share a burger, or have one each?"

Keeley giggled. "One each, of course, and chips each, too."

"And chips, too. Next, you'll be telling me you have a whole cup of coke to yourself."

"We do, it's a treat. Or we might have one big one and two straws."

"Sounds like you're going to have fun for the rest of today, Keeley. Here's your drink, you can drink it on the way downstairs. We'll go and find your mum."

Chapter 19

It was pitch black. All Mack could see were tiny, skeletal hands: babies' hands. They clutched randomly at his hair, but as fast as he prised open the bony fingers they grabbed desperately at his clothes, yanking at him from every direction. Then he was naked and they clutched at his skin, digging in and clenching, wrenching out chunks of his bleeding flesh that were held fast in fleshless palms, his blood spilling downwards. Little white skulls split into two, three, four pieces, sharp, nestled tight into his chest. Blackly bottomless eye sockets pleaded. Toothless baby jaws screamed in an endless howl of fear. The wailing bounced around his bedroom, still echoing when he woke to the loud sparkle of a little girl's shoe that exploded into his face.

He was in a hot sweat, paralysed, heart thudding, not able to move even an exposed, unsafe foot back under his duvet. The weight of dead children was heavy on his chest. A song circled around his mind, a comfort from Sunday School days: "Jesus, Jesus loves Mack, yes he does, yes he does; Jesus, Jesus loves Mack, yes he does, yes he does, oh yes he does. And Jesus know Mack loves Jesus, too." He let the ditty play on and on and on, until his heart resumed its normal rhythm, the weight lifted, and he could move his foot, hunkering down into his mattress, despite the muggy, stifling heat of the still night.

Mack hadn't had nightmares for years. In fact, he reminded himself, he hadn't had dreams for years. He'd made a conscious effort and achieved a hard-won victory over the nightmares that had plagued him as a child and teenager and to a large degree, had been successful. He groaned into his pillow; this was the one time in his career when he so didn't need his sleep to be any more disturbed than it already was.

He looked at the clock: two a.m., prime nightmare wake-up time. He got up, went to the toilet, made a couple of slices of toast and marmalade and drank a cup of cold milk, got back into bed and dropped off into a second, uneasy sleep. The alarm jangled at five a.m. He had to be at the station for Kennedy's six a.m. briefing.

The Superintendent was there, he walked over to Mack. "The DI told me about your suspect yesterday, Wiltshire, that he went no comment regarding the abduction. Was there no way of moving it forward?"

"Sir, really, he was adamant. We had him in the room for an hour and a half. The brief was arguing that we only had the nebulous word of an eleven-year-old, traumatised girl, etc, etc."

"Was there any DNA from the girl's clothing that could link him?"

"No. Not on the dead girl's clothing and not on Keeley's. The only thing he's said is that he's homeless at the moment, so nowhere to search for other clothing. In any event, Keeley said that it was the other guy who'd made a lunge for her, anyway. The fat guy."

"Ok, Wiltshire's still in the cells, is he?"

"Yes, Sir, we're waiting for confirmation from forensics regarding Scott's murder."

"Good, good. Keep me updated. If Kennedy can't call me, or he's tied up, then you can come to me direct, Sergeant. I'm all over this. You have my full support. We have to find this girl."

"Ok, thank you, Sir."

There were twelve other officers in the room, Mack found a familiar face. "What's going on, Dave?"

"No idea. It's all been hush-hush, I was told yesterday that I had to be here and that I wasn't to breathe a word. Do you know?"

Mack didn't but guessed once he heard about the secrecy. Kennedy stood up. "Right, folks, this briefing is strictly confidential. And I mean that. No blabbing to your mummy, daddy or bestie from school. You're going to split into three teams to raid three properties. We have search warrants. You're looking for the proceeds of crime. I want every room, nook, cranny and garden of each property searched. Don't forget attics, lofts, toilet cisterns, under sofas. Everywhere. None of these properties has children under sixteen and to the best of our knowledge, none has dogs. We don't anticipate there being any guns, but make sure you're all wearing body armour. And if there are dogs, don't be babies about it. The animals will be taken by surprise just like the humans, so don't start fussing if the dog barks, it's normal." A ripple of laughter went around the room like a Mexican wave; everyone across the county had heard about the officer who'd panicked during a recent raid and had subsequently been bitten on the backside by a tenacious chihuahua.

"We're planning to execute these raids at seven thirty a.m., so we need to get moving. Sergeant Sumerson, you're taking the Poplar property." Kennedy assigned teams and gave copies of the search warrants. Mack guessed that Kennedy was saving James Brown's property for himself: he didn't blame him.

Mack's team arrived at the Poplar address at seven twenty-five a.m. At seven thirty precisely, Mack started knocking. A bleary-eyed, sleep-in worker opened the door after three minutes, looked at the warrant, phoned his boss and duly let them in.

Four grumbling residents were woken up and moved into the downstairs sitting-room. The whole placed had been kitted out with IKEA flatpack furniture, easy to look in and under. The staff quarters were in the attic: kitchenette, bathroom, two bedrooms; the officers searched systematically from there downwards. The only noteworthy find was a stash of booze at the back of the airing-cupboard and then only because it turned out to belong to the worker, who said that he was an alcohol counsellor.

There was a padlocked door in the ground-floor hallway. Mack returned to the worker, "What's behind that door, mate?"

"It's the basement. We don't use it."

"When was the last time someone went down there?"

"No idea, it's not been opened since I've been here."

"Got a key?"

"Nah, sorry."

Mack got some bolt-cutters from the police van. The lock was ferocious. A voice behind him made him jump. "Do you need a torch?" The worker had a huge flashlight in his hand, it would beat Mack's puny, police-issued job any day.

"Cheers, isn't there electric?"

"Dunno. But if there is, it'll be ancient; this place was re-wired last year and I know for a fact that they didn't do the basement, so don't switch anything on, you could send the whole place up."

The door to the basement opened outwards, back into the hall. Mack shone the flashlight down. Dark, wooden treads disappeared into a pitch-black space. Large particles caught in the draught from the door's opening. They swirled around in his beam of light like the tail of a wraith from a child's story-book. Scott's words rang loud in Mack's head, spooked his heart into a faster beat. Telling the worker to stay put, he carefully descended, his fingers finding the dusty handrail of wobbly ban-nisters on his left. A damp mustiness hung in the air. Each step released a cloud of something that tasted of more than dust. It made him want to choke.

Once downstairs, he found he was standing on compacted and hard, bare soil. He swung the light around. It was a large area, he reckoned it probably ran under the entire footprint of the house. Lime plaster covered old brick walls. In places it was cracked and flaking and randomly stained, like the building's life-blood was seeping through. Gas lamps were affixed to the walls at regular intervals. A couple of them still wore the rotting remnants of old and blackened mesh mantles. Silvery, dusty cobwebs draped and clung to each lamp and swung between them, a faded parody of old-fashioned Christmas paper-chains. A cast-iron mantlepiece stood against the chimney-breast, a rusted, soot-blackened grate in the manhole, the hearth of pat-terned tiles just visible under detritus. Mack turned his light to the wall opposite, let it rest there like an illuminating full moon for a few seconds. His stomach lurched. He had seen enough. He shouted up the stairs, asking for the large flashlights to be brought in from the van and for SOCO to be alerted. "And be careful, don't trample down. Come one at a time, the stairs are fragile." A further thought occurred to him, "We need to check that there's not a gas supply still coming down here." Kennedy wouldn't appreciate it if he blew up half the street.

Next to the fireplace, a three-legged chair leaned into an alcove corner. It was a standard, honeyed pine one, with a rounded seat, not even antique, its broken, fourth plinth resting a few inches away against grubby skirting.

In the other alcove was a dark wood blanket box, one of its three, rusted, iron hinges had come off, leaving the top laying askew to its base. Behind the box was a bundle of cloth. He crouched down and carefully lifted it. A baby blanket, old and peppered with moth-holes, unfurled into his lap, its faded yellow wool rough on his palm through the latex glove and bordered with smooth satin. He laid it gently to one side. It had been covering a new-born's cradle, tiny wrought-iron spindles intact and rust-free. He nudged it. The wooden rockers seesawed obediently, almost smoothly over the soil floor, as though moving in familiar, time-worn grooves. Dim light was seeping down from the open door above. The tips of the rockers blinked up at him rhythmically. He swung his torch down. There was only dust.

Mack lifted the blanket box lid and rested it against the edge of the cradle. Inside, he found a screwed-up bundle of rags. He disentangled them. They were various items of baby and young children's clothing: rompers; tiny t-shirts; a rotting, red cotton skirt, with faded frilly petticoat still attached; a child's shirt; knitted baby bootees and tiny cotton socks, all grubby and moth-eaten, some stained.

A distorted, small face lunged into his mind: tongue bulging through pale lips; eyes swollen and the blue of the sea; hair straggly-wet and matted with blood.

He left the rags untangled where he'd found them and walked to the other side of the room. He had saved the worst until last. Opposite the fireplace, against the wall by the stairs, was a cast-iron, double-bed frame. The top bar of the ornately scrolled headboard was several centimetres deep in undisturbed plaster dust Four of the wooden struts from the bed's base were intact, those that had split and rotted were propped against the wall. Around the outer posts of the headboard – on either side – dangled loops of old rope, the ends frayed, the separating fibres stiff with age.

He went back upstairs to call Kennedy. His lips were rough with a dry powder and a bitterness lined his mouth.

After that, the basement was declared a crime scene. The charity would have to vacate for the foreseeable future.

When it was properly lit, it was clear that the basement had an outside door and bricked-up windows at either end. It didn't take too much investigation to discover that the door led to a small, outside yard below street level. It had been filled in with soil and turfed over, creating the appearance of a neglected front garden.

Some hours later, the room started yielding its secrets, disgorging victims through the soil floor, Mack thought, as though desperate to vomit them into the light. The graves were shallow and perfunctory, their contents were the bones of infants, and older children. The search, evidence-gathering and logging would take weeks, possibly months.

After SOCO had arrived, Mack was redundant. He wandered back into the sitting-room, where angry residents were waiting for a lift to an alternative property. He addressed the nearest one. "Upstairs, on that first landing, on the left, there's a wall, but when you look through the landing window, there's a structure over the downstairs bathroom, like the bathroom has got a room on top. "Yeah, what of it?" The bloke wasn't going to bend over backwards helping a copper. "Don't worry," said Mack. He ran back up the stairs. The wall was artexed over and painted the same colour as the rest of the landing. He tapped gently. It was hollow.

Descending the stairs two at a time and running out to his car, Mack grabbed a claw hammer from the small toolkit that he always carried in his boot, thundered back up the stairs and swung at the wall. It caved in after just a couple of hard blows.

Beyond the exposed doorway was a small, dark room. Mack

donned fresh gloves and shoe covers and stepped cautiously over the threshold. He still had the flashlight. He flicked it on. His stomach, just starting to recover from his jaunt into the basement, clenched again.

Bloody hell! Did the death in this place never end?

Chapter 20

Tim Kennedy was having the best day of his professional life. All his suspicions, the evidence that had been ignored - more than ignored, kicked into the gutter; the damage to his health and marriage, it was all pay-off for a priceless moment.

Kennedy had waited in the car as Dave Cooper banged with a consistent thoroughness on James Brown's white PVC front door. Eventually a bleary-eyed Brown had answered, clad in blue and white stripy dressing-gown and furry, flip-flop slippers. He squinted down at the search warrant. His face had paled. Kennedy watched as the cheek veins and bulbous nose brightened exponentially. Rudolph. In the end, Brown had no choice but to let them in.

Forty minutes had passed. Kennedy had been getting fidgety, counting the petals as they dropped from Brown's roses to a pavement grave. Then his radio crackled, Dave Cooper at the other end. They had found child abuse images in the loft, old fashioned photos, polaroids, not on a computer. The stash was tucked right away at the back of the space, under one of the eaves. Did the DI want to make the arrest? Oh yes.

Kennedy had sauntered into the house, taken the envelope from Cooper and shuffled through the photos, not lingering, just looking long enough to get the gist. Then he had looked Brown in the eye, dangled his handcuffs and allowed himself a long, slow, smug smile right in Brown's fat, double-chinned, clean-shaven, terrified face. "I'm arresting you," handcuffs on, "*Sir*", click, "For being in possession," etc, etc. They put Brown in the back of a squad car, drove him the slow way back to Chelmsford station and booked him into custody. Jenkins had also been found with child abuse photos and taken to Bellington police station to keep them apart. They had let them call their solicitors and then left them to wallow for a few hours.

Kennedy felt for Brown's wife and believed her when she said she had no idea, never went into the loft, couldn't use the ladder.

The woman was white with shock. And there were two little grandchildren: oh dear, from now on, life was only ever going to go downhill for James Brown. Kennedy made the referral to Social Services himself.

He was surprised at the depth of his delight and the level of his malice, but didn't feel the need to censor himself: Brown, the bastard, had nearly ruined his life, caused him a lot of misery and was a nasty, child-abusing crook, to boot. No: what went around came around, now it was Brown's turn.

So, when their murder suspect, Michael Wiltshire, asked to speak to Sergeant Sumerson and got Kennedy instead, his day got even better.

"What can I do for you, Mr. Wiltshire?"

"I seen someone I wanna talk to. You want me to talk, I will. But only to him."

"Who? Who have you seen that you want to talk to?"

"Inspector Brown. I seen him through the window in the cell door. I know he's around."

Kennedy's heart stopped for a fraction of a beat. "Ok, Michael, I'll see what we can do."

The Superintendent looked at him as though he were mad. "Don't even think it, Tim. Brown's in custody. Even if he wasn't suspected of being involved in police corruption and possibly even a paedophile ring and in police cells to boot, he's retired, no longer a serving officer. He absolutely cannot interview a suspect. The Inspectorate would be all over us like a rash." Another objection occurred to him. "And we haven't interviewed him yet about his own sodding crimes. Anyway, how do we know that our prisoner doesn't know that Brown's retired or even arrested and that he's playing us? Can't be done, Tim."

"I don't think he'd be asking; in any event, we've had Wiltshire with us, no-one could have told him about the raids and arrests and it hasn't hit the news. Maybe Brown didn't tell his criminal mates that he's retired, might have been useful for them to keep thinking he was a serving officer."

The Superintendent was still scowling.

"Sir, this is the best chance we're got so far. Wiltshire clearly has strong ties with James Brown. He trusts him. What's more important: trying to find a young girl, possibly saving her life, giving her back to her family, or dealing with bureaucracy, well, bending the rules?" (Breaking the law, more like.) He gave his manager a reminder for good measure, "And we've yet to solve Samantha's murder."

He watched as the Superintendent's face battled for several seconds, before he responded irritably. "Oh, all right. Go and get him. Put him in that side room next to the interview suite. We'll brief him there. Let me think about what to offer."

James Brown was full of bluster and indignation. Kennedy didn't engage, nor offer an explanation. It'd be interesting, he thought, to see how his manager's interviewing skills had weathered behind his big, fat desk.

He guided Brown over to the table and nodded towards the chair.

"So, James, sit down, please." The Superintendent waited whilst James lowered himself into the plastic chair, the legs squealing briefly across the hard floor. He folded his arms.

"You're here because we need a favour. And we think, all things considered, that you owe us one."

"Fuck off!"

"That's not nice, is it, James? Not when I might be able to offer you a very, very, tiny deal?"

"There's nothing you've got that I want."

"Oh, ok" said the Superintendent, turning to Kennedy. "He's not interested, Inspector. Put him back in the cell. Cuff him, we don't want him getting any funny ideas." Kennedy hauled Brown to his feet and yanked one of his hands behind his back. Brown pulled away, glaring at Kennedy. He grinned back.

"All right, all right: what? What's this deal?" The Superintendent nodded at the chair.

"First of all, let me tell you what you've got to do for us, James. It's actually not that onerous. We need to you to employ all those skills that the good British people paid to have you trained in,

James and that you saw fit to waste. This is your opportunity to give something back, makes amends a bit, if you like. We need you to interview someone for us."

The back of Brown's chair creaked as he settled.

"Know a Michael Wiltshire, James? Tall, lean guy, black curly hair, blue eyes. Got a conviction for kiddy-fiddling?"

"The name might be familiar. What's in it for me."

The Superintendent's face hardened. "Listen to me, James. You're actually not in any position to bargain. I'm offering you this deal out of the goodness of my heart. We're gonna have you, anyway. You wouldn't believe the evidence that's stacking up against you and your comrades in crime; we've got information that the good people of the jury are going to find very interesting. You're facing a lot of charges, looking at a long sentence." He paused for a few seconds, stroked his chin. "Ever seen what they do to coppers in prison? Especially coppers there for kiddy-fiddling." The Superintendent tutted sadly, "Nasty, nasty stuff." Kennedy was mildly impressed. "But today, and today only, James, I feel like being your fairy godmother. I'm going to offer you some protected accommodation when you get there. Keep you away from all the nasties who'll want to chop off your ghoulies. Might be able to find you a comfy bed in solitary somewhere, recommend you for an open prison even, in the long and distant future, if you really play ball." Kennedy watched Brown's face; his lips tightened and his eye whites showing slightly more than was normal. In the end, all that was left was defeat. He sighed.

"Go on, then. What's happened?"

Kennedy sat in on the interview and gave the caution. "So, Mr. Wiltshire, as you requested, here's Inspector Brown, ready for you to talk to."

"I only talk to him, not other coppers."

Brown interjected. "It's ok, Michael," he looked meaningfully across the table. "You can talk in front of him. What did you want me for?"

"What about the tape?" Wiltshire nodded at the equipment.

"Don't worry about that, it won't be going anywhere." Brown gave a practised, reassuring smile. "Go on..."

"A kid's identified me as taking those girls, ain't she? I'm fucked here. You know what he's like; I'll be fucked more inside. I need some protection."

"Michael, I've been out of the country, only came back last night. You were lucky to get me. The Inspector here has briefed me a bit, but you'll have to fill me in. What's happened?"

Wiltshire sniffed hard and settled into his story. "He needed some new blood, for a mate. His last lot of regulars was getting too old, one off'ed 'isself. He wanted us to find a couple that would be easy to take, told us it was summer holidays; best time, he said, kids out and about, no school teachers noseying around at the school gates. He told us which ones it was. So we watched for a few days. Saw these three girls, pretty-like, two blonde, one dark. They was always hanging around, but the dark one used to go home before the others, about tea-time. The other two used to stay out, doing their own thing. Anyhow, we planned the date. It was a good time. The council was doing work on the flats, so we got a white van, so we could look like workers if we needed to. Only on the day, the third girl was still there, had stayed out late, like, s'pose cos it was school holidays."

Brown gave an encouraging smile, Kennedy had to admire the sheer audacity of the git. "Go on, what happened then?"

"Well, we had to go ahead with it, didn't we? We had all the stuff, to quieten them, like, and this bloke was getting desperate for some new kids, supply and demand, didn't want to lose any business. So, we decided to go ahead and take them anyway, all three. Thought he'd be pleased with extra. Only one got away and now she's identified me and now I'm in the shit." Wiltshire paused for breath. "You know what's he's like: if I talk, he'll get me on the inside; he's got people everywhere. If I don't talk I'm fucked anyway, cos of the kid's ID."

"Yes, I think you're right to be worried, Michael." Brown glanced briefly towards Kennedy. "All right, I'll sort something, but finish telling me what happened."

"Well, it all went belly-up. Tony killed one of the kids – she tried to escape and then her screaming brought on one of his heads – you know how he gets. That's the one what's been on the tele."

"Where's Tony now, Michael. Why is he letting you take all the crap?"

"Legged it abroad, went that night, before it all hit the news, Ibiza, I think, not sure. That's where he normally goes, got some bird out there. I should've gone too, don't know why I didn't, now that I'm caught up in all this mess."

"So Tony killed the other one and what happened then?"

"Well, he came, didn't he? Wasn't best pleased. Took the other kid. Not seen him since. Spoke to him on the phone the day that the other kid's body was found. He told me to deal with Scott, that retired copper. So, I did and that's when your mate, wanker here, got me. Now I'm in the shit: murder and kiddy-abduction."

"Why did you have to deal with Scott, Michael?"

"I dunno. I never ask why 'bout nothing. He told me to look for any papers and deal with him. I just do what I'm told."

He looked from Kennedy to Brown in quick, darting movements. "You gonna help me? He'll have me, you know that! Get me off, or something? Please?"

Next to him, Brown had slumped slightly. His left hand was trembling in his lap. Good, Kennedy bet Brown's own fate was making itself felt. He stepped in. "We need to find this girl, Michael. We need to be seen to try, to avoid suspicion. Where's he taken her?"

"I dunno. We take 'em to that underground lock-up. Meet him there. It's always the same. Don't know where they go after that."

"Where's the lock-up, Michael?" Kennedy kept his voice light.

"Well he knows," Wiltshire nodded towards James Brown.

Kennedy looked at Brown, who inclined his head slightly.

"What about me? I've seen what he does. You can't let him get to me. You'll sort me? Please?" His voice was trembling as much as Brown's hand.

"We'll see what we can do, Michael, leave it with us." Kennedy motioned to the custody officer waiting outside to take Wiltshire back to his cell. He felt almost sorry for the bastard.

James Brown said that he knew the rough location of the underground lock-up, but wasn't prepared to give any details until he got a deal. He categorically wouldn't give the identity of the mysterious man who'd collected the girl and of whom the criminal fraternity were clearly terrified. Brown wanted more of a deal than just a bed in solitary confinement. He wanted a written assurance of protection for the duration of his sentence, which meant an extra screw just for him. And he wanted an open prison. Neither the superintendant nor Kennedy understood the open prison part: Brown would be more vulnerable in an open prison, not less; until their joint eureka moment when they realised how easy it would be to escape, especially given how many contacts he would have that the police would probably never uncover.

Brown was adamant: if he got the deal, he'd give more. And he wanted it signed by the chief constable.

Chapter 21

Emma was fading away in front of his eyes - and not particularly slowly. In all his years, and with all the children who had passed through his hands, Reggie had never had one who reacted this badly. It was like she'd retreated into some type of netherworld. The puking had stopped, but he was sure that was only because she was hardly eating.

She was wan and her eyes had sunk into their sockets. Her hair was lank. He must've been going soft in his old age, because he'd taken to feeding her by hand. After a couple of days of struggling, she'd suddenly become very compliant: opened her mouth, chewed, swallowed, took sips of water, swallowed. She wet the bed every night, but she was drinking so little, it barely registered.

He didn't need the stress, not now, not ever, but particularly not now, when he was comfortably retired. Recently, he'd even been toying with the idea of moving abroad, fancied Barbados, thought maybe the heat would be good for his arthritis. And now he was saddled, with limited options to call upon for help. It was a big, major fuck-up, that needed a fast solution.

According to his contact, and he had no reason to doubt him, Tony was now languishing at the bottom of the med with the fish feeding off the contents of his jugular. Michael, the half-wit, had got himself arrested after having been caught at Scott's flat. Reggie knew that he wouldn't talk. Anyone who worked for him knew the deal: get caught, you're on your own; blabber and there'll always been some prison officer, doctor or priest who owed a favour.

Reggie still had some relatives who might take her off his hands. He thought about just leaving the house and her with it, scarpering. But the house was registered in his name, eventually, some nosey bastard would come sniffing. And it would mean getting fake passports, opening up different bank accounts, travelling under a different name: in one word, hassle.

On the bright side, he'd found her a new ribbon. It had been hidden, languishing, just waiting to be found, right at the back of his cabinet; an exact replica of the first one, maybe even part of the first one, from the same spool - thinking about it, he was sure that was the case. He'd washed her hair specially and now she wore it all the time. It pleased him. If the bloody doctors hadn't mucked around with his prostate, he'd be making good use of her compliance.

Speaking of doctors, one of his old clients had been a paediatrician. Reggie prided himself on meticulously recording all his clients' details.

He called him.

Chapter 22

In the hidden room, the skeleton languished on a grey plastic chair.

A white cotton shirt, the collar blood-stained, hung from milky bones. Black polyester trousers draped down over flesh-less thighs; the underside of the fabric had rotted and dangled in shreds. From under the shirt collar hung a lanyard, its ID card still attached.

Mack stared at the skull. A policeman's cap leant jauntily over one side of the smooth and bony sphere; it had obviously been perched on the body's head, slipping down as the flesh had disintegrated.

Fuck, those bastards had been arrogant; or maybe they still were, maybe they were still around, watching him now. Mack didn't know what to think anymore. Finding his phone, he took a photo, just for his own peace of mind.

He moved forward cautiously to look at the ID card. The photo, unfaded - protected by its plastic sheathing - showed a youthful, handsome young man, hair neat and smiling for the camera. Stephen Clarke had worked for the local council. All bright-eyed and bushy-tailed, thought Mack, poor bugger, bet this was his first job.

He jotted down the details from the ID in his notebook, careful not to touch anything and upset SOCO. And for the second time in ten minutes ran downstairs - this time to announce that they had another crime scene.

He phoned the DI to tell him. Mack was exhausted from the disturbed night and early start. Kennedy said that he could go home and get some rest, as long as he started the checks on his skeleton's ID and stopped off at the council housing offices to get as much information as they had on the Poplar house. "Oh, and Sergeant," the DI was unusually buoyant.

"Sir?"

"No more bodies today, ok? Haha."

Yeah, hafuckingha. The dust was still on his lips.

He phoned the office and got someone onto checking out Stephen Clarke. And then stopped off at the delapidated building that was Tower Hamlets Council Housing office.

The council's filing system was a hybrid of paper and electronic. An older admin lady, whom Mack judged had probably been around for donkey's, eventually found an old file in a large box marked 'pending'. The file was sparse, only containing two tenancy agreements, the first between the council and a couple, Mr. and Mrs. Peter Knatchbull, dated 1975 and the second between the council and Mrs. Chastity Knatchbull, dated 1978. There was a note scribbled on the back: husband deceased, tenancy reverted to widow.

Some more rummaging around an old cabinet produced another file for the Poplar property. The Admin lady was happy to leave Mack to his own devices.

The file went back to the 1940s and was very detailed; obviously, public servants had at one time been more thorough. Scott had been right. The house had been acquired by (what had been) the Metropolitan Borough of Poplar just after the Second World War. It had been purchased from the Bull family for a cost of five hundred pounds.

The house was described as comprising three floors and a basement. According to the paperwork, the basement was unremarkable and the council hadn't sought to modify it, leaving its dirt floor and rough-plastered walls for tenants to use as they saw fit. The council had installed a privy in the old scullery, running water and a gas meter.

After having bought the house from the Bull family, the council had let it to them. The meticulous worker had detailed that the family hadn't been able to afford to maintain the house after the war, they would have been homeless and the council would have had to house them anyway, so it was clearly a logical solution. The tenancy had been handed down to successive Bull generations, until the tenancy agreement with the Knatcbulls. So was this a completely new family who moved in, wondered

Mack, or was there a link to the Bulls.

A successful trip to the Registry Office ensued. A Mr. Peter Knatchbull, deceased 1978, had married Chastity Bull in 1975. She was seventeen years old. Chastity had died in 1983 following complications with an abortion. The house had fallen into a state of disrepair during the Bull/Knatchbull families' tenancy; so, after her death, the council had been happy to dispose of the property to a local charity working with the alcohol dependent – the property had become their halfway house.

Scott had possibly been right all along about Reginald Bull's link to the house and its nefarious past.

And Mack would lay a bet that Keeley's dad was dead Peter's son.

A search on the Police National Computer revealed that Stephen Clarke had worked in the Poplar housing office and had been sent to inspect the house and make an inventory prior to its being sold to the charity. When he didn't arrive back at work or turn up home that night, he'd been reported as missing. However, the missing person's report was shut down three days later, the notes showing that Stephen Clarke had gone out with friends straight after inspecting the house and had too much to drink, hadn't wanted to return home and slept if off at his friend's house. The police report stated that the young man was very sorry, embarrassed, but all was well. A subsequent, second missing report made by the family a week later had also been shut down, recording that the police had seen Stephen, he was safe and well and didn't want to go home. In fact, he didn't want to see his family again – a fact that was relayed to them. The case was closed.

Mack found a number and called Stephen's mum and immediately wished he hadn't: another bout of maternal bereavement that his audio system wouldn't drown out; the family visit and possible viewing of the remains would be a job for Jenny and her womanly tenderness.

Mack wasn't shocked, or even surprised, to see that the case had been dealt with by Inspector James Brown.

And another body was added to the mortuary inventory.

He was running, panting, sucking decreasing oxygen around his body. His heart was drumming out a rhythm that his lungs couldn't sustain. This time it wasn't baby hands that ripped out lumps of his flesh. Vicious claws chased him. They tipped hands that were huge, bloodied and fleshy; the fingers were splayed and then clenching towards him, gaining ground. He raced onwards through dangling, eviscerated entrails. His head was hitting beating, harvested, hearts. His rubber shoes were no protection against slipping in blood and slime and vomit. He knew that capture would mean the talons rasping down his back, tearing paths through to his white, knobbly spine and ripping out his lungs, leaving ragged wounds weeping poison in blood-hot globules that dripped wetly down his back.

He woke up twisting and turning, chest heaving, panting, desperate to wipe off the blood, the poison, taking seconds to realise it was only his sweat running down and soaking his pyjama bottoms. He ripped them off and threw them across the room and then scrambled up against the headboard, hunched up, duvet up to his chin. There was no Sunday school ditty this time, no comfort to calm his heart.

Chapter 23

Brown's twenty-four hours in police custody had been extended for a further twelve by the Superintendent; it wasn't going to be enough, so Kennedy had applied for and been granted an extension of the arrest warrant, the Magistrate surprisingly accommodating when presented with the details - maybe he didn't like child-molesting, corrupt ex-coppers, either. The charges against Brown were growing longer by the minute. Kennedy, who was humming as he prepared to go to interview, wasn't sure where exactly to start: suspected murder of Stephen Clarke, Mack's body in the attic (well, almost); possession of child abuse photos; misconduct in a public office. Kennedy intended to devote a lot of time to his preparation, there would be no holes for Brown and his no-doubt slimy brief to crawl through.

The Superintendent had spoken at length with the Chief Constable, who decided that he didn't have the authority to agree Brown's request for a deal and was waiting for a decision from the Home Office.

Following his trip to the Housing and Registry offices, Mack had phoned Kennedy to suggest that he start trying to trace males in the Essex area with the surname of Bull who fell into the age range of sixty to eighty, on the rationale that the abductor from the 1980s, described as late-thirties then, would be within that range, now; he also suggested that they bring in Knatchbull. "For what, Mack? We can't arrest him, he hasn't done anything."

"No, but I think he's the child of the Knatchbulls who last rented the Poplar house, he needs to be helping us with our enquiries, Sir." Kennedy had thought both suggestions an excellent idea. Emma had been missing for eight days, but they were finally making headway and Kennedy was determined to find her - whatever the outcome.

It was whilst Kennedy was still preparing that the Superintendent called. The Home Office were offering to drop any potential charges relating to misconduct in public office and to fund an extra prison officer in acknowledgement of the risk to Brown.

"I want that in writing, signed by the Chief Constable and a Home Office minister."

"And you think they'll do that, do you? Write that down, sign it and give to a corrupt, shit-scared ex-copper, who's going to sell it to the press at the first opportunity." Kennedy was getting seriously pissed off with Brown's negotiating style.

"Look, I think you're being a bit previous, anyway, Kennedy. You haven't even bloody interviewed me yet and you're already talking about charges. Even if I show you the place Wiltshire talked about, it won't be admissible as evidence. There's no way that I'm going to admit to it in interview."

"I don't think there's much doubt about what's going to be on your charge-sheet, do you? And even if you don't admit to it in interview, your brief's going to sign an agreement on your behalf talking about this place that you're going to show us. That's the whole point."

"No, she's going to sign an agreement saying that in exchange for certain information, that I will give to the police, regarding the location of a venue that I may, at some point in the distant past, have heard about in the execution of my duties, I will be exempted from any possible future charges of misconduct in public office and guaranteed a screw on my wing in the event of my being remanded or sentenced."

"Whatever that agreement says, we're going to have you, Brown."

Brown glared at him. "Screw you, you bastard. You always were a cocky git."

"Well that's as maybe, James. But I'm not the one in a police cell, am I? And that, James, is because, as far as I know, cocky gittiness isn't a crime. Now, do we have an agreement?"

"Yes. If it's written down. They don't have to give the paperwork to me, they can give it to my legal representative, can't they?"

So, Kennedy had trotted off back to the Superintendent, who'd gone back for more negotiations. Eventually, after a couple of hours of further wrangling, they reached an agreement with which even Brown's brief was happy. The interview was postponed, so that Brown could show Kennedy where the underground chamber was.

Kennedy called Mack to co-opt him into the search party. Brown sat in the front of the car in handcuffs with Kennedy and directed him.

They joined the A127 and turned onto the A13 to London. After about five miles, they turned left onto a slip road that took them down a track, unmade, but the hard, compact soil indicated a level of regular usage. On either side, grass and bushes had been roughly hacked down. Kennedy reckoned they were heading out towards Purfleet. It was the direction down which the white van had disappeared and an area which had already been searched thoroughly. The abandoned, red brick farmhouse was on the left, the shards in its windows glinting sharp in the twilight, the front door split and yawning and police-taped over. Two ramshackle barns behind were similarly marked off. On the right was a small clutch of trees. The track gradually disappeared into grass, "Keep going." They continued forward over another three miles of rough, abandoned land, until the suspension of Kennedy's car was groaning and his vertebrae were coming out in sympathy. Kennedy slowed on approaching a wide ditch, a deep, gaping gash in the earth that blocked their way. Beyond the ditch was dense thicket. "This is it," said Brown, "Get out here."

He led them down a narrow dirt path that ran along the side of the ditch until a small, grass-covered hill emerged from the vegetation. Kennedy, Mack, two PCs and a K9 officer followed Brown round to the other side. There, set into the side of the mound and amidst long grass, was a door-sized metal grille. The dog was getting excited, indicating to his handler, who let him off the lead. Immediately running to the mound, he pawed it, whining. "Go on," said Brown, "It's open."

Kennedy didn't know exactly where they were, but in any event, he recognised an army bunker when he saw one. He pulled open the grille and shone his torch downwards. Brown nodded towards Kennedy's right. "There's electric." Kennedy reached down and his fingers found a light switch. He flicked it. A couple of square lamps came on. They were fixed onto old, concreted walls, the bulbs an inch-deep in dead and skeletal insects. Kennedy turned to Brown. "Where's the electric feed from?"

"That old farmhouse still has a supply, it was rigged up to reach out here years ago."

"What, and the electric company hasn't cottoned on?"

Brown shrugged. "How would I know?"

A metal staircase led deep into the earth. A light had come on down in the bunker; from above, all Kennedy could see was some cracked, filthy, screed floor. The German shepherd, alert, ears forward, panting with excitement, drooling, looked at his handler and then bounded down the stairs, his claws clanking against the metal. Seconds later, he re-appeared, a little's girl's sparkly summer sandal dangling from his mouth.

The inside was a cold, damp place, rectangular, Kennedy estimated it was probably about ten feet by fifteen. It stank: mould, urine, dirt, BO, cigarettes all hung in the air in a cloud of grime. Kennedy had been in a lot of filthy, unhappy places in his time; he knew the miasma of fear and sorrow - this place had it in spades.

There were rough wooden pallets dumped randomly. A couple of the them were pushed against the wall, piled up and two dirty single mattresses slung on top. Kennedy was pretty certain that SOCO would tell him that the fresh stains on one of the mattresses was Samantha's blood. The dog had already worked it out. Kennedy turned to Brown, "So this is serves as a drop-off point, does it? Wiltshire and his mate take the kids, bring them here and your mysterious benefactor picks them up?"

"Yeah, that's the sum of it."

"And where to after that?"

Brown shrugged, "Dunno."

"Yes you do, you lying bastard! Look, this is your chance to redeem yourself a bit, James. That girl could still be alive, do you honestly want her death on your conscience?"

"Look, *Inspector*, I don't want my own death on my conscience. I've got a family you know, I need to think of them."

Kennedy took deep breaths. "I very much doubt that your family give a shit about what happens to you after what they've just found out. Don't give me all that. You know where he takes them, just give it up. Be a man for once, do the right thing."

"No. I've done my bit, exactly as we agreed and as written down. He'll have me. You honestly don't know what you're up against, Kennedy. This is someone who's got links everywhere. In fact, you need to watch your own back. Scott could've told you all about that. Oh yeah, except he's *dead*, isn't he? So, sorry, no can do. You're the detective, so fucking detect!"

Kennedy turned to Mack. "Can you phone and get SOCO here, pronto, please? We'll stay 'til they arrive. Go outside and wait for them. Here," he threw the car keys over, "Tell them to call when they're near, they'll never find us otherwise, you'll need to take the car and get them to follow you."

Brown motioned with his handcuffed fists, "Ok, if I go up for a puff? I'm sure Sergeant Sumerson won't mind holding the lighter for me." He took a couple of steps towards the stairs to follow Mack. The German shepherd, still off his lead and having a good sniff around, turned instantly towards Brown and growled a low, rumbling warning. "I think that's a no," said Kennedy. What a good dog.

Chapter 24

Kennedy and the Superintendent started James Brown's interview at ten a.m. the following morning. Sergeant Jenkins was being interviewed separately at Bellington station at the same time. The Superintendent dropped down a thick buff file on the table between them and placed a large brown bag under the his chair. Kennedy went through the preliminaries and then the Superintendent took over.

"So, James, you're being interviewed with regard to the photos of child abuse found in your loft."

"Don't know anything about them."

"You sure about that?"

"Yes."

"Well that's weird, then, cos we've lifted one of your prints from a couple of them."

"No you haven't, because I never touched them. Didn't know they were there 'til you lot came raiding my home, upsetting my wife."

"I don't think we're the ones who've upset her, James." The Superintendent pulled out a polaroid photograph and placed it on the table in front of Brown. "For the tape, I'm now showing James Brown a polaroid photo of him standing on the doorstep of an address. Is that you in the photo, James?" Brown picked it up, gave it a cursory look and threw it back onto the table.

"Yes."

"Know where that was taken?"

"Yes."

"Where?"

"In Poplar Square, East London."

"And what were you doing there, at that address?"

"I was there doing my duty, investigating allegations of a crime."

"Remember the details?"

"There had been two attempted abductions of children. The

135

car of the alleged perpetrator was registered to that address."

"Get anywhere?"

"No, it was a false lead. As you know very well, Superintendent."

"Oh, Ok. Remember the date?"

"1981."

"You've got a good memory, James, anyone'd think you'd rehearsed this."

"Yeah, well, with the history of false allegations that've been made against me in my time," he glared at Kennedy, "It's not surprising, is it?"

"The problem is, James" said the Superintendent, leaning back in his chair and crossing his fingers over his stomach, "The problem is, that a very expensive forensic test has shown us that this particular type of polaroid film stopped being produced in 1980."

There was a pause. Brown's solicitor looked at her client. "Yeah, well, must've made a mistake. I must've gone to that house in 1980, then."

"Oh, no, you went there to investigate the alleged abduction attempts in 1981 – that's definite. DI Kennedy's sergeant spent a whole afternoon at Upminster nick searching for the file, took him hours. But's he's a tenacious one, isn't he Inspector?"

"Very thorough, Sir."

"Yes, indeed, but he found it eventually, buried under a whole heap of irrelevant documents out of date order, even out of alphabetical order: shocking filing. No, you were right the first time about the date, James. And in case you're still worried, let me reassure you by saying that we have independent corroboration of the date of the alleged attacks and they were in 1981. Don't worry, your memory's intact.

So, let's try again. Given that the polaroid was taken before 1981, it's clear that you were at number nine Poplar Square before being required there in the commission of your duty. Why were you there?"

Brown's solicitor leant forward. "Superintendent, my client

is here in the belief that he is being questioned about indecent photos found in his loft, of which he denies all knowledge. Can you tell me what relevance your questions have?"

"I know where I'm going, Ms. Montgomery."

"Maybe, Superintendent. But we don't."

"Well, it will become clear. And I'd like your client to answer my question."

"Yeah, I'll answer your question. That house was alive with kids, running around everywhere. We were always getting calls from the neighbours about them. Chances are that I was there just responding to some of those."

Kennedy wasn't having that. "No, that's not the case, because we ran the address through the PNC and there were no matches. There were no recorded attendances to that address before 1981."

"You know as well as I that there are still paper files waiting to be uploaded, Kennedy. So your argument rests on nothing. If your tests are accurate and that photo was taken before 1981, then it was as part of my work. I would have had no other cause to be there."

"So you had never visited that house before that point?"

"To the best of my knowledge and as far as I remember, no."

"And have you ever been inside that house?"

"Again, to the best of my knowledge and as far as I remember, no. But I may have stepped into the hall at some point. Thinking about it, I possibly would have, if I didn't want to discuss a complaint on the doorstep."

The Superintendent moved on. He pulled out a sheet of paper from his file. "I'm now showing the suspect a print-out of a police record entered by him." He slid the page across the table. "Do you remember that case, James?"

Brown lifted up the print-out and studied it, "No."

"Well, I grant you, it's hard to remember all the missing persons who get reported to us. But I'm sure you remember Stephen Clarke? Young man who was reported missing by his family in February 1983."

"No, that isn't familiar to me. I don't remember anything about that case. Why what's that got to do with anything?"

"Well, regrettably, he's dead. His skeleton has been found at that Poplar address, James." He turned towards Kennedy. "That was your tenacious sergeant again, wasn't it, Inspector?"

"Indeed, Sir."

Brown leant forward. "Now listen, I don't know what you're getting at, but you've got no proof that I was in that house. Sure, there's a photo of me on the doorstep, doesn't prove anything. And I certainly don't know anything about any skeletons. And I want to know why there are photos being taken of me at all, whilst I was in the execution of my duty."

"We're asking the questions, James. That's how it goes when you're the suspect and I'm the interviewing officer. I don't recall saying that you were in the house, just asking if you were. Now, your name was on that police misper report regarding Stephen Clarke. You recorded that you saw that young man and that he was fine and didn't want to return home."

"Yeah, well, that's what happened then. I can't remember every case that passed through me, can I?"

"No, for sure, wouldn't expect you to. But I think you must remember this one, because you gave the unfortunate Stephen Clarke a present to remember you by. Didn't you?"

Kennedy was watching Brown intently. The man's left hand was shaking, Brown moved it off the table and into his lap: yeah, bang to rights, you bastard. The solicitor scribbled something and passed it to Brown. He shook his head. She looked up. "Superintendent, can we stop the wordplay please. What are you talking about?"

"Does your client need a reminder?" The Superintendent leant down, picked up the brown bag and laid it on the table in front of Brown; he removed a police officer's cap. "This was found on the skull of Stephen Clarke." He paused. Kennedy could feel the vibration of Brown's hand through the table leg. "It's full of your client's DNA, Ms. Montgomery, we even found a couple of his hairs." He looked at Brown's head, "Bit lacking in that department lately, though James, eh?"

"I think I'd like a word with my client, now Superintendent. We could do with a break and a cup of tea."

"Certainly, I'll get someone to bring you one." He looked at his watch. "Interview suspended at eleven thirty a.m."

Half an hour later, the solicitor was ready to resume. "Right, Superintendent, do you have any evidence that my client has ever been in the property where the skeleton was found?"

"His cap was on the skull, Ms. Montgomery."

"His cap could have been stolen."

"Well, he never reported an item of his uniform stolen, which a responsible officer would have, don't you think?"

Ms. Montgomery sniffed, "Had that been the case, I'm sure that it would have been merely an oversight on the part of my client. Do you have physical proof that my client placed the cap on the body's head?"

"You know that we wouldn't be able to do that."

"Exactly. You have one old polaroid showing that my client was on the doorstep of the property in the proper remit of the execution of his duty. Any potential charges relating to murder, Superintendent, are not going anywhere. Furthermore, we would like to get our own testing conducted on the photographs. Now, do you have any further questions for my client?"

Kennedy looked at the Superintendent, he was surprisingly calm, like he knew something that no-one else did. He looked at Brown, who was smirking at him from across the table.

"No, not for the moment."

"Are you going to release my client?"

"No, I'm going to speak to duty CPS."

"Very well. Perhaps you'll make sure I'm told as soon as they've made a decision. And you'll be hearing from me regarding the fingerprints on the photos."

Afterwards, the Superintendent pulled Kennedy into a side room. "Tim, go back to the testing lab and see if they've managed to pull any prints off that chair the skeleton was on. That was an oversight on our part."

"Well, surely they did that anyway, didn't they?"

"Private labs, not like it used to be. Check in with them. I'll speak to the CPS, but we'll go with charging for the child abuse photos. Whatever Brown says, we have his prints. That's enough."

"Have we got enough to get him remanded, though, Sir?"

"Don't know, but we've got the warrant extension haven't we, so we've still got him. If we can get him linked more tightly to that Poplar property, we'll go for a murder charge, too. Then he'll be remanded. We've got to hear about Jenkins' interview yet, there might be something useful from that. And it will really upset me to have to let that smug son-of-a-bitch go."

Chapter 25

Mack found a website that had a better-than-average search engine to use for filtering the electoral roll. In all, there were six males in Essex who met his criteria. They were scattered far and wide, from Stansted near the airport, out towards Great Wakering in the south-east of the county; visiting all of them would take days. He made a list and emailed his schedule over to Kennedy. An email pinged back. Kennedy wanted him to prioritise talking to Knatchbull, whilst Kennedy was interviewing Brown.

Mack dug out a mobile number and called his new best friend.

"You're having a laugh, right?"

"No, I'm not. But really, Mr. Knatchbull, this will only take an hour of your time."

"Well tell me what you want now, on the phone."

"I'd rather not, it's quite sensitive. It would be better in person. I understand that you don't want your family involved more than necessary. I can pick you up somewhere if you like, meet away from home, or you could come to the station."

Knatchbull tutted. "Bloody hell, ok, I'm finishing work at midday. I'll meet you at the nick. Which one?"

Mack roped in Dave Cooper and met Knatchbull in the front office of Bellington police station at twelve thirty p.m.

"Very many thanks for coming, Mr. Knatchbull."

Knatchbull was his usual self. "Whatever. What do you want?"

"Let's find a room, shall we?" Knatchbull grumbled down the corridor and followed Mack and Dave Cooper into a free side room. They sat down.

"As part of our enquiries into the abduction case, we've found your surname linked to a property in Poplar, East London. We wondered if you could explain that?"

"Poplar Square. Number nine?"

"That's the one."

"My parents lived there, before they died. I was born there.

What of it?"

"So your dad was Pete Knatchbull? Your mum Chastity Bull?"

"Yeah. That's right. Although I don't see what business it is of yours."

"Were there any other relatives who lived there, Mr. Knatchbull?"

"I was an only child. My dad died when I was a toddler and my mum a few years later, when I was seven. I was brought up in care. I don't have much memory of my parents, or of my home before they died."

"You were raised in care? Weren't there any relatives who could step in to look after you?"

"Well, clearly not, otherwise they would've, I suppose. Look, I don't see what this has got to do with you, anyway. Bloody police, always noseying around other people's business. What's this all about?"

"You still in touch with your foster home?"

"No."

"Can you remember the address?"

"No. Pitsea, somewhere."

"Are you in contact with any of your parents' relatives, Mr. Knatchbull?"

"No. Why?"

"You sure about that?"

"Course I'm bleedin' sure."

Cooper joined the conversation. "Then can you explain how you were given a six-month suspended sentence for assaulting your cousin ten years ago, Mr. Knatchbull?"

Knatchball cursed. "Yeah, I can explain. Look, *Sergeant*, you asked me if I'm in contact with any relatives. I'm not. That bloke, Willian, was a wanker who found me and asked for some money; he thought that my dad had left some and that he was eligible. My dad left nothing. That William wouldn't have it. We had a punch-up. End of. I haven't seen him since. And I don't want to."

"Why was the case heard in Poplar?"

"Cos that's where I met him, it's where he hangs out. Now unless you tell me what this is all about, I'm off."

"I can't tell you that, at the moment, Mr. Knatchbull. But you're certain that there were no relatives around when you were a child? No-one visiting the house? Friends of your parents or wider family?"

The chair screeched back. "I'm done here. I don't need to answer these questions; you're not prepared to tell me what this is all about, so I'm off, I've done my bit. Am I free to go?"

"Know anyone by the surname of Bull?"

Knatchbull paused. "Was my mum's maiden name. You just said it yourself."

"Know anyone else by that name?"

"No."

"One final question Mr. Knatchbull. I'm curious about why you have so many locks on your door. Even your windows are high-grade security. Are you worried about anything?"

Knatchbull sat back down, crossed his arms, rested his elbows on the table and leant forward into Mack's face. "You really have got some front. I thought you were an idiot the first day I met you. Trust me, Sergeant, if you lived on the Mead and had a wife and two daughters to protect, you'd be security-minded. Look at what's just happened."

"Yes, of course, Mr. Knatchbull. Many thanks for dropping by."

Knatchbull pushed his chair back again. For the first time, he looked directly at Dave Cooper. "Do I know you, copper?"

Cooper held his gaze and shrugged, "I don't know, Mr. Knatchbull. Do you?"

Knatchbull grunted, "Ever been in Poplar?"

Cooper shook his head. "Nope, wasn't me who arrested you for thumping your cousin."

"All right, whatever, all police look alike to me, anyway."

Mack stood up. "Would you like a lift home, Mr. Knatchbull?"

"Are you having a laugh? Me in a cop-car? Do one!"

Mack saw Knatchbull out of the station and went back to the side room to see what Cooper made of it all. "He's an aggressive bastard, isn't he?"

"Yeah, what's he like to his kids?"

"Actually ok. I think he really loves them and his wife. Just doesn't love us, or Social Services."

"No Social Services involvement with his kids?"

"No, they checked. Why?"

"No reason, was just curious, given how forceful he is, makes you wonder how he relates to his children, that's all."

"He's got two girls, maybe it'd be different if they had boys." Mack rubbed the back of his neck, the blood vessels leading to his brain were threatening to expand into a migraine, something he didn't need ahead of a busy afternoon of driving. "You got any painkillers on you, Dave?" His colleague rummaged around a trouser pocket and found a couple of grubby paracetamols amongst some change. They would have to do.

After he had gone, Mack pulled out the records regarding Knatchbull's conviction for assault. The cousin was listed as having No Fixed Abode.

He went back to his list of people named Bull and started to plot his visits. He asked Kennedy if there was someone to share the load, but all the PCs had been sent to an incident in Chelmsford. Mack was on his own.

Mack managed two visits, one in Stansted and one in Harlow. Both men had passports and family history to demonstrate that they'd never had any links to the Poplar address and didn't know anyone by the name of Knatchbull.

The paracetamol barely touched the surface; maybe the layer of grime had reduced their efficacy. He got home just before emptying a non-existent lunch into the toilet and collapsing into bed, managing to text Kennedy to say he was sick before falling into a fitful sleep. He woke up at midnight, forced down some buttered toast and took two more paracetamol with coffee, followed up with two ibuprofen for good measure.

Chapter 26

Mrs. Knatchbull had agreed for Keeley to have another visit with Clarence, on the Friday before the start of the new school term. Clarence settled the student and prepared the room, all the while wondering if she needed to check in with Mrs. Knatchbull about what she wanted said to Keeley about sexual abuse and Emma, because there was no doubt that Keeley would be thinking the worst, especially given how long her friend had been missing and oblique comments in the media.

"If you think that I want my daughter knowing about the birds and bees from you, Mrs. Hope, you've got another think coming."

"Mrs. Knatchbull, I'm not offering to give Keeley sex education. I'm asking *you* what *you* want me to say to her in the event of her asking me if Emma could be at risk of that."

"Well just tell her she isn't."

"But do you think that's an option in this day and age, Mrs. Knatchbull? This stuff is all over social media. And they're taught about protecting themselves in school. What does Keeley know?"

"She just knows the basics, about periods and stuff, what they're for, how babies are made."

"So, she understands the rudiments of sex."

"Yeah, I suppose."

"And you're happy for me to have a conversation about sexual abuse if the subject is unavoidable?"

"If you must, but I want to be told about it afterwards."

"Absolutely." Why was the ruddy woman always so difficult?

After choosing her drink and biscuits, Keeley sat in the same chair as before. Bertie was already waiting for her. She picked him up and cuddled him under her chin.

"I really like coming here, Clarence."

"I'm glad about that. What's good about coming here?"

"I can say things that I'm not allowed at home and I can cry and no-one tells me I mustn't."

"Ok. What would you like to say here today, Keeley?"

Keeley paused and looked across to the office's open window, the leaves rustled gently in a light breeze. "There's no-one who can hear us, is there Clarence?"

"No, there's just you, me and Donna."

"No-one's listening under the window?"

"I promise, no-one's there. It's too high up, Keeley, for anyone to hear what we're saying. Why don't you and Bertie go and look?"

Keeley picked up Bertie, walked to the window and peered through and down.

"See? It's high up, isn't it?"

She nodded and sat back down. "But could someone be listening at the door?"

"They could if they wanted to, but no-on will want to, Keeley. Why don't you go and look there, too?" She watched whilst Keeley opened the door and looked each way down the corridor. She closed the door firmly. She and Bertie sat back down. "Clarence, I'm scared of something."

"What's making you scared?"

"You won't tell?"

"Um, I might have to if it means keeping you safe. Can you explain what's making you worried?"

"That the men will come back and take me, too."

"What makes you think that could happen?"

"Cos my dad has put an extra lock on the front door. We've got three already, now there's another one and Mr. Bridge came round and I heard him say to my mum and dad that we have to be careful."

"Mr. Bridge? Who's he?"

"My old headmaster, at junior school."

"Ok and he sees your mum and dad outside school, does he?"

"I didn't think he did. My mum and dad never go to anything the school does for parents, but he came round a little while ago."

"When was that?"

"Wednesday, the day after I came here."

"Has he been round before?" Keeley shook her head. "What happened when he came round?"

"Me and Claire got sent to watch the TV in mum and dad's bedroom. We had to close the door. Mum said it was so they didn't get disturbed by the tele, but I think it was so we couldn't hear what they said."

"So how did you hear?"

"I went to the toilet and when I came out, I heard Mr. Bridge's voice and he said 'you have to be careful'."

"Sounds like that's worried you." Keeley nodded glumly. "But Mr. Bridge could have been talking about anything," said Clarence. "It could have been something about your new school, how to drive a car, there are lots of things that we need to be careful about, aren't there?"

"Yes, but then he said something else."

"What was that?"

"He said 'he knows'."

"Did he say who he was talking about?"

"I went back to the bedroom then, I knew if I got found out, mum'd be cross. But if he wasn't talking about the men who took Emma and Samantha, why did my dad put another lock on the front door?"

"Keeley, listen to me. If the police thought that the man or men were going to come back, they would've told your mum and dad that and made sure that you were safe. I promise."

"My dad wouldn't listen to the police, he hates the police, he calls them pigs."

"Yes, I know your dad feels like that, but he would still take their advice if they were worried about your safety, Keeley. Honestly, he would. Your parents love you very much, they wouldn't do anything to put you at risk."

"You sure?"

"Yes, I am sure. Do you want me to tell your parents how worried you've been about this?"

Keeley shook her head vigorously. "No, please don't Clarence.

147

I'll only get told off. You won't, will you? My dad's already cross about me coming here."

"I thought your mum wasn't going to tell him?"

"Yeah, so did I. But she must've, cos I heard him talking about..." she paused, "Am I allowed to swear?"

"Yes, if you want to."

"I heard him and mum talking about bloody Social Workers and then they said your name."

Clarence smiled. "That's ok, Keeley and I won't tell them if you don't want me to."

"Are the police near to finding Emma? My mum and dad don't tell me and I'm not allowed to watch the news."

"Your mum and dad won't know, Keeley, that's why that don't tell, because they don't know."

"Do you know?"

"I know that the police are still looking, all the time. They're doing their very best."

"Will you tell me if you know anything? You're the only grown-up who talks to me about it."

"If I can tell you, Keeley, I will. But at the moment, all I know is that the police are looking very hard. Is that ok?"

Keeley nodded. "Is there going to be a funeral for Samantha?"

"Yes, there will be at some point. Would you like to go?"

"If I'm allowed."

"Do you want me to try to find out when it will be and let your mum know?"

"S'please." She gave big yawn. "Is my mum here yet?"

Clarence looked at the clock. "She will be soon. Is there anything else that you'd like to talk about today, Keeley?"

"Can I come again?"

"I spoke to you mum on the phone about it. She's worried that you won't be able to fit it in with your new school times. What do you think?"

"I think I will. I know that I'll get lots of homework and there might be after-school clubs that I want to join, but that won't be yet. Could I come at least one more time?"

"Ok, I'll talk to your mum. I'll call her later today. Would you like another drink?"

"No, thank you, I'm tired."

"Ok, we'll stop in a minute. How are you feeling about starting your new school?"

"I'm still upset that I won't be going with Emma and Samantha."

"I know you are. But there will be nice things about it, won't there?"

Keeley gave a little grin. "I am a *bit* excited. My new uniform is all ready. And I've got a really nice new schoolbag and an ipad." She yawned again. "I want to go now."

Clarence opened her office door to find the records clerk just about to knock. She had the Knatchbull empty file. "I was passing, thought I'd drop it off."

"Oh, thanks Amanda. Can you just leave it on my desk somewhere."

"You'll have to sign for it, first." Clarence took the proffered pen and scribbled her signature resting against the wall. "Cheers, just dump it anywhere. I need to take Keeley downstairs to her mum." She would never hear the last of it if Mrs. Knatchbull was kept waiting.

Chapter 27

Jenkins hadn't been as savvy as Brown, or maybe he had a less vigilant brief, or maybe the interviewing officer had just been better, but in any event, he'd done what Brown hadn't: squealed. He had admitted to the possession of polaroid images of child sexual abuse, was bang to rights anyway, given that his fingerprints were all over them. What Kennedy really wanted to know, though, was whether Jenkins had named or implicated Brown, or mentioned anyone with the surname of Bull.

"No, sorry Tim," the Inspector who interviewed Sergeant Jenkins was apologetic. "Not a dicky about anything else. Just admitted possession of the photos, said it had been a blip in his life, a mistake a long time ago when he was going through a bad patch. There was nothing on his home computer, nor his work one. And never any involvement from Social Services with his kids or grandkids."

"Why did he still have the photos if it was just a blip?"

"Said he didn't know how to dispose of them, was too scared to put them in the rubbish. Said it hadn't occurred to him to burn them til today."

Kennedy took the phone from his ear and looked at the screen as though it were malfunctioning, he put it on loudspeaker. "And you believed him?"

"S'not about what I believe, is it? Sorry, Tim, I know you've got a hell of a situation on your hands, but we had no other evidence against him."

"Did you ask him if he knew the Poplar Square address?"

"Yep. He said only from the investigation into the attempted abductions in the early eighties and then only vaguely, cos he hadn't been part of the investigation."

"Did he say where the photos came from, where they were taken?"

"Nope, said that the risk to himself and his family was too great to give any further information, said he'd rather go to prison than do that. He was bailed."

Kennedy had phoned the forensic lab after finishing with James Brown - at least being charged with possession of child abuse images had wiped the smug look for his fat face: small mercies.

The lab hadn't tested the chair for prints – no-one had asked them to. It depressed Kennedy; in the old days, jobs like that would have been done automatically by professionals who knew their job. "Yeah," said the young technician on the end of the phone, "And that's why the national testing service became un-viable, mate. Course we'll test it – now you've asked. When do you want it for?"

"Well, now would be good."

"Now? It's four p.m., I'm the only one here, going home, unless your manager wants to pay the overtime, mate." He wouldn't. Kennedy supposed it could wait until tomorrow. "To-morrow's Saturday, mate, skeleton service."

Kennedy sucked in a deep breath, bloody Tories and their pri-vatisation agenda. "Ok, fine, do it now then please, we'll cover the overtime." He would just have to face the his manager's wrath.

"Need an email pinged over to authorise that."

"Don't," said Kennedy.

"Don't what, mate?"

"Don't call me mate again. How long will it take?"

"Not long."

"Ok, can you call me on this mobile that's calling you as soon as you know? It's urgent."

"Yeah, so I gather."

"What's your email address?"

He sent the email, cc'd in the Superintendent and texted Mack to see how he was. There was no response. Kennedy resisted calling him; his sergeant had more than earnt his money lately and was long overdue a rest day. He hadn't known Mack got mi-graines, but he wasn't surprised, the man did seem to get overly-anxious occasionally, although that hadn't stopped him making huge strides with this case. Kennedy was pleased, more than pleased – surprised.

The call came whilst he was eating his dinner. The technician had come through for him; *now* they could be mates. Kennedy phoned the Superintendent. To comply with the requirements of the Police and Criminal Evidence Act and the extended arrest warrant, they would be interviewing James Brown on Saturday morning.

Their suspect was woken up at seven a.m. by the custody sergeant, who rattled in with some breakfast and tea on a tin tray. Brown's solicitor arrived half an hour later ready for the eight a.m. interview. She was less than pleased.

"I hope you have a valid reason for getting me here at this hour, Superintendent. And I hope my client has had his full eight hours sleep entitlement."

Kennedy looked at her heavy eyes and scowling mouth. Stale alcohol fumes drifted towards him.

"I can assure you, Ms. Montgomery," replied the Superintendent, "Mr. Brown has benefited from the full entitlement of everything the law offers detainees. I'm sure you'll ask to see the custody record if you're worried about that. And I'm sure you would be the first person to complain if we weren't adhering to the PACE clock, hence the early start."

"So, James, I'm going to caution you again." The Superintendent went through the formalities. "Now, following our interview yesterday, do you have anything to would like to add, or amend regarding what you said?"

"No."

"Are you sure?"

"Yes."

"Ok, because this morning we're interviewing you regarding the murder of Stephen Clarke."

"Oh, really, Superintendent, not this again."

"Yes, again, Ms. Montgomery, because today we have further evidence." The Superintendent paused and shuffled a few papers, pulling out his notes from the folder.

"James, yesterday you said that you couldn't recall ever stepping into number nine Poplar Square, although you may have stepped into the hall in the execution of your duty. Are you maintaining that position?"

"Yes."

"And you maintain that you don't know anything about how Stephen Clarke's body came to be found in that house, with your cap on his skull?"

"Correct."

"When Stephen was found, his skeleton was sitting on a grey plastic chair in an upstairs, boarded-over, small room."

"So? What of it?" Brown was becoming fidgety. Kennedy watched his left hand start to shake. Brown clasped it tightly with his right.

"If you were never there and didn't know what happened, perhaps you can explain how your fingerprints have been found on the underside of the chair on which Stephen's body was found?"

His brief looked at Brown. Yeah, thought Kennedy, you didn't need this after your Friday night, did you? The situation was irretrievable.

"Ok, Superintendent, I'd like a word with my client, please."

"What was it, James?" The Superintendent ignored her. "Walk in on one of your little games, did he? See too much? Threaten to tell? It was his first job out of school: he was nineteen. Or was it simply sheer, bloody arrogance on your part. Just because you *could*?"

"Superintendent, I want to speak to my client. Now."

The Superintendent stood up, gathered his papers, and shuffled them back into the file. "Sure, have as long as you like, Ms. Montgomery. We're still going to charge him with murder."

Chapter 28

Mack woke up at ten a.m. on Saturday hungry and with a less sore head, but the ghost of the pain wasn't ready to move on and he felt like he needed at least a month's worth of sleep. The analgesics had suppressed the migraine, but had been ineffective against his dreams.

He couldn't fathom it, didn't know what was happening to him. He'd had everything under control for years: had denied, repressed, screwed it up tighter and tighter until it was just a little dot of scar tissue in the furthest corner of his mind, locked away and imprisoned in the smallest of cells. But the draught had been getting stronger since the start of the case, and a storm was gathering, blowing hard across old scar tissue that had inflated, re-energised and blasted open the cell door. The memories were full-screen again, running on repeat in technicolour.

Past was the past, done and dusted. Except now it wasn't, it was yelling in his head and screaming into dreams, demanding recognition, vengeance, its day in the light.

He checked his phone. There was a voicemail from his mum asking if he was ok, because she hadn't heard from him. He texted her to say he'd call later that day. There was a text from Clarence that had come the night before: she wanted to talk to him. Another one pinged in as he was looking at the phone, was Mack off-duty? Should she call Kennedy? Fuck, no. He texted her back. It was a Saturday, but he could meet if she wanted to.

Mack was already seated at the outside table farthest from the other drinkers with an orange juice and crisps when Clarence's two-seater red convertible pulled into the pub carpark. Two men drinking near the entrance watched her walk across the grass towards him, summer skirt swishing in tandem with shapely hips. They glanced at him as she sat at his table – lucky git, or more likely - how did *he* get *her*. Mack didn't particularly try to suppress his feeling of one-upmanship that he knew squared his shoulders and straightened his back. "What'll you have, Clarence?" He got her a drink and more crisps to replenish his salt levels and sat down opposite her. She looked at him closely.

"Are you ok, Mack? You look a bit peaky."

"Had a migraine. I'm ok now, it took me by surprise, that's all, haven't had such a bad one for a long time."

"That's horrible. When did it start?"

"Thursday night, I didn't get up 'til this morning."

"Poor you. What do you do you think brought that on?"

"Not sure: Knatchbull's constant hostility; tiredness; too much driving in bright sunlight; stress, or a combination of all of them, probably." He paused, "How do you do it, Clarence? How do you work with this crap day in, day out and not get stressed?"

"By crap, do mean child abuse?"

He nodded, "Yeah."

"The same as you work with murder, people being attacked and burgled, terrorists plotting to deliberately maim and murder hundreds of people. It's just a job, you have to go home and forget it."

"But this is different, child abuse. Kids've got no defences, no power, have they?"

"Well, no, they haven't. But neither has the old lady beaten to death for a tenner; or the poor bloke caught up in a terrorist's bomb. It's all crime. It's all nasty. It all results in damage to life or loss of life." She twizzled a discreet diamond stud in her right ear. "It sounds like this has got to you a bit, Mack."

"I just can't get my head around it. How people can do it to kids. If you could've seen Samantha's body, she still had her little sparkly sandal on. It's more than crime; it's a wickedness."

"Try not to see it as worse than any other heinous crime, Mack - it'll tie you in knots. It's easy for us to get caught up in public outrage about child abuse; of course, it's completely appropriate to be outraged. But sometimes, it reduces your ability to make unbiased and rational assessment." She looked him in the eye. "Try not to let it get to you. I know it's hard, but if you don't you just become ineffective as a professional and it spills into your personal life, as well."

"It just makes everything feel out of kilter, that's all." He stopped, stood up - he didn't need Clarence to work as his therapist. "Anyway, another drink?" He nodded at her glass. "Same again?" His eyes were stinging: probably just the migraine; that, the nightmares and sheer, bloody exhaustion. The blokes near the entrance glanced over again, their eyes lingering on the blonde curly head in front of him. He rubbed his eyes, manned up, ignored them as he went past. He returned to the table with the drinks and hoped that the subject had been forgotten. But Clarence had something else she wanted to say.

"Mack, it's just worth bearing in mind that sometimes, people find that working professionally with child abuse triggers stuff for them, could be anything – big or small." She looked and held his gaze, "Sometimes."

He looked away. "Yeah, well," he didn't need anymore, but asked the question anyway. "And what do they do about it?"

"They can see their GP, or maybe their employer has a counselling service. Mack," he looked up. "There's no shame in it. It's normal. It happens to most people at some point. It's just not talked about enough, so when he happens, it takes people by surprise. The important issue is to acknowledge it and get help if necessary. Sometimes just admitting it – to oneself or to others - helps enormously, not everyone needs counselling, some do, some don't, depends on the individual."

"But what if people don't want to admit it?"

She smiled. "I'll give you an example. You know I'm widowed?" He nodded. "For the first year, every time I had a client who'd had a death, I had nightmares, absolutely predictable. I knew that after our first session, I'd go to bed that night and wake up screaming." He was surprised. She always seemed so sorted.

"So, what did you do about it?"

"I had to let myself grieve properly. That's what the dreams were. Just my mind trying to grieve; but consciously, I wasn't letting myself acknowledge the loss. Still haven't, fully, still have questions, but at least it's a start. Dreams, crying, it's only emotional energy, nothing to be scared of. If you don't let it out during your waking hours, it'll find another way. That's often why we have nightmares and dreams, our unconscious mind trying to resolve problems. We just need to make the link." She finished her drink, put the glass on the table between them.

"Anyway, notwithstanding all that, I wanted to see you to talk to you about Keeley."

"Oh yeah?" Mack was still mulling over his nightmares; he dragged himself back.

"I've seen her twice, just to offer some support."

"Oh, did you tell us that?"

"No. Sorry. Should have done. The first session was only Tuesday."

"Crikey, I'm amazed. Did the parents ask you?"

"No, Keeley did. Phoned me herself. Anyway, I saw her for the second time yesterday and she said something rather odd. Do you know a Mr. Bridge?"

"Bridge...oh yeah, the headmaster of Mead Primary?"

"That's him. Well, apparently, he came to her flat on Wednesday just gone. Keeley and her sister got sent to watch tele in their mum's room and she overheard him saying something when she went to the loo and after Bridge had gone, her dad put another lock on the door."

"What did she hear?"

"Bridge telling the Knatchbulls to be careful, cos 'he' knows. Keeley didn't know who 'he' is. Scared her, though. She thinks the men are coming back for her."

"Yeah, I had a funny incident with him, too, went all weird on me when I asked about his kids. I was just being polite, but he practically slammed the door in my face."

"Well, I thought you ought to know."

"You got any witnesses to what Keeley said? S'pose not."

"Actually, I have," said Clarence. "I've had a student sitting in with me. She'll have written up the session. She's there precisely to cover me and act as a witness, as well as for her learning, obviously."

"Obviously," grinned Mack. "You think of everything, Clarence. Right, I need to think about whether this relevant and talk to Kennedy. Keeley say anything else?"

"Only that she'd had a dream about the two men and would try to draw them if she remembers what they look like. Any progress with finding Emma?"

"Yeah, we've located where the girls were held, but that's the sum of it. No more leads at the moment." He thought of something else, "Has Keeley mentioned anyone with the surname of Bull?"

"Bull? No, but if she does, I'll try to get more information and get straight back to you. Oh and Mack, Keeley was asking about Samantha's funeral and whether she can go. Do you know when it is?"

"I'll find out. I actually don't think a date has been set, yet." Mack stood up and walked Clarence to her car, knowing that the two blokes were watching again. "Thanks. For everything."

"I'm always here if you need me, Mack. Just call."

Mack phoned Kennedy from the car.

"How's the head, Mack?"

"Yeah, ok thanks, Sir, better." He relayed his conversation with Clarence. The Inspector had some news of his own: James Brown had been charged, not only with possession of child abuse photos, but also with the murder of Stuart Clarke. Brown had been slotted into the Saturday morning Magistrates Court and remanded. He still hadn't given any information about the mysterious criminal, though. Nonetheless, Kennedy was jubilant.

"Get whoever's on duty today to run checks on Bridge. Could be anything, but we can't leave any stone unturned. And Mack,"

"Sir?"

"Knatchbull's called again with this harassment issue. He's threatening to make a formal complaint about you if you don't stop watching his flat. You're not doing any surveillance that I don't know about are you?"

"Guv, I'm not. It's probably someone he's upset, wouldn't be hard, would it? When is it happening, does he say?"

"Said you were out there again last night."

"Well, as you know, Guv, I was in bed with a migraine last night."

"Mack, I believe you."

"And he's saying it's me, is he? I've seen the view from that balcony. It's a few feet of grass but it's got two or three huge trees at the end. They're in full leaf, now. He'll find it difficult to see someone in a car clearly, unless he's got binoculars." It occurred to Mack that Knatchbull probably had. "You know what he's like, probably just over-reacting to something. Do you want me to talk to him about it?"

"No, no. If he calls again, I'll see him and try to get to the bottom of it. Let me know as soon as about Bridge."

Mack had the luxurious prospect of a weekend without working. He phoned Susie, asked if she was free. She was. They met at the pub and went on for a pizza. She was good company: funny and witty and politically scathing. She was much shorter than him with a figure that was perfectly petite. He kept an eye on her drinking, had a good time.

Chapter 29

Clarence was restless. Saturday nights were the worst time to be alone, single, widowed. She called her sister, who was out to dinner with hubby: date night - yeah, great. Her best friend didn't answer. She knew that she hadn't been wrong about Mack and his anxiety and it wasn't rocket science to conclude that he'd had a bit of a rough childhood, or maybe more than a bit of a rough one, maybe a really rotten one. Talking to him about herself had been a judgement call, but she'd known that he was struggling and had felt for him. The payback was in her own battle.

She wandered into the kitchen. A bottle of perfectly chilled pinot grigio beckoned. She shut the fridge door forcefully: she was becoming too fond of dry and cold white wine. She hesitated, well, maybe just one for the garden. The weather-stripped pallor of the wooden table hummed through the bottom of her glass – a mirage in a wrong place. She pulled out a few weeds, deadheaded pinkly fading tea roses, gently tumbled the petals into an old, cream and patterned porcelain bowl for their scent. The sun was dipping quietly behind the garden wall, its rays retreating, seceding to shadows that inched across her lawn, biting away the light. The day was slowing, settling, stilling. The cats were sprawling in the grass, fat blobs of mellow ginger, too lazy to even chase butterflies after their dinner.

She sat down on the lawn, softly rubbed a hot, feline stomach, the deep, contented purring vibrating back down into her palm, a stark contrast to the high-octane pain that thrummed through her chest. Parched grass prickled her thighs through thin shorts. She ran a hand across it; the hosepipe ban was beginning to show. The lush, verdant, picture-perfect gardens that had surrounded her honeymoon hotel rustled into her mind. The short time in Italy had been the happiest of her life.

It had been raining on a day fashioned for autumn. She'd dripped into Social Services Reception and vigorously shaken out her trench coat, not seeing the person seated in the shady

corner behind, until the Receptionist caught her eye and nodded. He was there to see someone about a case and seemed to
have been forgotten. The rain droplets had landed and perched
perfectly on the weave of his woollen navy jacket. When the
sun broke free and shone through the grimy window, miniscule
rainbows shot through the water that freckled his right shoulder. He grinned. His eyes crinkled. And that was it. For ever.
Until it wasn't.

A large box on top of the spare room wardrobe held all her
wedding paraphernalia: photos, a still-wrapped cake slice, her
engagement and wedding rings. She'd put it all away after Ted's
disappearance – when she was alone, she refused to call it a
death. How was there a death without a body?

She debated whether to indulge her maudlin turn of her
thoughts, go upstairs, get the box, cry over the photos, eat the
cake; or whether to have a drink, mask everything, slosh it away.

The box won.

It could have been yesterday, the photos were that bright. Her
beautiful ivory dress (too old for white) that still hung at the
back of her wardrobe; everyone smiling, happy for her; parents
so proud, relieved she wouldn't be alone when they had gone.
And her handsome, wonderful husband. He wore a cravat that
matched the exact shade of his eyes and the emeralds of her engagement ring. His dark hair gleamed bright in the weak spring
sun. There was a photo of him lifting her into the train on the
way to Italy for their honeymoon – the only man who could ever
easily carry her eleven stone frame (probably more now, with
the booze). She moved on.

A second box, one she never allowed to intrude, held the me-
morial service details: the order of service, the photo of Ted that
had been at the front of the church, in the absence of a coffin. At
the bottom, underneath a pair of cotton black gloves she'd worn
that day, was another photo, one she didn't remember being
taken, didn't remember seeing.

It had been taken from the front of the church, looking out at
the congregation. The place had been full. Ted had had a long

career and colleagues wanted to pay their respects. She examined it, eyes blurred, reaching the point of emotion overload.

The security light outside her front door clicked on, shining brightly up into the bedroom window. The cats were sprawling on the bed; one of them opened a green eye. When Ted had died, gone, left her, she sold the large house they bought in Leigh-on-sea, the family home they planned to fill with children and terriers and, against her family's desperate advice, had bought the cottage, because it was closer to work and further away from everything else. Her brother-in-law had insisted on installing security. Consequently, the front garden was bordered with vicious holly hedging, there was a light at the bottom of the back garden, mounted high onto the brick wall that bordered farmland; a light outside the back door; a light outside the front door and two lights mounted on the wall pillars either side of a gravel drive. When the foxes were busy, the place was lit up like Wembley Stadium.

The light clicked off. She stood up, pulled the curtains and got ready to go to sleep. The cat sat up, rested on his hind quarters and lifted a back paw to scratch methodically and thoroughly behind a pricked ear. He paused mid-movement, paw hovering and looked at her. "What?" The outside light clicked back on. The cat opened both eyes, straightened and moved onto his two front paws, settling into a sitting position, weight forward, unusually alert. He stared hard at the window. The skin on the back of her neck prickled. "I do wish you wouldn't do that," she said, "It spooks me." She pulled back the duvet, lifted the cat out of the way and deposited him next to his brother on the other side of the bed: the cats' side. As she slid under the cover, she remembered she hadn't locked up. She sighed, debating whether she could be bothered to go all the way downstairs; the cottage was isolated, it was only ever passed by farm staff and residents travelling to and from the village, none of them would be interested in breaking in. She thought about Keeley and her friends, got out of bed. The cat moved purposefully back to her side and resumed his vigil. Loneliness bit again; with Ted, she'd never had to worry about being safe.

She went downstairs, locked the front door, the back door, the French doors in the small dining-room and checked the windows and turned back to the front of the cottage, towards the stairs.

The outside light clicked on. There was a noise from the front garden: a crunch on gravel, just once, like something had stopped dead suddenly and was standing poised, waiting, assessing, working out if she'd heard. She paused. Her heart fluttered. It had been a deep, heavy, thorough sound, almost a footfall, too sturdy for a badger, or a fox. She padded into the dark front room and stood to the side of the bay window, peering through the nets. But only a startled, adolescent dog fox was looking at her, his ginger coat rich and bright in her artificial light, tail bushy and proud. He turned away, trotted across the road and disappeared amongst the large harvested bales in the dark fields opposite. The light clicked off. Shivering despite the muggy heat, she went back to bed.

The phone woke her, her sister's jolly hockey-sticks happiness unwanted. She declined the offer of Sunday lunch - didn't want to play happy families. She fed the cats and decided to catch up with some work reports. Her notes were in the office. She found her bag and work pass and got ready to leave.

There was a folded sheet of paper wedged halfway through her letterbox. She pulled it out. Across the centre of the page were two words written in black felt-tip and bold, block capitals: 'BE CAREFUL'. She stumbled back and sat heavily on the stairs; the fox had been a latecomer to the party.

Clarence ran through a list of all her recent clients, but couldn't identify any who were angry, mad, or bad. She considered whether to call the police, but dismissed the idea; they would only ask about her clients, who she might have upset - if they were interested at all. And quite possibly it was just a crank. She put the note on the hall table, decided to talk to Mack about it when she had the chance. She made sure the house was secure and locked the cat-flap to keep her pets indoors.

The office building was open, the security guard wet in his dark blue uniform, his white and tan terrier under shade next to a bowl of water, snoring, whiskers and paws twitching. Clarence looked and grinned, "Yeah, don't" said the guard, "Who's the sensible one, eh?"

She spent a couple of hours report-writing and then started thinking about a late lunch. She gathered her belongings, walked to the door and looked back to check she's left nothing that she would need. She spied the edge of a buff folder that had been partially buried under some post on her desk. She had forgotten about the Knatchbull file.

Clarence didn't know why she asked for it. As the records clerk had said, it was empty. There was just the name and date of birth on the front, nothing else to see. She threw it back onto the desk, it landed upside down. There was some writing scribbled on the back in blue biro. She found her glasses. 'Foster home cancelled, gone to live with relative'. No name, just an address outside Chelmsford: bloody hell, what appalling recording. She circled the address, sat down again, turned her computer back on and pulled up the database search engine, ran the address through it, but there were no matches.

She supposed it wasn't particularly significant, but she made a note of the address to pass on to Mack when she next saw him, just to be thorough.

Chapter 30

The paediatrician had tried to refuse, told Bull to call an ambulance. But Reggie Bull had invested heavily in insurance over the years; it always paid out – in the end.

Bull watched the doctor's hands shake slightly as he opened his bag and pulled on some latex gloves. He lifted one of Emma's eyelids, then the other; she moaned slightly. Dr. Parmer softly stroked her cheek. Bull grabbed him by the shoulder and swung him round. "No fucking funny ideas, Parmer, she's not for sale and definitely not before my dibs."

"She's a patient, what do you take me for?"

"For what you fucking are. Get on with it." Parmer gave Emma a glucose finger-prick test, checked the result, then inserted a canula into the vein in the crook of her arm and set up a sodium chloride drip, hooking it over the high, scrolled iron bedhead. He watched for a few seconds, took off the gloves and pushed them into a pocket, nodded towards the corner and followed Bull over. "You're lucky, her glucose isn't too low, but she's dehydrated. I thought you'd given up all this? Is this the other child who was taken?"

Bull gave an almost imperceptible nod.

"So, you've already had one dead body to deal with – that clearly went badly wrong and now I'm the route to avoiding another?"

"In a manner of speaking."

"In a manner of speaking! You've got some front, Bull, I know I've had my weaknesses over the years, but I didn't murder kids, kidnap and traumatise them. I don't want to be involved in your crap. Not one bit."

Bull round himself mildly amused by the other man's indignation. "How long have we known each other, Parmer? Thirty, forty years? Where do you think all the kids came from? What do you think happened to them before you got your grubby little mitts on them? They didn't get flown in by the stork, you

165

know, pre-formed to accommodate your pleasure. Someone had to find them, get them, break them in. And that someone was me. I know I've been careless with this one, but there we are. It's what we do, who we are. You're no better than I am. You've had your fun over the years."

"Yes. And made you a rich man."

"True, but that's the name of the game, Parmer, isn't it? You like sex with children. You choose not to restrain yourself, you choose to break the law. I provided a service, you purchased it. End of. Don't bellyache with me because, all of a sudden, you've having to deal with the messy end."

"Messy end! I never signed up for murder, you bastard."

Bull snorted his laughter. "How many kids you gone through over the years, Parmer? High-days and holidays for you usually, wasn't it? As I remember it, your fiftieth was a bit of a celebration. Was it two, that night, or three? Although to be fair you've slackened off a bit over the past few years; in fact, thinking about it, I've not seen you for a long time, not since your retirement bash." Bull stroked his chin. "That was a big do, all the great and good – wonder if they knew about your little hobby. Should I call it that? At a conservative guess, I'd say, over the course of our working relationship, you've got through tens rather than just a few kids."

"Got through?" Parmer spoke through clenched lips. "I didn't murder them, or have them murdered, you bastard, leave them dying. They were all returned to you in one piece, unharmed."

Bull snarled scorn. "They're not unharmed. You're in fucking denial, Parmer. How many of those kids do you think went on to kill themselves? Do you honestly think, that after the likes of you and I have finished with them, they have a normal life? Don't tell me you're not a murderer; it's just that the sentence you give is delayed, it's still going to happen. A load of them will have ended up on wards like the ones you used to run: attempted suicides, self-harm, drugs, booze, bulimia." He breathed in through his nose.

"You're a nonce. You're like me, like all the other men who've come here over the years, crawling and whining, making excuses, pretending that they're not what they are. Just trying it out, just the once, blah, blah. In today's society, the likes of us, mate, we're the lowest of the low. It's not the seventies, there's no Paedophile Information Exchange arguing the toss. Now we're just the scum of the earth. Times have changed." Bull felt the beginnings of the familiar flicker of the tic at the corner of his right eye. "Do you know what we're called now? 'Minor Attracted Persons' - MAPS. The terminology has changed, but we haven't.

You're a professional, have social standing, but that would all go down the bleedin' pan if anyone got to find out about your little habits, especially you being a paediatrician. You're someone who's meant to make kids better, not rape them!"

"It was never rape. I never hurt them."

"Bollocks! It's rape in the eyes of the law, end of, whatever the kids did or didn't say and whatever you tell yourself. And you know it as well as I do. You'd lose everything. No more beach holidays with the grandkiddies in their cute little swimming trunks and bikinis, Parmer, they'd be whisked away quicker than you can call 999. Your kids would hate you, if they don't already. Were you ever able keep your hands off them? I doubt it, you must have had a little dabble at home. What does the wife think? Does she know about your proclivities, or just think that you never really fancied her? That you have a low sex drive?"

Parmer was breathing heavily. Bull watched the sweat gather on his upper lip.

The doctor walked over to the cabinet and found a cubby hole containing some good whisky. He looked at Bull, who nodded. Parmer poured a couple of glasses. "So why do you do it, Reggie? You're coming at me like you're all holier than thou."

"I don't do it any more, do I? Too old. Got prostate trouble. But why did I? For the same reasons you did. Because it's who I am; it's all that I know. It still turns me on, just can't do much about it now. And I'm greedy. I like it. It makes me feel good. I'm addicted. Just having her here pleases me. Just watching her sleep pleases me, knowing that I can do what I want, if I want. And ultimately, because I never fucking cared and still don't. The difference between us, Parmer, is that I know what it is, what I am and I don't pretend otherwise. I'm honest about it, at least with myself. I grew up with this. For me it was do or die. For these kids, now, when they're with me, it's do or die. But I don't want this one to die, it's inconvenient."

The tic was picking up rhythm, a desperate moth trapped under fine fabric. Parmer was no stranger to Bull's temper.

He went back to Emma, checked her pulse, felt her forehead. She was still asleep. He turned around. "I'm going to leave you a second bag. When this one's empty, just hook up the second one. When that's empty, gently remove the canula – the needle - just slowly slip it out and put a plaster on if it bleeds a bit. Do you understand?"

Bull nodded, "Course I do, I'm not an idiot."

"Well, make sure you understand this: this is a patch-up job. I've stopped her deteriorating any further, but it doesn't matter how many threats you make, I can't make this child better, because she's traumatised and malnourished. You need to keep her fed – even if it's just toast and butter - and hydrated. The best option would be to return her. Do you understand that? Do we have an understanding? About everything?"

Bull gave a nonchalant nod. "Sure, we have a deal." Parmer packed up his belongings, pulled out a pristine, white handkerchief from his pocket and picked up his empty whisky glass.

Bull burst into laughter. "Seriously, Parmer, don't bother. Do you honestly think I haven't kept insurance over the years? DNA, notes, photos. You don't need to worry. I asked you to treat her, you have. It's no use to me to dob in my clients."

Parmer walked towards the door. "Don't call me again. Ever. I've got myself under control, anyway - don't need your services anymore."

Bull's genuine mirth chased off his anger. "You've got old, that's all," he said. "Don't try and kid yourself, or me, that you've developed a conscience."

Chapter 31

Having Susie in his bed hadn't scared off the bogey-man. The nightmares had started shortly after falling asleep. In the end, embarrassed, Mack had got up and driven her home to the other side of Chelmsford. He'd been a gentleman and seen her safely into her flat, but had a feeling that he wouldn't be seeing her again. And he couldn't say he blamed her.

He needed to speak to his mum, no point denying it any longer. His nights were an unholy rotating trio of sleep, screaming and sweat over which he had no control; it was beginning to impact upon his daytime functioning. For the past twelve years or so, his home-grown method of denial and repression had worked, but Samantha's murder - the violence done to her, her dangling limbs and opened stomach - had torn up his self-help manual. In fact, if he was doing the past, he may as well admit that the pages had started to curl up after his baptism of rape. And now he needed a new, better, more professional manual, a new testament: Guidance for Fuckups.

He debated seeing his GP and ruled it out a second later; he didn't want his medical records recording that a version of insanity was temporarily engaging his brain. Talking to Clarence in a sane, rational way in bright and high sunshine was one thing, opening himself up to police intolerance of weakness in any future job applications was something quite different, whatever feely-feely pamphlets they gave out when you started the job; ditto the work counselling. He knew Clarence was right. What she said made sense. He needed to get his response to the case under control; he needed to get his mind under control, but he intended to take instruction from the re-write of his own manual.

All of it was about his dad, he knew. The anxiety that went straight to his head and stomach, his inability to challenge Kennedy to any effective degree – or any other male in authority for that matter - the violence of the re-born dreams, all of it stemmed from the tension and terror: he thought some more; horror was a better word - it stemmed from the horror. Probably, at some level, he'd always known, but had buried it away to bulk out the scar tissue. It had needed someone to point it out, make him face it. And he thought that maybe it was about his mum, too, for not protecting him, even though his adult self knew she never could have. All of it needed to face the light.

The police checks against Bridge had come back clear. He had no criminal record, not even a speeding ticket. Kennedy wanted Mack to try to have a casual conversation with him in the first instance - they had nothing to bring him in for. Mack planned to be at the school for the first day of the new term on Monday. He decided that he'd take Dave Cooper with him, thought that it would be useful to get another take on Bridge and that Cooper hadn't been himself lately. He hadn't bucked up much since their night in the pub. Mack wanted to check in with him.

He phoned his mum whilst his courage held and arranged to go for Sunday lunch.

When Mack had gone to university, his mum had given up the rented family home and bought herself a one-bed flat outright with a small surprise inheritance from Scottish relatives they never saw. The flat was on the first floor of a modern block. It had a little balcony that was just wide enough for a round table and two chairs and faced Chelmsford town centre. Mack parked in a visitor bay and rang the buzzer.

Every time he saw her she looked a bit shorter, a bit more frail. There were crows' feet edging her eyes, although she was only in her mid-fifties. Her short hair had greyed and maybe thinned. The guilt bit into his heart. He knew that she had a reasonable social life, played bridge, went to church and the inheritance had left enough to live on, so she didn't need to work. But she was so overwhelmingly happy to see him, it made him realise how lonely she was and how much she missed him.

She'd cooked a huge roast lamb dinner with all the trimmings and his favourite boyhood pudding: treacle sponge and custard.

Afterwards, he did the washing-up and slumped onto the

sofa, sated. He drew in a breath and took the bull by the horns. "Mum?"

"Yes, darling"

"Do you ever think about dad? Do you wonder what might've happened to him?"

She didn't answer his question, didn't meet his eyes. "What makes you ask?"

Shit, this was hard, his heart was already pounding thirty seconds in. "Well, um, we never talked about it, did we? Did you ever report him missing to the police?"

She stood up and got some chocolates from the sideboard cupboard, Roses, gave him the whole tin. He busied himself opening it, the sticky-tape tight around the lid and unnecessarily tricky, like the manufacturers expected the chocolates to make an escape bid. "No, I didn't report him missing." Her brown eyes, lighter with age, welled up. "Did you honestly think I wanted him back? I was just glad he'd gone. Why are you asking me this, Mack?"

He gave up on the sticky-tape, which needed a knife anyway, got up to sit next to her and put his arm around her shoulders. "I know, mum, I'm sorry, I'm really sorry."

"I don't want to think about it."

"I know, but it's just that I've started having nightmares about it all. And we never discussed it, any of it, did we?"

"What's there to discuss? He was big and brutal and nasty. I couldn't stand up to him. He was so strong. He would never get help with his drinking. Once, I left a couple of leaflets on the kitchen table, ones about Alcoholics Anonymous. When he saw them, he was livid, threw them in the bin and went down to the pub. I was too ashamed to go to the police, to even tell anyone at church – when I could go." Her sobbing ate into him. "I just wanted you to be happy and safe, to protect you. I'm your mum and I failed you. Badly let you down. It's all I think about, what he did to you, what I let him do."

Mack held her tight. "It's not your fault, mum. He was the one who got drunk and violent. Not you."

"It is my fault. I married him and had a child with him. I knew what he was like before I was pregnant. I thought a baby could change him. But he got worse, drank more than ever."

"You were young, optimistic. Lots of domestic violence victims think it's their fault." He recalled Clarence's words, "It's normal, the norm, what most people think. He was a horrible, violent drunk, we were better off without him. He did all of it, not you. The responsibility is his. It doesn't matter now."

After some minutes, she left his embrace, got up and went to the bedroom to fetch a tissue, came back, sat next to him and took his face in both hands, warming his cheeks, making him face her. "It does matter. It mattered then and it matters now. If you're having nightmares, it matters. What can I do to help?"

He hadn't planned for his own tears, hadn't planned for any of it; he wondered if anyone ever did – not even Clarence, apparently. But he especially hadn't anticipated his mum's response, her validation of his pain and the confession of her guilt. He hadn't understood it was what he needed to hear. He cried into her shoulder, great heaving spasms of backed-up despair that she absorbed and held. When he could finally stop, she wiped his eyes with her soggy tissue, which made them both laugh, stretched up and kissed him hard on the forehead and then they sat next to each other, holding hands, a new level of intimacy that was comforting and safe.

"I'm so proud of you, Mack. I tell all my friends that my son is a detective sergeant. My tall, handsome son."

"Mum..."

"It's true! You're a wonder, to have turned out so well after what you went through." She paused, "Is it this case that's brought it all back, the missing girls one?" He nodded. "I know that you're going to find that other girl, Mack - Emma, is it? You always were so clever, you'll work it out."

"I'm not that clever, mum."

"You were reading before you went to school. Do you know that?" He didn't. "It came really easily to you. You were way above all the other children your age. I think that your dad's behaviour stifled you a bit – maybe a lot, but still, you made up for it. At every open evening, the teachers sang your praises. You've achieved 'A' levels, a degree and you're a detective sergeant before you're thirty years old. I know you have to take exams for that – I googled it," she said, proudly.

"Crikey, well done, mum, you've finally moved into the internet age, have you?"

"Yes, I got myself an ipad so that I could learn about what you do. The phone screen was too small." He hugged her again.

"Cup of tea, mum?"

"Please, darling."

Later, when he was getting ready to go, she laid a hand on his arm. "Do you think we should report your dad, now, as missing?" Mack thought about it. He did something he never had before, something that had never been safe: he let his mind consciously return to the past. He remembered the shouting and thumping; the fear that she was hurt; the gut-clenching terror that she would be gone in the morning, or worse; the confusion and hatred; how everything used to get twisted and tangled up in the child's obligation to love. He remembered how his fantasies were watered by her tears and how everything had culminated at a tidal resolution.

He was a serving police officer, needed to be seen to have acted within the full remit of the law. He wondered what Kennedy would do. He could never ask. But that was ok. Because despite it all, he was moving towards a future. He was taking Clarence's advice: acknowledging the past, knowing it and leaving it behind. He didn't need to know what anyone else would do. It was time to be his own man, complete the process started with his baptism and be born again.

"For all we know, mum, he could've gone off with another woman, inflicted himself on some other poor family. There would be a whole heap of questions that we'll never be able to answer and you'll only get upset. It was nearly fifteen years ago. If his body ever washes up somewhere one day, or if he turns up on your doorstep, we'll deal with it then. But I think we would've heard something by now if any of that was going to happen." He kissed her cheek. It was as soft and fragrant as when she used to tuck him into bed. "Don't worry, mum. Leave it."

"Will you come next Sunday? For lunch?"

"I can't promise Sunday, it depends on work. But I promise, I'll be here every weekend at some point from now on. Sorry, mum."

"Perhaps we could go to church together?"

He laughed, "Yeah, perhaps. I'll speak to you in the week. Love you."

She saw him out to the communal door. As he got into his car, she called out, her voice breaking, "Mack – you will forgive me. Won't you?" He ran back to her, took her hand and pressed his lips to it, "Always, mum, always."

That night, he went to bed early and slept for ten hours of untroubled peace.

Chapter 32

Friday and Saturday nights had been the worst. When he was small, without the words for questions, Mack's mum had put him to bed early with cocoa and an audio book on a tape recorder. But it made no difference. He still jolted awake to the opening squeak and metal clank shut of the front gate and the uneven, scratching fiddling of a key trying to find a lock in the dark and the shouting and swearing if it didn't play ball. If they were lucky, if it was a good night, his dad would stumble across the doorstep and collapse in the hall, crawl through the spinning to a solid wall and sit tight against it until morning, when after bacon and eggs he would sprawl away the day in bed. If it was a bad night, if they were unlucky, if God wasn't smiling and was bearing a grudge, his dad would roar in, belt unbuckled and already half-off, ready to spew out his bitterness before the vomit cut him short.

Later, after, when it was over and he heard his mum trudge a heavy tread up the stairs, he would take his hands away from his ears, lie down again, listen for the shower running, and fall into a restless sleep. His dad was like God: he rested on a Sunday. Mack and his mum used to go to church, mum in best dress with matching make-up, standing tall and proud and straight.

The day after Mack had turned ten, become a big boy, he had tiptoed down the stairs and peered through the half-open living-room door in time to see a large fist open and then grip his mum's slender arm and twist backwards. He heard the crack. The screaming started straight after.

His dad was a tall, heavy man; his mum used to say that he was built like a packhorse. Mack had landed hard against a wall. The blood stain never completely faded. After that, Mack was a target, too. As he got older, more angry, bolder, bigger and stronger, he tried to save the both of them, but could never match the strength of a large man full of drink-fuelled, spiteful fury and was always the worse for it.

His dad had gone when Mack was fifteen, making his Friday night trip to the pub and never coming back. He didn't show up for work on the Monday, had never been popular on the building sites, they didn't much care. The hours of absence morphed into days, the days into weekends, the weekends into a whole month, the months into half a year. At first, for days, his mum had cried every night. He could almost feel her sobs juddering through his mattress: relief or sorrow, he never knew.

Then there came a night when his mum didn't cry. For the first time, Mack began to sleep a deep, thorough sleep, undisturbed and restful. He and his mum fell into the type of life that they thought normal families had: families where people laughed together and loved, didn't flinch when they accidentally touched.

His mum started cooking proper dinners, huge affairs, Sunday roasts and mid-week shepherd's pie; she fed his mates, too. They both put on weight - they both needed to. He'd go out at weekends like normal teenagers did and took sharp control of a new and acknowledged propensity for alcohol. His mum took on extra work hours to save for his university fees, wouldn't let Mack take a Saturday job, wanted him to study.

And so it was. The past was the past. Mack and his mum never talked about it. The violence, the memory of brutality, was relegated to the shadows, lurking in the darkness, never brought into the light to be named and then banished. Bruises faded and her untreated broken forearm healed slightly crooked, a reminder of how their lives and minds and souls had been warped.

His mum's tears watered fledging, timid, night-time fantasies. They speedily grew bold and greedy, sprawled outwards into his waking life and claimed hours of daytime dreaming. The permutations of his dad's death were endless, the planning and intricacies full of precise detail, the possibilities electrifying. The best fantasy, his favourite method, was that his dad had toppled drunk over the sea-wall somewhere and splashed into the Thames - its juncture with the North Sea creating an inescapable current, that he had fallen from such a height that his stomach ruptured open, spilling his guts to float away on the ebbing tide like a mass of fleshy, tubular jetsom. Or even better, that he'd tumbled onto the stony and hard-littered mudflats at low tide and lain alone, broken, helpless, screaming and hearing no-one respond, knowing the inevitability of the water, dreading the moon's tidal call, anticipating death and the manner of its coming. And then it would start. First there would be a lapping, a soft stroking of ears, mouth and eyes, the gentleness of the water offering a stupid hope of redemption, salvation. Then would come the waves, pushing harder, surging into every orifice and staking a claim, each ebbing allowing for only seconds of spluttering and desperate gasps of oxygen. The finale was almost orgasmic: a flooding, salty, violent tsunami into the lungs, banishing air, bringing death, washing a finally dead, dead, dead, obliterated body out to the North Sea to be nibbled and consumed, liquidated and cleansed.

Mack tunnelled his sadness, shame and horror way into the back of his mind, deep into his unconscious. Soon, it was so well controlled he didn't even dream. At university, he couldn't relate to male tutors, or any adult men, so was either scornful and challenging, or scared. He didn't know how he was meant to be, what a man should do. He developed a hashed-together persona that got him by: defensive and not too deferent. A belligerent protection of females, construed as gallantry, and his obvious intelligence, kept him on the right side of popular. His tall good looks helped. Mack settled into an adult identity: joined the police, made his mum proud, made sure he kept to the Friday night phone call, tried to be a good son.

But Samantha's death, the violence done to her, had torn off the scar tissue and revealed soft, tender wounds that were readily ruptured to weep mercurial poison that scalded a route backwards through his brain and lit up the past like a tube map. The images were so vivid, so alive, so replete with rich and satisfyingly violent vengeance, that Mack wondered if they must be somehow burnt into his brain cells. They were so clear, in fact, it was like they'd morphed into a memory.

Chapter 33

Kennedy sent Cooper on an errand on the Monday morning, so Mack was at the Mead Primary school bright and early by himself. He took the opportunity to have a good look around. The school was a modern, one-storey building, screaming seventies construction, design and lack of imagination.

It was an ugly, uninspiring structure. The pebbledash that had been pummelled into the brickwork was coming loose, so had dropped away in places and the shape of the place was a stuck together combination of squares and rectangles in weather-dulled, primary colours. The overall impression was one of shabbiness and neglect.

He knew that the estate had been built on Mead Farm, left abandoned after the second world war – named for the drink made there for centuries. The village itself, Bellington, was named after the celebrated church bells that had used to ring out on Sunday mornings, calling farmhands to worship; like the farm, they were gone. He wondered where the bee hives had stood. The only nod to the area's past was a tall oak with a huge girth that stood to the edge of the small playing-field - and that had been fenced off to stop the pupils climbing it. It was shame; as a child, navigating himself to the top of the world had given Mack hours of respite, the chance to practise being in control of a disturbed and confusing life. Now health and safety had gone mad – no wonder all the kids were getting fat. Mack was still gazing up at the high and ancient branches when he saw Bridge's small, grey fiat pull into the car park.

He wandered over as the headmaster unlocked the main school door. "We're actually not starting term until tomorrow, Sergeant Sumerson. Perhaps it could wait 'til later in the week? I have a lot to prepare – new school year, I'm sure you understand."

"I can imagine, Mr. Bridge. But my Inspector wanted me to pop by to run a couple of points past you. I'll only need a few minutes of your time." He stepped over the threshold straight after Bridge. "Shall I come in?" Mack followed the other man down the main corridor to his office. School smell hung in the air. The door to a small, windowless room next to the headmaster's office was open, a couple of cleaning ladies had just arrived, too, and were starting their day.

"So, Sergeant, how can I help you?"

"Well, a couple of things, really. Just wanted to update you about Emma, in case the children ask you any questions."

"Well, that's very thoughtful of you, Sergeant. I must admit, I was feeling anxious about what I would say to them. I was going to address it during the first assembly. What do you advise?"

"Just say that the police are still working very hard to find Emma. Would that be ok?"

"Yes, I'm happy with that. What about any after school clubs. Should they start up?"

"They can, however, it's on the proviso that all the children are collected and not left to go home by themselves. I know that it's tempting, when the school is so close to the estate, but it's not worth the risk. Make it a condition of attendance. Are you in contact with the police school liaison officer?" Bridge nodded. "Ok, well if you have any problems about that with the parents, why not get him to speak to them. You could even ask him to be there after school the first couple of days, to push home the point."

"Excellent idea, Sergeant. Was there anything else?"

"Yeah. I wondered if you've seen any of the girls' parents since the incident, Emma's or Keeley's, I mean, whether they've said anything interesting, or significant that could help us."

"No, I haven't seen anyone. Obviously, we sent a card from the school to Samantha's parents. And I'll be at the funeral. When is that, by the way? Do you know?"

"No, I don't. Sometimes, the body can't be released for a while, depending on how the case progresses. Ok. Well, thanks Mr. Bridge." Mack turned to leave, then turned back. Bridge already had his back to the door and was leaning over his desk. "Oh, one other thing: do you know anyone by the surname of Bull?"

The headmaster didn't turn around. "Bull? With a 'u'?"

"Yes."

"No, can't say I do. Sorry."

Mrs. Knatchbull dropped Keeley off for her final session with Clarence at the end of the first day of the new school term.

"So, how did your day go at your new school, Keeley?"

Keeley smiled, "It was really good. I made a new friend on the bus and we came home together."

"That's great, Keeley. That's something that you were worried about, wasn't it?" Keeley nodded. "But in the end, it was ok. What's your friend's name?"

"Jane Spencer. It's funny, Clarence, cos that's the same name that my mum had before she married my dad."

"Oh really, that's a coincidence, isn't it?"

"Well, it was my mum's name, but before that she had another one."

"Your mum had another surname?"

"Her first name was always Janice, but before she was Spencer, I think she had another last name."

"How do you know?"

"Last year, in the summer holidays, we went to Disneyland. Mum told me to get the passports from the drawer. But there was an extra one, underneath all the others, from when mum was a little girl. In that passport, she had a different name, before she was called Spencer. I think she must've forgotten about it. Actually, I forgot about it 'til just now, I think cos I was so excited about going to Disneyland. I've never heard of anyone else who's called Clarence. I thought it was a boy's name, anyway. Why did your mum call you that? Did she want you to be a boy?"

Clarence was glad that Keeley was so happy and chatty, not so glad she'd asked about her name. She gave a practised explanation. "No, it wasn't because my parents wanted a boy. There used to be a programme on the television – a very long time ago – about a lion called Clarence. When I was born, I had loads of blonde, curly hair and my mum and dad thought it looked like a lion's mane. Do you know what I mean?"

Keeley nodded, "Yeah, the fluffy big fur around a man lion's neck."

"That's right, so they called me Clarence." She'd obviously piqued pity, Keeley's mouth was a perfectly formed open circle. She straightened her lips.

"Oh well, you've still got lots of blonde hair. And it is quite curly. And you're still not very old, so it'll probably be ages before it goes grey. I think Clarence is a nice name, anyway."

Out of the mouth of babes: Clarence changed the subject, "So, school was good?"

"Yep, I'm in the same class as Jane. I think we'll be besties."

"That's really great that you've found a new friend. And right at the start of term, too."

"She lives near the school, so she got off the bus before me. But we've got each other's numbers. I told mum. She said that I can have Jane over to tea one day."

"Did you have school dinner or packed lunch?"

"School dinner."

"And what was that like?"

"S'ok, fishfingers, mash and peas. After, me and Jane sat with some other girls and watched some of the big girls play hockey on the field."

"That's so good, Keeley. I'm pleased you enjoyed your first day. Do you think you'll join any clubs?"

"Probably. We haven't got a list yet. But I probably will. Maybe a dance one, that would be really good."

"Sounds like you like dancing."

"I used to go to ballet when I was little, but my mum stopped it. I think it was too far away."

"Ok. So, you know that this is the last time we're going to meet?"

"Mum told me."

"And how do you feel about that?"

"Ok, but can I come back if I want to later?"

"Yes, as long as your mum agrees. You can call me, or she can, anytime - I'll be here."

"Will Bertie still be here?" Keeley picked up the stuffed bear and gave him a kiss on the head.

"Everything will be the same, nothing changes here, Keeley, except Donna won't be here."

"Where is Donna today?"

"She had to go to a meeting this afternoon. But apart from that, nothing'll be different if you come again." Out of curiosity, Clarence asked a final question. "So, what was your mum's first name, then, before it changed to Spencer?"

"I think it was Ball...no, that's not right, I remember that it was like a cow." She looked down, frowning and then looked up again, triumphant. "Bull. That was it! Bull. Like a boy cow." She giggled. "That's funny, isn't it? My mum was called after a boy cow and you're called after a boy lion. Maybe they knew that mum was going to marry my dad and that would be really confusing, wouldn't it? Then my mum would be Mrs. Knatchbull and my nan and grandad would be Mr. and Mrs. Bull. That would be funny. Yeah, I expect that's why it got changed."

Chapter 34

George was playing him up. Given that they were half-brothers, Reggie was hurt: he had expected at least a modicum of loyalty. He scowled down at the screen of the mobile phone and fruitlessly stabbed some buttons, bloody useless things, he could never work out how to turn up the volume. "George, it's going to happen. It's got to happen. End of. The family has to be protected. I don't care how you do it, just make sure you stick to the rules." He paused, pressing his ear against the phone, "Look, don't bellyache about your family. You've been mostly left alone all these years. If you don't play ball, you know how it goes. I'll call it in, George, and then you *will* be worrying about those pretty girls. Just do it."

He threw the phone onto the sofa and poured himself a long whisky. One thing – he had asked for one thing from his half-brother - and all he got was whinging and whining. George knew the score, what was expected.

Reggie's paternal grandad had died at the ripe age of ninety-seven. Typically, he had lingered with a cancer that would have killed most people within a year: grandad had lasted for ten. Reggie had read somewhere about the strength of mad people, their proclivity for lingering, why the psychopath in films kept getting up. And by the world's standards, even by Reggie's if he was honest – and Reggie's baseline was low - Grandad was mad. Towards the end, he'd had his bed moved into the front room of the Poplar house, where he could watch the comings and goings through the window and monitor everything that went on. The old man had had a lot of time to think about and plan his legacy.

It had been at about the time Reggie started to have some success from his own, private business. He had branched out from the family, running a few things on the side, mainly drugs and then guns; IRA activity was at its height and he found a niche market.

He had seen the way the East End was going and got out, made provisions for himself. He'd already accrued enough money to buy his nice, private, secluded house in Essex, back when house prices were still reasonable. He had it modified to suit his needs and used it as a base for business and never left; he valued consistency. It had been a cash buy from a client, no need for a mortgage, questions, officials.

It had been the seventies: gentrification was coming. The other houses in the Poplar terrace were gradually vacated as all the old residents, war survivors, like the houses, died. Ever since Reggie could remember, children had taken over the running of the houses from their parents, but inter-generational living was coming to an end and landlords and bereaved relatives took their opportunity. Young people moved in, relishing the unchanged, period features, loving having a Regency house slap-bang in the middle of the East End, prepared to spend the money that previous owners could never afford. They weren't going to put up with the state of number nine Poplar Square: all the busyness of the property, kids running around, people always coming and going; peeling paint and cracked windows. And unlike the old neighbours, who lived and let live, the new ones took an active interest in who was parking in their little street. They walked their dogs in the park opposite, played with their pretty little kids there - there was always at least one of them keeping out a nosey eye. In the end they even started a Neighbourhood Watch. It had spooked the clients and marked the beginning of the end for the family home.

Reggie found himself another niche market. He took the richer, more powerful clients, men scared off by the changes in Poplar, and he offered them a superior service. After a few false starts, he learnt how to safely obtain suitable children and he provided them clean, disease-free, fed and trained to please, compliant children, unlikely to attract the attention of Social Workers, teachers and any other (normal) adults who might encounter them. And when he told clients that that the children's education didn't suffer – that Reggie himself, a once Oxbridge candidate – was providing them with an education whilst they were in his care – he knew that he had found the magic formula. Men queued up to buy a golden ticket, to purchase the deletion of guilt and the normalising of perversion. Reggie was choosey about his clients and he knew the clients would always be necessarily discreet about him. And so he made his fortune.

A few months before he passed, grandad had demanded regular visits from his older male relatives, including Reggie and made it clear that he was considering his legacy. He called a family meeting to make the announcement. On the day, the house had been put into lockdown, the kids confined to their room, no visitors, front room curtains drawn like he was already dead: the old bastard always had been a drama queen. By that time, the cancer was eating into his throat. He had been propped up on pillows, fussed over by the women, and then wheezed through his speech about who was to take over as Head of the Family. It wasn't to be one of his sons, or any of his younger brothers, or any of Reggie's numerous cousins. No. The chosen one was Reggie. According to grandad, his grandson was forward-thinking, dependable, loyal and bright – intelligent even. Reggie's dad had brought fresh blood into the gene pool when he married Reggie's mum, which meant that Reggie didn't suffer from the inbreeding stupidity that afflicted much of the family. Grandad passed two days later. His was no burial in the basement: he went to the family plot in a large Poplar church to join his dad and his father before him.

Things had changed swiftly after that. After the war, when the house had been sold to the council, but rented by the family, they had been given a lifelong tenancy. Reggie didn't want the privilege, thank you very much; it was his habit to ensure that his name wasn't recorded on any official documents and he had bitterly regretted being stupid enough to have registered his house in his own name. There was a young couple living in the Poplar house, the tenancy went to them.

The family had never used their money wisely, spent it as quickly as it came; even after the war, when business picked up a bit, the family never invested in the house, or kids. Reggie changed that. He took and kept control of all the money, paying family members regularly, like a salary. And then he gradually shut down the business side of things that ran out of number nine Poplar Square. The police, regular clients for years and broadly useful in keeping him and the family out of the spotlight and out of trouble, had become too demanding for Reggie's peace of mind, thought they could run the show, take the power away from the family. The rise of the computer age, meaning easier cross-referencing and tracing, was making everything too risky. He found other accommodation and then moved family members out. When Chastity died, she and the kid were the last ones there. Reggie had doled out the family savings to each relative and sent them on their way, the house had gone back to the council. It had been a shame. His family had lived there for generations, nearly two hundred years, since the house was built. But needs must, it was a different world.

Reggie had worked in a more arms-length way from then on. But everyone in the family knew the deal. They had their dosh and were secure. But there was one condition: if Reggie called it in, he expected a swift response. George was out of the habit, having gone and got himself fostered and then adopted when he was ten, squealing little pig. But Reggie firmly planned to lick him back into shape, this would be a good test of his abilities – and loyalty. And after all, there was no-one else.

Chapter 35

Clarence was trying to work out what the hell was going on. One minute she was getting into her car to go home from work and trying to get hold of Mack on his mobile and the next she was in someone's kitchen with her wrists tied together in her lap and her ankles lashed to the legs of a wooden dining chair.

She squinted through blurred vision. A short, tubby man was sitting a few feet away. He had greying hair, a face wet with sweat and bright blue eyes. He was watching her intently. "Would you like some water?" She nodded and winced - the movement kicked into motion a throbbing that galloped across her forehead. He got up, filled a glass from the tap and held it for her whilst she sipped, "Better?"

Her buttocks felt glued to the chair. She let her eyes drop down and saw that the crotch of her trousers was damp. She looked back at the man and felt her heart start to race deep in her chest. His fingers were tapping out an uneven beat on the surface of a large, glass dining-table next to him. By his hand lay a needle and a syringe half-full of amber liquid. It chattered against the glass to the vibration of his rapping. She stiffened.

"What's the t...", the corner of her mouth drooped downwards. She ran her tongue around her lips, looked at the glass. He held it for her. She tried again, "Whad time's it?"

"About six a.m., you were out for ages, longer than I thought you'd be. Sorry, your head must really hurt." He nodded at the syringe. "I think I gave you more than I should've, but I'm not used to all this."

Clarence raised her tied hands to her mouth, plucked at her lips, pushed up the sagging corner. "What given me?"

"Don't worry. It's temporary, your speech will be fine."

"Where am I?"

"Ah, can't tell you that. He wouldn't like it."

"Who wouldn't?"

He took a deep breath and sighed out. "I'm sorry about this,

Mrs. Hope. I didn't want to do this. I know you're just doing your job. I like Social Workers, in the main they're very helpful people, good people. Unfortunately, you've just been in the wrong place at the wrong time."

She shook her head carefully, closed her eyes and tried to focus despite the cotton-wool that appeared to have lagged itself around her brain. "I don't know what you're talking about. Who are you?"

"You've heard the wrong things, know the wrong things, Mrs. Hope. It's not your fault. But there are consequences." He paused for a few seconds, staring at walls that were painted bright white. He turned back to face her. "I did try to warn you, but I don't think you realised."

"Warn me? How?"

"I put a note through your front door."

"That was you?"

He nodded. "Couldn't do any more than that, was risky as it was. And now it's too late. He's got you."

"Who's got me?" There was no response. "Who's got me, because from where I'm sitting, it's you."

"No, no, no," he shook his head vigorously. "Not me. I would never have done this if he hadn't made me."

Clarence was trying to think about what she could have heard. Fear was drenching the cotton wool and plastering it to her brain. And then it dawned. The last thing she remembered before waking up was trying to ring Mack to let him know about Keeley's Bull connection. This was about Keeley, who'd been so scared that someone was listening. Shit.

Mack had never spoken to Clarence's supervisor. Warren called him at ten a.m. on Tuesday to ask if Clarence was with him. "With me, no, why?"

"She hasn't arrived for work and we can't get hold of her on the landline or mobile. She had an early, before-school session with a child and her ten a.m. has arrived. We wondered if she was with you, working on your case."

"No, not at all. Have you been round to her house?"

"No, we're only just beginning to worry."

"Is there a next of kin on her staff record?"

"Yes, her sister, Erin."

"Why don't you call her, see if she can get hold of her. Can you let me know?"

Warren called back ten minutes later. He had spoken to Clarence's sister, who couldn't shed any light. She had a key, would go to the house and check that everything was ok. "No, don't let her do that alone," Mack was twitchy about it and didn't know why. "Can you call her back and ask her to wait outside until I get there and give her my mobile number?"

"Sure," said Warren. "She's not in any trouble, Mack, is she?"

"I'm sure there's a reasonable explanation, just being cautious." He took the address from Warren and found Clarence's cottage by satnav. It was an isolated spot for a woman by herself, opposite farmland and probably a hundred or so meters down from its neighbour on the other side of the road that meandered into the village.

A tall blonde woman was waiting for him in the drive, Clarence's sister by any name. The little red convertible wasn't there. "Mack?"

"Yeah, hi. You got a key?"

She handed it to him. "There's something wrong, the milk's not been taken in and I can hear the cats meowing inside."

"Ok, wait here." He let himself in and walked through the ground floor, checked upstairs and then the garden. Two fat ginger cats trailed him everywhere, asking for breakfast. He went back to the front door. "Ok, you can come in now, Erin." He nodded at the pile of post on the hall table. Can you go through that, make sure there's nothing significant?"

"Let me just feed the cats, otherwise they won't shut up." She went into the scullery, where she found the cat bowls and filled them with biscuits, changed their water, emptied the litter tray and re-filled it. She went back to the hall table. She called out to him. "Mack," her voice was tight, "What's this?"

He went back down the hall. "What?" She handed him a sheet of paper.

"Where the hell is she then, Mack? Something's happened, hasn't it?"

He blew out his breath. "Don't know. Do you think you'd feel able to call round local A&E departments? See if she's been in an accident? Has she got a boyfriend or friend she might have stayed with?"

"No boyfriend, but I'll call her best friend." She made the call, shook her head at Mack. "No, she's heard nothing."

"Ok, can you phone around the hospitals?" He called Warren back. "Who was Clarence seeing recently, Warren. Anyone controversial?"

"Well, only that girl from your case, Keeley."

"When did she last see her?"

"It was her last appointment yesterday, after school."

"And did everything seem normal afterwards? Was Keeley collected ok, no trouble from the parents?"

"I didn't see Clarence afterwards, but just stay on the phone, Mack and I'll check with Reception." Mack heard the other man walking swiftly through some rooms and then an exchange. "Brenda, did Clarence's client get off ok yesterday afternoon - her last appointment?"

"Keeley?"

"Yes, was she picked up on time? Any trouble with the parents?"

"No. I saw the girl leave with her mother. Everything was fine."

"Was it just the mum, or was the dad there, too, or anyone else?"

"Just the mum. She's usually quite brusque, but she was reasonably pleasant yesterday, actually."

"And did Clarence leave on time?"

"No, she stayed after us. Said that she had reports to catch up on."

"And what time did you leave?"

"Seven p.m."

Warren went back to Mack. "Did you hear all that?"

"Yeah, ok, I'll get back to you. Have you got CCTV there, Warren?"

"Oh, yes, good point. We have."

"Ok, go to see if you can see her on last night's footage. Will they let you view it, data protection and all that?"

"I'll go to the security office now. I'll get back to you."

Hanging up, Mack turned to Erin. "Anything from A&E?" She shook her head. "Ok, don't worry, we'll get to the bottom of this. There's probably a simple explanation."

"Well, there's no simple explanation regarding that note, is there Mack? I've always said she shouldn't get involved in all this police stuff. I've always thought it was dangerous."

"Erin, we'll find her. I promise. Let me just update my manager." He called Kennedy from the garden. "She last saw Keeley, Guv, I think we should be concerned."

"But you asked her to let you know if anything significant came up, didn't you?"

"Yeah, of course. But Keeley was her last appointment yesterday. Maybe she hadn't had the chance. Hold on, let me try her number." A terrible thought occurred to him. He checked his phone. He had had a missed call from Clarence at eight p.m. By then, he'd already been in the land of nod. He put Kennedy on hold and called Clarence's number.

"No response, Guv."

"Ok, Mack, let's get things moving. I'll get her listed as a missing person this end. You need to go round to the Knatchbulls, see if they say anything about Keeley's appointment that can shed any light."

"I think I'll go to her office first and see if there's anything there, any notes. She had a student sitting in, she might have a view."

He saw Erin on her way and then drove to Bellington Social Services. Warren met him at the second floor lift. "Was the student sitting in with Clarence for her session with Keeley yesterday, Warren?"

"No, she had a meeting with her course supervisor. And I think Clarence was pretty reassured that she wasn't going to have any problems. The whole point of the student being there was to act as a witness in case the parents made any allegations. And to record and observe, obviously. Anyway, here we are." He opened the door to an office. Warren leafed through the papers on Clarence's desk. He picked up the Knatchbull file. "This is Keeley's surname, isn't it? What's this address on the back?"

Mack took the file, saw what Clarence had circled. So, Knatchbull had been telling porkies. Mack wasn't surprised. He wrote the address in his notebook. "Anything look out of place here to you, Warren?"

"No, apart from that file. Nothing in it, though, don't know why she's got it. Ok, let's look at the CCTV."

The security guard pulled up the footage from the night before. "We've caught her on the camera leaving the office at just before eight p.m. Then she disappears round into this side road. See? I think she must've parked there. I don't know if the police have any cameras around there?"

"Is it just a residential road?"

"Yeah, staff often park there if the work car park's full, wouldn't be surprised if the residents start asking for parking permits, soon."

"No, there'd be no reason for a police camera, then. Where does it lead to?"

"School playing fields. It's only a short road and the entrance to the fields is at the end."

Mack turned to Warren, "Is the field quite open, would she be visible if she was there?"

"I would say so, and it's used on a daily basis, but do you need to check?"

"Yeah, I'll drive round there now. Ok, thanks Warren. Keep me updated." As he turned to go, Mack caught something out of the corner of his eye and turned back. "Could you play that couple of seconds again, please." The guard rewound. "And stop just there. And then rewind a few seconds. Stop. Can you enlarge that?" Mack peered at the screen. Bloody hell: he recognised that car – and the driver - making drive-pasts and watching Clarence intently as she was leaving.

She was drawing in steady breaths, in through the nose, out through a still-floppy mouth, trying to bully her heart back into a normal rhythm. You're a psychotherapist, talk your way out of this, build rapport, remember your training. She closed her eyes, consciously dropped her shoulders, looked up and relaxed her face into a neutral expression, then raised her hands and propped up the side of her mouth with one finger. "What's your name? You know mine, it would be good to know yours."

"You don't need or want to know my name."

"I think I do. You're holding me hostage. It would be nice to at least have a name to address you by."

"Hostage?" He focused on her, blinking rapidly. "You're not my hostage." He looked at the syringe.

"Ok. How would you describe the situation we're in?"

He fell into silence and dropped his face into his hands for some seconds, then he sat up straight, wiped his palms against his trouser leg and ran a forefinger under a damp shirt collar. Without looking at her, he stood abruptly and crossed the kitchen floor. The light went out. The door closed. A second door slammed shut. The syringe was still on the table. She strained her ears, listening for any new noises. A large, cream American fridge/freezer hummed quietly on her right, to her left was a shiny green range cooker sitting centrally in a length of expensive fitted cupboards and cabinets, overlaid by a dark wooden worktop.

She had been placed facing tall and wide French doors overlooking a large, neat, bland garden. It was bordered by a substantial brick wall, itself dwarfed by tightly-packed and starkly clipped giant leylandii growing behind. Dawn had come, through the trees she could see a red sky - Shepherd's Warning.

The kitchen scene from the film 'Hannibal' - in all its brainy gore - was creeping into her mind. She watched the garden, concentrated on the birds that swooped and soared and sang silently through the double glazing, kept up her breathing. A robin landed right outside, his breast reddening in preparation for the cold, defying the lingering summer. He opened his beak to the sky, little breaths ruffling his brown throat feathers. He finished his song, watched her intently, head to one side, then flew away, disappearing into dark-green foliage.

It occurred to her that someone could be watching - a maniac getting off on her heavy breathing, sweat and damp crotch. She pursed her lips, opened wide, grinned hard, lifted her bound hands and felt her face - both corners of her mouth had moved upwards. She scrutinised every corner and crevice for a camera, or a pinprick of light, or suspicious object. Certain as she could be that she was alone, she jerked her hips forwards and propelled the chair, inch by inch, towards some drawers set into one of the cabinets. The wooden legs bumped and then screeched across the ceramic floor tiles like fingernails down a blackboard. The top drawer opened silently and smoothly. She chose the sharpest-looking knife. She twisted and contorted her arms to stab the silver tip into the bevelled wooden edging of the worktop, then slipped her bound wrists over the handle, so that it was wedged fast in the knot of the rope. She took deep breaths, pulled the knife out, bent over and gently edged the blade between the chair leg and her ankle; the steel was razor-sharp, the ropes gave way almost instantly. The blood rushed to her feet, making them tingle.

Mack sped out of Bellington High Street, siren blazing, calling Kennedy on the way. He was at the Mead school in five minutes. A squad car pulled into the car park behind him. Mack and two uniformed officers moved down the corridor to the Headmaster's room. It was empty. Mack found the secretary in the school office. "Where's Mr. Bridge?"

She was startled. "In his room, I think. I actually haven't seen him today. Why? What's happened?"

"He's not in the office. Where else could he be?"

"Well, he could be anywhere in the school, couldn't he?"

"Ok, we'll look."

"No, please don't do that. It'll alarm the children. I'll call the deputy head." She lifted the phone. There was a noise coming from outside the room, along the corridor. Mack followed the sound to the windowless cleaning room that he had seen when he visited the day before. He opened the door and found a light switch to his left.

The headmaster was squeezed in a gap between the wall and an old butler sink. A tap was dripping rhythmically. The sharp tang of disinfectant hung in the air. Bridge's knees were under his chin, arms grasped tightly round them. He was rocking and keening. Mack walked up to him quietly and crouched in front of him. In the background, a constable was radioing for an ambulance.

"Mr. Bridge, where's Clarence, Mrs. Hope?"

Bridge looked up with glazed eyes. His tie was loose, top button undone, the chest and underarms of his shirt were stained yellow and soaking wet. His hair was plastered to his head. Mack tightened his throat and resisted the urge to move away. "Mrs. Hope? Dead now, dead."

Mack stared at him. "What do you mean, dead? Where is she?"

"At his house, I was supposed to do it, but I couldn't. But he will. And then he'll have my girls. He will and he'll violate them. My beautiful girls." He clutched Mack's arm. "You can protect my girls, you're a policeman, don't let him get them."

"We will protect them. But where is she? Where is Mrs. Hope?"

Bridge's eyes darted around the room. "Is he here? Can he hear me?"

"No, no he can't hear you or see you. I promise. You see this policeman?" The constable stepped forward. "He'll look after you, keep you safe."

"And my girls. He'll go to their school."

"Mr. Bridge, tell me where Mrs. Hope is, then tell this police-man where your girls are and we'll get the police to them. I promise."

Bridge looked at the constable. "Police were bad when I was a boy. Are you good?"

Mack dug clenched fists into his trouser pockets, waited a few seconds, kept his voice even. "Yes, he's a good policeman. I'm a good policeman. Can you remember where Mrs. Hope is?"

"29 Old Dukes Road, Little Baddow, near Chelmsford." It sounded familiar, Mack pulled out his notebook; it was the same address as the one written on the cover of the Social Services Knatchbull file.

Once both ankles were free, Clarence lodged the handle of the knife into a decorative rut that bordered the hob of the cooker, so that the blade was upright. She held it steady with her forearms and then slowly slipped her bound wrists downwards over the blade and started to seesaw the rope against the cutting edge. She stopped. Turned her head and wiped her forehead against her shoulder. Inhaled, exhaled, started again, moving the rope against the blade in tandem with her breathing. A single drop of sweat dripped from her temple. It was enough to make the handle slip out of position. In an instant, the knife twisted and a vein in her right forearm spliced open. The bleeding was im-mediate. Within seconds, blood had started to pool on the tiled floor. She stumbled, the back of her hand smacking hard against a sharp edge of the cooker as she went down, her shoulder taking the force of the fall.

Mack drove out of Bellington, through Stock, turned onto the A12 and found the address via satnav. It was a large house, se-cluded from distant neighbours by high hedging and back from the road at the end of a long, curving drive. He parked opposite. A squad car pulled up behind. Leaving uniformed to bang on the door, he ran around the side of the house to the back garden, looking through every window.

Clarence was lying on the kitchen floor, blood smeared around her, blonde hair matted. Mack rattled the handles of the French doors, sprinted back round to the road, yelled to the constables and lifted a battering-ram from the boot of the squad car. The house security was as thorough as Knatchbull's.

Chapter 36

George had fucked it, bottled it. Reggie's tic was in overdrive, pulsing so hard that it was obscuring his vision. He was spitting with anger. His kitchen was like a war zone, the Hope women had bled everywhere, he'd nearly slipped, for fucks sake. He was sure that some of the blood was on the sole of his shoe. Reggie hated mess. He'd told George clearly: no blood; strangle her, suffocate her, give her an overdose of the drug, anything. But No. Fucking. Mess.

As usual, Reggie had prepared. None of this could be laid at his door. Emma had been fed, the rope and ties had been left ready for the Hope woman. He'd even left the sodding chair in the right place. He'd wanted to show George that he trusted him, wanted to welcome him back into the bosom of his family. He understood that George had been a child when he left, had been at the mercy of do-gooders, he couldn't be entirely held to blame for going. It was fitting that George's re-entry into family life was by knocking off a Social Worker. But George had failed. And Reggie had come home to *that*.

A whole host of possibilities went through his mind when he realised that George had run out on him. The woman was already halfway free and she tall, strong, a good match for Reggie, who was old, out of practise, had back pain and prostate trouble. She was on the floor by the time he got there, slipped in her own blood most likely, but conscious and still alert, with a determined, fierce look on her face. The bitch had been kicking out at him, randomly, but with strong legs, long ones that could reach far, certainly as high as his arthritic knee if he got too close. Thankfully, George had at least taken her shoes off, got one thing right. Reggie had had to think fast. A long knife on the floor nearby – fuck knew how she'd got hold of it - presented a solution. But the blood, no, he'd needed to find another way.

A saucepan, one of his set of copper ones, was the most obvious choice. They hung precisely on matching hooks just inside the kitchen door: large to small descending. In the end, he'd stepped in the mess just to get close enough to wallop her round the head; she'd kept spinning round on her buttocks in the wet every time he got near. He was sure that she somehow realised that he wanted to avoid stepping in the blood, it was smeared it around her like a bloody voodoo circle. Eventually, he managed a whack across her temple with his milk pan. It would have germs on it and would have to be sterilised, but at least the bitch was quiet and those long pins were still. And then, the worst possible betrayal – and it could only have been George – the police had come.

Before Reggie'd had time to plan, to think, to even squirt the milk pan with disinfectant, he heard the sirens and had to make a speedy exit through the back, locking the French doors behind him and taking the key. He hadn't like just leaving all that mess; it worried him, made him fret. There was a gate in the wall between two of the trees. He locked it behind him, squeezed through the branches and was in a field that was still his land. A landrover was parked there. He had sped away before the police even pulled up.

Reggie had been daring to think that everything would settle down once the threat of the Hope woman was dealt with, that he could have some type of normality again. All the stress and running away was exhausting for someone his age. And in what he could now see was clearly spectacular stupidity on his part, he'd been starting to hope that George could begin to bear some of the load. George was bright, like Reggie, brighter than all the others, a teacher, headmaster, no less. And Reggie had grown fond of Emma, had even considered keeping her as a companion for his old age. Sure, he was too old for sex, prostate knackered, but she was a pretty little thing to have about the place and he was sure that she was starting to love him. She had perked up over the last few days - the visit by Parmer had been a genius idea on Reggie's part. Emma was eating by herself, starting to watch a bit of kids' television – no news of course, he made sure he controlled what she saw. He had given her some Enid Blyton books -

traditional ones, proper children's books - and drawing pads and crayons and felt-tips. She had even drawn a picture of him. It wasn't great, didn't capture his best features, but he was willing to overlook that; she was a child, after all. He'd been touched, had blue-tacked it above her bed. It was the first thing he looked at after her. Yeah, things could have been good, he could even have home-schooled her – he would have liked that. Well, soon Emma would have one or two little playmates. George had known the score. Reggie had forgiven him once, but George had blown this gift, he would need to learn his lesson. It would be all his fault.

Reggie pulled over and waited for his tic to slow down, deliberately breathed in and out to get his heart under control and glugged down from a bottle of water.

He took out a small notebook from his jacket. He always wrote everything down, never kept anything on a mobile or computer. Bloody new-fangled, modern stuff: he didn't know much about it, but he knew that whatever you put on it lasted forever and could be seen by any noseying bastard who cared to put in the effort. No. It was the paper way for him: safe, controllable, disposable.

There was nothing for it. They were all getting too used to a respectable two point four kids life, it would be good for them to have a reminder of where they belonged, what Reggie could do, who was boss. He pulled out his phone and chuckled to himself: insurance, always insurance; it paid off – in the end.

Chapter 37

By the time the paramedics arrived, Mack had checked Clarence's airway and put her in the recovery position, cut the rope that bound her wrists and found and wrapped one and then another tea-towel tight around the seeping vein. There was a large bump and a small cut on the back of her head and a gash to her right temple. The ambulance whisked her off to A&E.

Mack was waiting to hear back from police control about who the owner of the house was. He felt twitchy, prickly with desperation; if it did turn out that the house still belonged to Knatchbull's relative, well, he'd at least be onto something. There was a fluttering in his stomach, the sense he was close to a breakthrough, maybe he was turning into a proper detective - Kennedy would put out the banners.

More uniformed officers had arrived and were searching the house and neighbourhood for Clarence's attacker. A K9 unit was already deployed. It didn't take long for the German shepherd dog to find the trail to the locked gate in the six feet high back wall. He scrambled up a police ladder and negotiated the drop of the wall and the gap in the trees in one smooth leap and kept running, nose low, following two sets of tyre marks across an open field that lead to a road bordering land belonging to a plant nursery. A white van was parked tight against a dense hedge. The dog sniffed loudly around the back doors, pawed at the handles and sat down, waiting for his handler, who was panting more than several yards behind.

Mack joined in with the search. Whoever lived in the house liked luxury: the bathroom towels were white, thick and sumptuous; drinks trays with good whisky and cut crystal glasses were in both reception rooms; the four beds were dressed with high-quality, Egyptian cotton. Only the master bedroom and en-suite held anything close to personal effects: expensive toiletries and a wardrobe hung with sharply-pressed shirts and jackets, drawers lined with exquisitely folded trousers, t-shirts and pullovers, as though they had just been taken out of their shop bags and kept in the neat arrangement that no lay person should ever be able to mimic, and socks and pants separated with little plastic dividers and placed evenly. Mack compared it to his own random clothing arrangements - he accepted that he might be a bit of a slob, or maybe a lot of a slob, but for sure, this bloke was obsessive. Otherwise, there were no photos, or bills or papers, not even any books. The bureau in the dining-room was empty. The large loft was bare, there was no door to a cellar. And there was no sign of Emma, no indication that a child had ever stepped foot in the place.

He was busy rifling through vertiginously stacked towels and bedding in the airing-cupboard when his radio crackled. Control had the answer to his question. The address was registered to someone called Reginald Bull, born 1943.

You bastard, thought Mack, got you.

He phoned Kennedy. "I don't think we should leave any tape or sign of police presence here, Guv, we need to lure him back. And I've checked in with control, they haven't picked up any cars on CCTV in the area and have traced them, none belonged to anyone called Reginald Bull. Ideally, we need someone camped out in the fields opposite, watching, or in a neighbour's upstairs room."

"Yes, I agree. Any more thoughts about whether this bloke's linked to Emma?"

"Can't prove anything from what's here. The place is virtually a show-home, spotless. But I think this has to be our main lead, now."

"We haven't got any others, Mack. Ok, I'll get Cooper onto some surveillance. Are you going to see Knatchbull now, talk to him about his link to the house, what he knows?"

"Yeah, I'm wondering if it'd be worth another visit to that bunker out near Purfleet, see if there's any sign of Bull there."

"Go to Knatchbull, Mack, I'll get someone to check the bunker. And then we need to interview Bridge. He's still at the hospital, being assessed. In fact, can you check in with them and get an update, see when he'll be fit for interview?"

"Did you get his kids?"

"They're at Chelmsford station now with their mum. Goodness knows what all this is about. But I hope it ends up being about Emma."

There was no-one home at the Knatcbbulls', or at least no-one answering the intercom. Mack peered up at the third-floor flat; as usual, all the windows were shut tight, he couldn't see any movement. He phoned and left a message on Knatchbull's mobile. Then he drove to Chelmsford hospital.

Clarence was in theatre, having her wounds stitched. He found Erin waiting in the relatives' room, huddled into an armchair. He sat down next to her. She straightened up, glared at him and folded her arms. "You police have got a bloody nerve, getting my sister involved with your antics. She has a serious injury. And she was drugged. Goodness knows what else could've happened."

"I know. You're right to be upset and worried. I would be. What's the doctor said?"

"He said she's lucky you got to her!" Erin paused, tears lit her eyes. "But she'll be ok." She glared again. "No thanks to you! She slashed her vein trying to cut herself free. Have you got him?"

"We've got the man who took her initially, but we don't think it's the same man who attacked her at the house."

"Who? Who was it?"

"Can't say that at the moment, Erin. Did she say anything about any of it?"

Erin uncrossed her arms. "Well, she wasn't totally coherent when she was talking to me - she came round in the ambulance and they only let me see her briefly, before they took her into theatre. But she was clear that there were two different men. The first man is the one who put the note through her letterbox. He left her tied up and then went and a second man came."

"How did she know it wasn't the first man coming back?"

"Said there was definitely a second man, that he was taller and thinner... she didn't remember more than that." Erin pulled a tissue from a pocket. "I think by then she was probably already losing consciousness, even without being walloped again, cos she said her vision was going blurry. Maybe due to blood loss. That's really pissed her off, being knocked out twice. She said she was drugged, Mack."

He nodded. "There was a syringe at the house. It's gone for analysis. How's her head?"

"Concussion, but no permanent damage. She badly bruised her shoulder too, as she fell, I think. She told me that she heard someone on Saturday night in her front garden."

"How does she know the man who took her put the note through her door? Did she see him?"

"No, she thought at the time it was just an animal. I don't know how she knows it was this man who took her. Wasn't 'til the next day, when she saw the note, that she realised that someone had been there."

He stood up. "Ok. I'll come back later to see how she is."

Erin grasped his arm. "I mean it, Mack, please keep her out of your business from now on. She's had a really, really rough couple of years. She doesn't deserve this. It's not fair. She's a Social Worker, not a detective."

"Clarence is very good at her job, Erin and she's pretty strong-minded, isn't she? I wouldn't want to try to dictate to her."

"I'm not saying to dictate to her. I'm saying don't ask her in the first place!"

Mack went to find the psychiatric registrar to get an update on Bridge. He felt guilty, guilty and stupid. Her sister had been right to ask the police to keep Clarence away from their business, she wasn't trained to manage the danger that she had been exposed to, not in this case, not the last one she'd worked with them; Kennedy had been right.

The psychiatric registrar was irate with the police, the constables waiting with Bridge had tried to get an update from police control without success.

"He's not fit to be formally interviewed, Sergeant."

"Ok, why is that?"

"Mr. Bridge is suffering from a very high level of trauma. He's barely coherent. He's experiencing flashbacks to childhood abuse. Do you know his background?" Mack didn't.

"He was adopted when he was ten. Had gone to school after having been buggered at home the night before. There was blood on his seat, the teacher called Social Services."

"Who did it to him? Was anyone ever arrested?"

"No. He says that he was always too scared to say, knew that they'd get him."

"Is he prepared to say now?"

"Only on the condition that his family gets protection."

"We've got his children and wife safe at the station. Sorry, someone should've told you, but it's been a bit chaotic."

"Yeah, I heard about that Social Worker being abducted and attacked. She's here, isn't she? You got whoever did it?"

Mack looked at him. "Didn't anyone tell you? Bridge took her."

"Mr. Bridge?" The doctor stared at Mack over his glasses. "That's why there's police here?" Mack nodded. "Well," said the psychiatrist. He tutted, "I wish your colleagues would do a proper handover. Are you sure about that? The man can barely think straight."

"Yeah, I'm sure. I was there when he admitted it. Looks like he knocked her out and may have drugged her. There was a second man, too, who came along after. Bridge took her, he told me that he'd been expected to kill her, but couldn't go through with it. He was talking about someone else who would come along and do that."

"And do you know who that is?"

"Got an idea – probably."

"So Mr. Bridge knows who it is?"

"Yes. And I'm certain that the man who's controlling Bridge may have links to the missing girl we're still looking for. Can I just see Bridge? Not formally, I know I can't do that. But just for a chat - with you, obviously. A missing girl's life is at stake."

"Well, it's a bit unorthodox, but, ok, let's go to see him and tell him that his family is safe and see if he's prepared to talk to you."

Chapter 38

Bridge was huddled into a cushioned chair next to the bed in one of the A&E cubicles. He looked small and shrunken and defeated. The smell of him filled the whole space, drowning out the sterile smell of hospital. He was hunched and shivering, despite the rough hospital blanket draped around his shoulders. He didn't look any better than when Mack had seen him a few hours ago. A nurse was trying to coax him into drinking tea, but his hands were trembling too much to keep the flimsy plastic cup steady. In the end, she held it for him and he sipped like a child.

The doctor pulled up a chair for Mack. "Mr. Bridge, do you remember Sergeant Sumerson. You apparently met him earlier?"

Bridge turned dull eyes towards Mack. "Is my family safe?"

"The police have got your children and wife at the police station. Do you feel able to talk to the sergeant?"

"Police station's not safe; there's police involved, too." The doctor glanced swiftly at Mack.

"It's ok, I know what you mean, Mr. Bridge. We're onto that. We're onto all of it."

"You know? About the house?"

"Yes. Tell us, Mr. Bridge. Tell us about Reginald."

He closed his eyes. "What do you want to know? You already know what he is, you must do by now. He's a monster, that's what. They all are. They're everywhere."

"Who's everywhere?"

"The family. They're spread out everywhere. You can't escape."

"You were adopted, weren't you, Mr. Bridge? Is that your adoptive parents' name?"

He nodded. "My birth name was George Bull. But I got taken into care when I was ten and my name got changed."

"But you stayed in touch with your birth family, did you?"

"Didn't want to. They found me, later. Reggie found me, don't know how, but he did. He's kept tabs on me over the years, promised to leave my girls alone as long as I agreed to step up if the family ever needed me. Never thought it would happen."

"But it has?"

"He wanted Mrs. Hope dead."

"Do you know why?"

"Said she knew too much. From Keeley."

"Keeley?" Mack's guilt stung again – the missed phone call. "What did Keeley tell Mrs. Hope?"

"I don't know. I really don't. But obviously it made him worried. He expects you to just do as you're told, like it's a test, or something."

"Does he have Emma, Mr. Bridge?"

"Yeah, I think so. I can't say for sure, but almost certainly."

"And do you know where he's keeping her?"

"It'll be in his house somewhere. You seen it?" Mack nodded.

"Well, then you know he likes his comforts. She'll be there, somewhere."

"We searched everywhere, we couldn't find her."

"You need to go back. Look harder. If he's got her, she won't be anywhere else."

Bridge clutched both sides of the blanket and pulled it tight around him, leant back in the chair and closed his eyes.

"Let him rest now, Sergeant. We're going to admit him. Who do I speak to about getting more information about his wife and children?"

"Just ask the officers outside. I'll make sure they stay briefed."

Mack sprinted back to his car, jumped in, barely buckling his belt before speeding out of the hospital car park. He turned on the siren. Radioed for back-up. Went through a red light. Left a centimetre between him and another car who'd pulled over, ignored the honking. He arrived back at Bull's house twenty minutes later. He flashed his warrant card to the constable standing outside and ran upstairs, this time starting from the top down. By the time Kennedy arrived with two uniformed officers, Mack was back on the ground floor. He had flushed cisterns, checked behind bath panels, trodden around and checked under rugs for loose floorboards and found and emptied a chest freezer in the utility room. There was no sign of anyone.

Kennedy was as desperate. "We must've missed something, Mack."

Mack should his head. "We haven't. Has someone been back to the bunker?"

"Yeah, nothing." Kennedy's entire face was wet. He undid his top button, ran a finger around his collar, eventually he yanked off his tie and stuffed it into his trouser pocket. He had sent the constables on another search of the grounds. "Let's go through the house again."

"It's pointless, Guv. She's not here." Mack realised he hadn't had time to even pee since finding Clarence earlier in the day, his bladder was excruciating, fit to burst. "Excuse me a minute." He used a downstairs cloakroom. The liquid soap was luxurious. He ran the hot tap; the water was scalding. He rinsed his hands, dried them on the white fluffy towel. It was a big house, he wondered how many sinks there were, how powerful the boiler would have to be to service them all and provide such instantly hot water. He sat down on the toilet seat for a few moments. There was a sense of something lost whirling around at the top of his mind.

He got up and went to the foot of the staircase, stood for a few seconds, then took the treads two at a time, found the airing cupboard again, opened the door and stepped back to look at the immersion tank. Kennedy was thundering up the stairs behind him. And then the thought was there, landing safe and clear, showing itself. Finally. He had noticed something earlier in the day, but not registered it. There was no electric feed. There were no water pipes. The tank was a dummy. Sweat prickled his back.

He emptied the shelves around the tank of towels and bed linen, throwing them onto the floor. Then he carefully slid his hands around the length and girth of the tank and felt along the wall behind it. His fingers found a switch. He pressed it.

The floor juddered. He jumped back. The tank moved slowly downwards into a shaft and came to a gentle halt. A neatly cut square of floorboard on top of the tank slotted across the top of the shaft, forming a floor. Behind it was a plain wooden door. There was a large window in the top left quarter. There was no keyhole, no bolt. Mack stepped across and turned the handle.

Emma was sitting on a double bed pushed against the far wall in a large windowless room. She was wearing a red dressing-gown over flowery white pyjamas. A blue ribbon tied back her blonde hair. The room was lit by a bright electric light hung from a central ceiling rose, wall lights were dimmed. A long and wide flat-screen TV rested on a low table at the foot of the bed and was playing cartoons. Opposite the bed was a sturdy cabinet, mahogany, the glass-doored top half lit with three inset spot-lights. Inside were several wooden rods, moveable ones that swung out horizontally from a central vertical spine. They were hung with tens of ribbons neatly arranged in shades of myriad colours. To the left of the cabinet was a door, ajar and showing the rounded edge of a white sink and a large, mirror-fronted wall cabinet. Behind him, Kennedy was urgently talking into his radio.

And then there was frantic activity: whispered phone-calls in the room; shouting from the bottom of the stairs; the pulling up of vehicles and doors slamming outside; a female PC gently moving him to one side; an ambulance crew. But the detail of those conversations, the décor, the rest of the room's furniture, were a blur for Mack in the years to come. What stayed with him and re-played in his dreams even into old age, were the child's words, as she looked at him and whispered, with the TV remote in her hand, pointing at the television, frozen in time. "Is my mummy here? Has she come now?" And his own reply, in a voice that he didn't know could be his own, "Shhh, don't worry now, don't worry, soon, soon, you'll see mummy very soon," and the tears as they ran down his cheeks. After nearly two weeks, they'd found her. And she was alive.

Mack followed the ambulance back to the hospital to give A&E the update and handover himself. Emma's family liaison officer met him there with her parents. Their overwhelming joy and prolific thanks embarrassed him and made him want to call his mum. He did. He wanted her to hear it from him and not the news and to reassure her that he was ok.

He stopped by to check on Bridge, who was in a side room with his wife and daughters, two PCs outside, asked them if there had been any trouble. "None, all quiet and let's hope it stays that way." Then in the hospital foyer he bought himself a giant-sized decent coffee from the commercial outlet, some grapes and a large bar of chocolate in the shop and went to find Clarence.

She was sitting up in bed, her injured wrist stitched and dressed. He left the grapes and chocolate on her side table, pulled up a hard, plastic chair and sat down heavily.

"So, how's your head?"

"Sore, thumping, but I'll survive, just got a gash and a bit of concussion that's all. The bastard really bashed me."

He nodded to her arm, "How many stitches?"

"A couple in my temple, that wasn't too bad, but ten in my arm. You know I did it myself, trying to cut off the rope? The knife slipped."

"Erin told me." He gave her the news about Emma.

"She was in the house all along? While I was there?" He nodded. "Has he assaulted her?"

"Don't know. She's still being assessed and examined. At least she's alive. She actually looked ok to me in that she wasn't really thin and I didn't see any bruising. But who knows? We'll know more tomorrow." He paused, "I'm sorry, Clarence. None of it should've happened. Has anyone taken your statement?"

"Yeah, earlier after I woke from theatre."

"Did they go through any mug shots with you?"

She nodded. "Neither man was in any of the photos. But to be honest, I don't remember much anyway, specially about the second one. They said the efit guy can come when I'm feeling better."

"Well I didn't expect Bridge to be in any of them, his record's already been checked."

"The headmaster? Who Keeley talked about?"

Mack nodded. "He's the one who took you originally. Do you know why you were targeted?"

"I think it's because of what Keeley told me in our last session. Did you know her mum is related to this person by the name of Bull that you've been asking about?"

"Not her mum. Her dad. The address you and Emma were held at is the one you saw noted on the cover of Knatchbull's empty social services file. The house belongs to someone called Reginald Bull, so Knatchbull, mister, is related to Bull, isn't he, if what's written on the file is right - that Knatchbull went to live with a relative?"

"No, Mack. I was trying to phone you to tell you when that bloke got me, Bridge you say, the headmaster?" Mack nodded. "Her mum is related, too. Keeley saw an old passport belonging to her mum when she was a child. She was called Janice Bull."

"But I thought her maiden name was Spencer?"

"It was. But that's because they changed it. Keeley's mum and grandparents had the surname of Bull. That's what Keeley told me. I think we have to presume that's what they didn't want us to find out."

Mack leant back in the uncomfortable chair, scraped it back across the hard floor to give himself more leg room, winced at the sound and realised suddenly that he was exhausted, head threatening. "And Mr. Knatchbull's mum's maiden name was Bull. So, they're all bloody related?"

"Looks like it, doesn't it? So, is Bridge related to this Reginald Bull? Is he the second bloke who came and knocked me out?"

"Yep, I think so, to both questions, but no proof at the moment that the second guy who attacked you was Bull, but it's certainly a strong possibility. We'll uncover more when Bridge is properly interviewed. He's too unwell at the moment." He looked at her pale face. "I should go, Clarence, you must be exhausted. When will they let you out?"

"Tomorrow, all being well. I'm only here tonight for observation."

"We'll need to talk about your security before you go home."

"I've got security – holly and lights."

"I mean whether you go back home initially. Bull's still at large. And someone knows where you live, don't they?" She looked at him blankly. "The note: I saw the note."

"Oh, that was Bridge. He told me when we were at the house."

Mack stood up. "Ok, well, there's a constable outside your door here for tonight and we'll re-visit the rest in the morning."

"Mack, before you go, there's something I wanted to say to you." He sat down again. "First, thank you for today. The ambulance crew came to see me earlier, told me what you did."

Mack briefly brushed the heat off his cheek. "Clarence, you've nothing to thank me for. It's our fault this happened to you. Your sister's really cross."

"It's not your fault. It's Bridge's fault, Mack and maybe this Reginald Bull's if he was the bastard who coshed me the second time. And just ignore Erin. She's a teacher, thinks she can talk to everyone like she talks to her pupils, has never learnt it doesn't work on grown-ups." Mack wasn't too sure about that - it had worked pretty well on him. "But there's something else." He watched her uninjured hand rise up to her ear and lower again when she realised she wasn't wearing any earrings. "I'm going to see out this case with you, but then I'm taking a sabbatical. It's been agreed, before all this, not because of this. I need to get my head together." She nodded at the side table. Mack passed the grapes. She shook her head, "No, the chocolate." She unwrapped the foil with her good hand and started breaking off squares, offering some to Mack.

"When Ted, my husband, died, my heart broke, Mack. People tell you that, but you can't know what it means until it happens. I loved him so much. It was like my soul was ruptured." She blinked a few times. "You know they never found his body? We were in Italy, on our honeymoon. I don't know why he went for an early-morning bike ride, motor-bike, but he did. The bike was found several hundred yards down the road from the hotel.

There was just his helmet, with a load of blood, his blood."

Bloody hell, that was a story and a half. "Clarence, I'm so sorry, I didn't know all that."

"The coroner ruled death by misadventure. It was a rural hotel, there were forests nearby. The general conclusion was that there'd been an accident and that the wolves had taken the body."

The wall light over the bed caught the hint of red in her hair, the glistening in her eyes. "I think I love you." He didn't know whether exhaustion was firing off song lyrics in his brain, or whether he'd learnt to be honest with himself, or whether the intimacy of a small room on a hot evening with dark lapping through the window and marooning them in an island of soft lamplight was sending him into lala-land. But her wisdom, her knowledge, the hips that convention would say were too broad, the kink in her nose, the thick, blonde hair - all of her was suddenly dear to him. "So, what are you going to do?"

"I'm going to find out what happened to my husband. What really happened. The explanation never sat right with me. Everyone said I just had to get on, but I can't settle back into a normal life: work, home, bed. I'm too unhappy, need to find out for myself." She paused, broke off some more chocolate, proffered it. "Shall I let you into a secret?"

Her eyes were the grey of storm clouds, their light the glint of gulls swooping and keening, the draw of nature. He could only nod.

"I'm not even sure that he's dead." She held his gaze for a long moment. In the end, he had to look away, bring it back, eat the chocolate melting onto his fingers.

"Well, you need to do what you need to do, but I'll miss you, Clarence. If I can do anything to help, I will, you know that." The chocolate was all gone, her eyes were closing. A nurse came in and closed the blinds and gathered up the foil, throwing it into the bin. Clarence slid under the covers, blonde hair billowing, mumbling into sleep.

"Do me a favour before you go? Text Erin on my phone? Ask if she's remembered to feed my cats?"

Mack sent the text, a response pinged back immediately. 'WTF. How many times? I've fed the friggin cats, they're locked in and I've left a camera at your house linked to my phone so that I can keep an eye. I've even left the tele on. They're fine. Stop worrying!' He turned to read it to Clarence. She was already asleep. He clicked off the light on his way out.

Chapter 39

The following morning, Kennedy and Mack met with the consultant paediatrician, a duty Social Worker and Emma's parents and their police liaison officer. The paediatrician was optimistic.

"She hasn't been sexually assaulted and is in reasonable physical health. Whoever had her fed her. She has lost a bit of weight, verging on being too light, but she'll easily make that up with proper eating again. We've got her on some glucose, her blood sugar was a bit low, but that's about it."

Mack was astounded, given what Bridge had said about the assault when he was a boy. "No sexual assault. That's definite?"

"As far as any physical injuries go, yes. Obviously, there may have been inappropriate touching, and Emma may disclose more further down the line, but there is no physical damage in the genital area and no bruising to the upper thighs, buttocks or hips or stomach, which would be an indication."

"What about bruising or injuries to other parts of the body?"

"She was tied around the wrists, she still has some faded contusions, she was tied tightly, probably with plastic and it broke the skin. And she has fading finger mark bruising around her upper arms and on her collar bone, probably about ten or eleven days old, it's barely visible now."

Mack opened his mouth, but the paediatrician had anticipated his question. "Yes, Sergeant, all the photos were done and have been uploaded. We did a paper body-map, too. I'd suggest she was held down, which is where the finger marks come from. She doesn't seem to be able to remember a lot of the first few days."

"You think she was drugged?"

"We're waiting for toxicology. It's obviously possible that she was drugged. But most of those types of date-rape drugs," he glanced at Emma's parents, "Sorry, I know this is hard for you to hear. Sometimes they're called knock-out drugs, they don't stay in the system very long, so unless something was given to her in the last twenty-four hours, max, it's not going to show up in her blood or urine." He paused, "And there's something else. We think she's been cannulated."

Kennedy frowned, "What do you mean?"

"When we inserted the needle into her arm for the drip, we noticed a very faint mark. She said she remembered the man doing the same thing to her."

"What, to administer drugs?"

"Well, I can't see why else someone would, Inspector, unless he's just a sadist."

Mack glanced at Emma's mum. She was pale, drawn, eyes rimmed in red. Her life would never be the same. He remembered the mother of that first abuse case, how she'd waited until her child was sound asleep, walked stoically down the hospital corridor, into the car park, unlocked her car, got in, closed the door and screamed and screamed.

"So how do you tell if drugs have been used, if these types don't stay in the body that long?"

"As well as the canula mark, Emma said something about being made to drink some orange juice that tasted funny. Even though those drugs don't stay in the body long, they might show in the hair after it's grown out. We'll do a hair strand test in a couple of weeks. But I am optimistic about her physical health; I think she'll make a full recovery."

"But what about her mental health?" asked Mack.

"Ah, well, that's a different matter. Almost certainly, she'll need specialist psychological support."

"Has she talked much about the man who had her?"

"She asked where he was, whether he was ok."

Emma's dad was stony-faced. "I don't understand why she's worried about that bastard. After what he's done, why's she asking about him?"

The paediatrician answered. "Sometimes, kidnap victims identify strongly with their abductor to make themselves feel safer. It is a common response. It doesn't mean that Emma loved him, or even liked him. It's just a psychological response in an attempt to keep herself safe. I'm not an expert, but we can access people who are, if need be. Sometimes, it's called Stockholm Syndrome. Have you heard of that?" The father hadn't. He turned his attention to the police.

"Have you found this bastard yet?"

Kennedy responded. "We haven't, but we will."

"Well, make sure you do, before anyone else's kid goes missing."

"She's been asking to see Keeley." Emma's mum's voice was shaking. "Do you think that would be a good idea? They're good friends. I think it would help her."

"Keeley's the girl who was present when the abduction happened, is she? The third girl?"

Mrs. Downs nodded. "Maybe in a couple of days or so, Keeley could come and visit? I'd like to get some semblance of normality back for her. Although, I suppose, she'll never be normal again..." She buried her head in her husband's shoulder.

The doctor turned to Mack. "Would Keeley like to visit, do you think? You've been the one keeping contact, haven't you?"

"I think Keeley will be desperate to see Emma. Once you think she's ready, let me know. I'll speak to the parents. They don't know that Emma's been found yet."

"How long before Emma will be fit for interview, doctor?" Kennedy moved the conversation on.

"Not yet. Maybe tomorrow. You'll need someone good, though, who can be patient and who understands the psychological processes. I'm waiting for Emma to be seen and assessed by the child psychiatrist. I'm hoping that will be later today."

"Would she be well enough to just see the facial recognition officer and look through some mug shots?" asked Mack. "We still don't know what this man looks like." He saw their confusion. "The efit guy..."

"Oh, well, let's see what the psychiatrist says. Emma's had a very traumatic experience. And she's got to be told yet that her friend's dead, hasn't she?"

"We think she might have been there when that happened.

We found the place where they were taken to initially. Their DNA was all over the place and the murdered girl's blood was there, we think that's where she was killed, so Emma probably witnessed that."

The paediatrician raised his eyebrows. "Oh, really, well then, there's a lot to deal with, isn't there? She'll need ongoing sessions, maybe for years."

"She's being difficult about it, Mack." Erin had brought some of Clarence's clothes in and was trying to persuade her sister to go to stay with her and her family for a few days. "Just until they've caught this other bloke, Clarence." She turned to him, "You tell her."

"Erin's right. We haven't interviewed Bridge, yet. We don't know if he told Bull where you live. You're quite isolated there, Clarence. If you dialled 999, it might take a good ten minutes for a response car to get to you. By then it could be too late."

"Bull can't possibly know what Keeley told me about her mum's surname. And even if he does know that I know, why does it matter?"

"I don't know why it matters, but he clearly does know, Clarence, or he guessed, or he just got spooked that Keeley would. Somehow, he knew that she was seeing you and was worried about what she might say, because that's why he took you in the first place. Your seeing Keeley is the only link between you and this case, it must have something to do with that."

"No, Bridge took me."

"Yeah, and maybe it was Bridge who told him that you were seeing Keeley. And if he did, it's highly possible that he told Bull your address, too. Bridge took you to Bull's order. There's no way Bridge would've done this by himself. He told you that. Remember? It's in your statement."

"If he did know, how did he know? Bridge, about Keeley, I mean - I missed that part," said Erin.

Mack sat down. Something was niggling. He tried to reach out and snatch it from the maelstrom that lately rotated constantly around the top of his brain. He remembered Clarence's account to him of her second session with Keeley. Erin wasn't the only one who'd missed it. He needed to go back to see the Knatchbulls.

Clarence remained standing by the bed. "Can't you come and stay with me, Erin? I just want to be in my own home, with my cats. The house is really secure, no-one can get in."

"Clarence, term's already started. I'm meant to be in school today. They've had to get a supply in."

Clarence's face was set, her eyes unmoving, lips taut in a straight line. Mack watched her twiddle the earring that was back in her lobe. He found a word for her expression: stubbornness and maybe more than just a touch of stroppiness; he guessed that was what fuelled her dogged determination to deal with every case she came across and her resolution to find out what happened to her husband. Clearly, Erin was used to it. She sighed. "I suppose I could take emergency leave for a few more days. How long before you the police get this man, Mack?"

"I don't know. And it's not safe for either of you to be at that address, anyway."

"Well, that's what happening, Mack," said Clarence and gathered her belongings. "I'm going home."

He suspected she would be capable of a full-blown argument if he pushed it and given what she'd just been through, he could hardly blame her. But there would need to be protection in place, whether Clarence liked it or not. "Do you want a squad car to take you both there now?"

"No, I've got my car. I'll need to go to collect some bits and pieces, let the kids and my husband know what's happening," said Erin. "Actually, Mack, I've got an idea. I left one of those home cameras at Clarence's – you know the ones that are linked up to your phone, so you can see what's happening when you're out. I left it there so that I could keep an eye on the cats. We could send the link to your phone, too, so you can check in."

"No," Clarence said flatly. "Not happening. It's not appropriate for Mack to have to watch us parading around in our dressing-gowns, Erin."

"For goodness sake, it's on the mantlepiece in the dining-room, opposite that old sofa that the cats sleep on. It's not in the loo! And you can set it so that there's a sound function, too. I'd rather be seen in my dressing-gown than dead. At least if we scream, there'll be someone to hear us."

"I'll think about it. But no-one's going to be screaming. We'll be fine. Now, can we just go? I want to get out of here."

Mack caught Erin's sidelong look and briefly nodded. "Ok. Clarence, the squad car will take you home, but it'll be on the understanding that officers stay with you until Erin arrives. And there will be a police car driving past your house every hour," or more frequently if he could get it past the Guv, "Until we've got this man that's what will be happening." He saw Clarence's throat muscles twitch, but he wasn't taking no for an answer, "That's the deal." He walked them out to the car park, saw Erin into her car and handed Clarence over to the constables. "Before she goes in, check the house and garden."

"And Clarence, I mean this. Keep your doors locked." He had a further thought: he had recently been on some training about personality disordered people, the emphasis had been on psychopaths. "And keep your cats in." Then he texted his number to Erin.

The Superintendent was trying to keep his blood pressure under control. The Poplar skeletons had been hived off into a separate investigation, but Bull's secret room had yielded another treasure-trove of criminal activity. And the investigating of it was going to cost a fortune.

He could see his budget speeding into the red at an unstoppable rate. There would need to be an investigation into the bastards who had been using Bull's services over decades and a load of forensic testing to sort out. Since the abolition of the Forensic Science Service in 2012, the Superintendent had been careful with his budget, managed not to overspend, but he could see that was going to change rapidly - what with that and the overtime. The strain on his budget was going to make it snap.

Samantha's murder wasn't resolved, but there was progress. The same day that Emma was found, the body of the suspect in Samantha's murder, Tony, Michael Wiltshire's partner in crime, had been found in dense scrubland on the north coast of Ibiza – throat slit - and the island's boys in blue weren't up to the job, in the Superintendent's opinion. Nor was the lowlife, it seemed: there were no keys or wallet, but Tony's driving license had been stuffed deep into a back trouser pocket. And now Kennedy and his sergeant wanted protection for the Bridge family and for the Hope woman: not that he couldn't see why.

The large wooden cabinet in Bull's secret room – a rape suite in the worst possible sense - had held in excess of two hundred ribbons, a lot of good whisky and two boxes of old-fashioned card indices. Each card held the name, address, age and crudely detailed sexual preferences of visiting males; some had polaroid photos attached, capturing the men in flagrante, their victims' faces never showing, only the bodies, mainly young teenage, some pre-pubescent. A few of the cards, happened upon by an unfortunate SOCO, had used condoms stapled to the back. There was a hook on the side of the cabinet, on which hung an old, but still operating, polaroid camera and in a small fridge in the en-suite were canisters of polaroid film. Bull was neurotic, para-noid, thorough, or just plain mad - the Superintendent couldn't decide which.

Chapter 40

The psychiatric registrar had cleared Bridge for interview, on the condition that he be given an Appropriate Adult and that the police be mindful of his emotional fragility and the fact that some prescribed tranquilisers would make him a little slow and sleepy. Bridge agreed to attend the station voluntarily if he could first be taken to the safe house to see that his wife and children were protected.

"I'd like to go to see the Knatchbulls, first, Sir, before we interview Bridge."

"Surely that can wait, Mack. I agree that the links there need to be explored and cleared up. But our priority has to be finding Bull. Bridge is the route to that and I want to get him interviewed whilst he's agreeable, I don't want him to be waiting and getting stressed again. You saw what he was like. Won't look good if he ends up back in hospital, will it?"

"I think that the Knatchbulls could have more information than we know about, Guv. And now we know that Mrs. Knatchbull and her parents changed their surname, clearly, there's something going on."

"Well, we've made that assumption based on what Keeley told Clarence. We haven't seen the passport, have we? Keeley could've got it wrong. Clarence could've got it wrong, although I know that's unlikely. Look, we've got Emma. We've got Bridge's kids and his wife. We've got a car that's going to be keeping an eye on Clarence, plus she's going to have her sister with her. Everyone's safe. Let's get Bridge interviewed, see what he has to say and then follow up with the Knatchbulls. They'll have no beef with protecting Bull. I know that mister is hostile, but if Bridge is telling the truth about Bull and if Knatchbull knew that Bull was behind all this, and knew where he was, don't you think he would give him up? Knatchbull's not a monster, is he?" Mack shrugged his shoulders: he wasn't sure about that.

After his arrival with his solicitor, Bridge was arrested for kidnapping. The Appropriate Adult arrived ten minutes later.

Kennedy opened the interview. "So, Mr. Bridge, we know you've had a very difficult few days and we don't want to make you more stressed. If at any time you feel you need a break, please just say." He paused and waited for Bridge to settle in his chair. "So, in your own time, can you tell us what happened to make you track down and take Mrs. Hope?"

"Reggie told me I had to."

"And Reggie is..."

"My half-brother, same dad, different mum."

"But you were adopted, weren't you? Reggie is a relative from your birth family, is he?"

"Yes, I was adopted when I was ten. But Reggie always knew where I was. Don't know how, he made contact when I was at university."

"And what did he say when he made contact?"

"That I needed to remember where I came from, that if he ever needed me, I'd be expected to do what he said. Otherwise, there'd be consequences."

"Did he tell you what those consequences would be?"

Bridge shook his head. "But I knew that it would be something nasty. The family's just a bunch of criminals. I always knew that if I had my own children, he would use them against me. And that's what has happened."

"Can you elaborate on that, Mr. Bridge?"

"That's the deal. If you play ball with Reggie, your own kids get left alone. If you don't, he'll get them."

"He actually said that to you, did he?"

"He didn't need to. My family are a rotten, horrible lump of humanity. When I was a little boy, I used to see them rape the other children in the house."

"The house in Poplar Square, you mean? Is that where you grew up?"

Bridge nodded. "For the tape, please, Mr. Bridge," said Kennedy gently.

"Sorry, yes, the house in Poplar Square. That's what happened. You didn't have any choice. And then other people came and did it." He looked them straight in the face, "Including police."

"Yes, we know about that, Mr. Bridge. We've got them."

"Have you? You sure? You can't have all of them. There were a few. Although most of them are probably dead or retired now."

"So, when did Reggie make contact with you about Mrs. Hope?"

"Last week. Reggie wanted to know if anyone knew about the links between me, him and Janice and Pete. Whether Keeley knew anything and might mention it in her counselling sessions."

"Janice and Peter Knatchbull?"

"Yeah."

"And what are the links?"

"Janice was born a Bull. I don't know the exact relationship between her and Reggie and me. The family is massive. But for sure we're cousins, once or twice removed. I don't know. The actual relationship won't make any difference to him, the fact that you're born into the family is enough for him to expect your loyalty."

"And Janice's parents changed their name, did they?"

"They just wanted to get away from him, from all of them. Janice's grandparents first moved to the Mead after the war, they were in the flat that Pete and Janice live in now. I expect they wanted to get away, too."

"But why does it matter, Mr. Bridge, if anyone knows the link. Why would that matter to Reggie?"

"It reduces his power base, doesn't it? And it gives power to the relatives, might mean they could walk away from him. He relies on threats and loyalty to keep everything together. There's power in secrets. That's how he keeps control."

"But what are the secrets, Mr. Bridge?"

Bridge sat back in his chair. He blinked several times. His eyes were sunk into dark bags, they draped down his cheeks like polluted, fleshy tears. He looked at his lap. When he looked back up, he was weeping. "You really don't know, do you?"

Kennedy looked at Mack, who shook his head. "No, we don't know, Mr. Bridge. You're going to have to spell it out."

Bridge took a laboured breath and licked tears off his lips. "We need to be wiped out, Inspector. The whole lot of us. All of the Bull family. It's a gene pool that needs to be exterminated. We're a blot on the landscape of humanity." He reached out a shaking hand and took several tissues from the box on the table. He rubbed his face roughly and thoroughly. The tears had dried up. "I need a break. Can I go to the toilet and have some water, please?"

"Yes, of course. I'll get someone to take you. Do you want your Appropriate Adult to accompany you?" Bridge shook his head. Kennedy paused the interview, nodded to the custody officer to get Bridge some water and watched as they shuffled out of the room. "Child abuse," said Kennedy, to no-one in particular, "It's everywhere."

Five minutes later, the custody officer came rushing back in.

"Sir, he's taken an overdose in the cubicle. I've called an ambulance. Someone's with him. I tried to get him to sick 'em up, but he was already losing consciousness."

The Appropriate Adult got up, "I'll go." He left the room running.

"How did he get them?" Kennedy had gone red in the face. "Was he searched?"

"He was, Guv, honest. But I think they must've been in his pants, individually, cos I couldn't find a box, I think he had them down there wrapped in bits of paper towel, cos that's all there was to see."

Kennedy looked at Mack. "The tranquilisers. Wouldn't take many of those to knock him out quickly. Can you make sure his wife knows, Mack? And find someone to accompany him to hospital." He rubbed his face, loosened his tie and undid his top button. "Damn it." He thumped the table. "We should've realised what he was planning with the way he was talking."

Mack stopped off at the hospital on his way into work the following morning. Bridge was alive and would survive, but the psychiatrist, less than happy with the police, was more than clear that they wouldn't be interviewing Bridge again for the foreseeable future.

Despite his boss' optimism, Mack was determined to follow up with the Knatchbulls. He got through his paperwork and arrived at the Mead estate at eleven a.m. He glanced up at their flat as he locked his car. And then he looked again. Every window of the Knatchbull flat was wide open to the air. He unlocked his car, found his baton (it would be a thumbs-up from Kennedy) and took a precautionary, careful look around. A woman leaving the block let him in through the communal door. He paused at the top of the stairs to the third floor, the Knatchbulls' flat door was ajar; he peered hard into the dark corners of the stairwell, got out his torch and swung the beam around, sweeping the ceiling for good measure. His phone rang. He ran back down to the landing below to answer it before it stopped. Essex control room was on the other end.

"Mack, we've had a report that Keeley Knatchbull isn't in school today. Duty sarge wants to know if you want us to go to the school or home to take a report."

"I'm outside their flat now. But why have the school called the police?"

"Think they were just worried, given her recent history. The friend she gets the bus with said that Keeley didn't get on it this morning. And they've not had a call in from the family saying that she's sick, which apparently is standard procedure."

"Ok, thanks. I'll see what's what and get back to you. Cheers."

Back on the third floor, he tapped gently on the flat door, keeping his baton behind his back. There was no reply. He edged it wider and stepped into the small hall. The door to the sitting-room was open. Mr. Knatchbull was slumped in an armchair, tightly cupping his face, shoulders hunched forwards. His wife was in the kitchen. She had one arm gripped around Claire's shoulders and was pouring milk from a bottle into a glass with the other.

He tapped on the door again. "Hello. Mr. Knatchbull. What's happened? Why're all your windows open? Where's Keeley?"

Knatchbull looked up. "Just piss off, copper. We don't need you. All the fucking times you sit outside watching me and the one time you would've been useful, you weren't there. Now do one. You'll just make it worse."

"Hasn't been me who's been watching you." He went into the kitchen. "What's happened, Mrs. Knatchbull? Has something happened to Keeley? Why isn't Claire at school?"

Mrs. Knatchbull opened the fridge door, put the milk back, took out some butter, all the while holding onto her daughter. "He's taken her."

"Who? Who's taken her?"

"Who do you bloody think? Reggie of course. This is his punishment for us and George not playing ball."

"George? You mean Mr. Bridge?"

"Yeah, him, whatever name you know him by."

"Not playing ball for what, Mrs. Knatchbull? You mean, regarding Mrs. Hope..." Mack stopped himself, Claire's eyes were fixed on him.

Mrs. Knatchbull nodded. The maelstrom in Mack's head was at galeforce. Suddenly it slowed, stilled, prepared to change direction and a nugget of treasure dropped straight into the front of his mind: Bull had never been after Bridge's kids. They'd all got it wrong.

"Mrs. Knatchbull. Tell me what's happened. We can find her."

"I don't know where she is. And even if I did, if I tell you, he'll kill her." She dropped a couple of slices of white bread into the toaster. Mack watched as she wiped miniscule crumbs off the work-surface with a cupped hand; they were dust before they hit the floor. It took her three attempts to depress the toaster's lever.

"Is that why you've kept Claire at home? Because you think he planned to take her, too?"

A hoarse, ripped voice came from the sitting-room. "Just fuck

228

off, will you! I told you right at the start of all this that we don't need coppers, but you wouldn't listen! You're only making it worse."

Mack moved rooms and sat down on the sofa opposite Knatchbull. "I can't just go. Your child is missing. We need to find her. Maybe it's Bull who's been watching you. Could it be him?"

He shook his head. "Not his way. If he does it, he does it. And now he has. You can't help us. We've got to deal with this on our own. Please, please, before you make it even worse, just go away."

Mack tried another road. "I know that you were sent to live with Reginald Bull when your parents died."

"It was when my mum died, my dad had died before that. And what of it?"

"And I know what Reginald did to Mr. Bridge, George, when he was a boy. So, I think it's a pretty sure bet that you were his victim, too."

Knatchbull roared out of his chair, towering over Mack, legs astride. "You have no idea, copper. No fucking idea what he's like. He's a monster!"

"Pete!" His wife's voice rang out from the kitchen. The toaster pinged, golden bread leapt into the air, chased by a blue spark. Knatchbull looked towards his wife and then at his younger daughter's pinched and wide-eyed face. He took some deep breaths, sat down again and took a roll-up from a tobacco tin. His fingers shook. In the end, Mack took the lighter and did it for him. Grey smoke made a slow meander towards the novelty of an open window.

Mack tried again. "I do know what he's like, Mr. Knatchbull. We know everything, now. I know that you're all related. And I'll tell you something else I know, Mr. Knatchbull and it's this: Reginald is not God. He's not all-powerful. He's not all-knowing. He hasn't got ears that can listen to you from wherever he is. I know that's how it feels and that he did have total power over you when you were a child. But now you're an adult. You can take back some control. Did you know we've found Emma? She's alive and she's fine. Wasn't sexually assaulted."

Knatchbull snarled. "Yes, she was. He wouldn't have been able to stop himself. It's like an addiction."

"No. She wasn't. He's not what he was. He's weakened. And he's old. We can get him."

"Listen to me, copper. We're a massive family, a huge criminal network. He's got contacts everywhere. He might have someone watching the flat now and know that you're here. That'll make Keeley even more unsafe. If he knows police are here..." Knatchbull stubbed out his cigarette. "You don't understand. No normal person could understand this." He looked at Mack, "Anyway." Knatchbull reached for his tobacco tin. "At the moment, we stand a chance of getting her back. We need to show him that we've learnt our lesson."

"What you need to do is to tell me what's happened. Now. And there was no-one outside watching when I pulled up. As soon as I saw your windows open I thought there must be something wrong, so I had a good look around. And there's no-one watching, or listening in this building, either." Mack waited for Knatchbull to look up. "There isn't. I checked thoroughly. I'll say it again, Mr. Knatchbull. Reggie is not that powerful. Not anymore. He hasn't got ears that can listen through walls, he's not all-knowing. Reggie is not God!"

Mrs. Knatchbull and Claire came into the room. The toast had been forgotten, abandoned where it landed, crumbs scattered. "Oh, just bloody give it up, Pete. Tell him. We've lived in this prison for years and in the end, what good has it done us, eh? It's done nothing, no good. He's got our daughter, now. It's all different. We need police help. We can't go on how we were." She turned to Mack. "All the locks, the protection, the worry and being careful and in the end, it was as simple as him snatching her on the way to school in broad daylight. It's not even a minute's walk to the bus stop from here." She nodded at the kitchen window, "I watch her. But this morning I looked away for just a few seconds... And he managed it." Her eyes were red and puffy, she rubbed them with her free hand. She went back to the kitchen and fetched a phone from a bag that hung on a door-knob, keeping Claire tight to her side, walking in step, like their ankles were tied. She held out the phone to Mack. Her hand was trembling, "Here, look."

There was a slightly blurred photo of Keeley. Her head was being held back by a gnarled hand pulling hard on ponytailed hair tied with a dark pink ribbon.

He stiffened, felt goosebumps crawl up his back. He looked at Mrs. Knatcbhull. "Did you put that ribbon in her hair?"

She shook her head.

In the photo, behind Keeley, was a greying old man, possibly tall but stooped from the shoulders and slender. A blade was held to her throat. "Is that him? Is that Reggie?" She nodded. "Who sent you the photo, Mrs. Knatchbull?"

"It came from Keeley's phone. He must've made her take a selfie. You can tell if you look at the angle." Mack stared at the photo. Most of the screen was taken up by Keeley and her aggres-sor, but he had a sense of recognition and couldn't pin it down. "Is there anything about that room that's familiar to you?"

She shook her head. "It can't be his house," said Mack. "I've been there and anyway it's still a crime scene. If he was back there, we'd know. This looks completely different. Does he have anywhere else he uses?"

"I don't know, I've never wanted to know anything about him."

Mack pinched and then enlarged the screen on the phone. His heart became a drum, his stomach spasmed into a tight knot, hot bile burnt up into his throat: oh please, please God, no, not that. The phone screen was showing part of a photo hanging on the wall behind Keeley. That could only be one place. He remem-bered Scott's words: "If you haven't got any kids, it'll be your old mum, or anyone you love."

Chapter 41

It was the second day of Clarence's enforced hibernation and she was already bored. The stitches in her arm were beginning to itch, showering and hair-washing was a kerfuffle - Erin would need to dry it for her. She eventually managed to dress herself and go downstairs. She peered through the glass in the front door. The ten thirty a.m. police car was parked opposite, pulled in tight against the expanse of harvested and stiffly yellowed fields. She opened the door, collected her milk and newspaper, gave the constables the thumbs-up and watched as they drove off. It was just after she had closed the door and turned the dead-lock, was looking forward to her coffee and reading the paper, that she heard her sister scream. The milk bottle shattered as it hit the wooden floor.

She ran to the dining-room. Erin was standing in the door-way, hand over her mouth. Clarence pulled her out of the way. The shock hit her heart. "Hello, Mrs. Hope, we meet properly at last." She recognised the voice instantly. His cursing was the last thing she heard before he'd whacked her with a hard saucepan. She raised a hand to the gash on her temple, waited until she had her voice. "How did you get in?"

He smiled thin lips. "You need to get better security advice, my dear. Especially living all the way out here by yourself. Has no-one ever told you how easy it is to climb over a back gate and use good bolt-cutters against a padlock? And that you need to remove keys from door locks?" He nodded towards her dining-table. "That little device there allows anyone who has one to make a hole in your double-glazing and slip their hand through. You leave the keys in and voila. You're lucky I'm not a burglar. The insurance would never pay out."

"So, what are you, then," she snapped, "Apart from a man holding a knife to the throat of a terrified child?" He was bending so close over Keeley's head that the breeze of his breath was catching and ruffling the loose strands of her hair. Clarence felt

Erin's hand reach for hers and gripped it tight. She looked at Keeley's stiff, white little face and forced a smile. "It's ok, Keeley. Everything will be ok."

"I don't know why adults always say that to children," he said. "Blatantly, everything is not going to be ok, Mrs. Hope. Do you think Keeley thinks everything is going to be ok? She's not stupid. Children always understand more than adults think they do. That whole 'seen and not heard' malarkey means that they hear a lot. Adults forget that." He glanced down at Keeley's head and yanked on her pony-tail. Her head jerked back. He grinned in her face. "Don't they, Keeley? Why should you believe the good Mrs. Hope here when I'm the one who's controlling the situation? Eh? When I'm the one holding the knife? She doesn't have a say about anything at the moment, does she?"

"Ok. Ok," said Clarence. She took a risk on the name, "Reginald, or are you Reggie? Why don't you tell us what you want us to do."

He beamed and released Keeley's hair. "Ah, my name goes before me. How wonderful. Good. You know who you're dealing with. Now I'd like you two ladies to come in here. Shut the door. That fucking whining cat is getting on my nerves." He swiftly pulled a dining chair into the centre of the room and forced Keeley onto it, a cupped hand smoothing the ends of the pink ribbon, keeping the knife against her pale throat. Clarence could see the pulse in the child's neck artery jumping wildly, but Keeley was otherwise still, eyes frozen on Clarence's face. She sat with Erin on the small sofa that faced the fireplace.

"So," said Clarence, "You finally got Keeley, then, after missing her the first time round."

"Missing her?" He stroked a clean-shaven chin with his free hand. "Oh, no, you've got that completely wrong. I never meant for her to be taken. It was always going to be Samantha and Emma."

"Keeley was in the wrong place at the wrong time, was she?"

"Keeley was a naughty girl who should've gone home for her tea when her mum told her to." He tugged on the ponytail again,

"Then she would've been out of the way."

Clarence tried to sift his words to find some logic, an equation starting to form. She moved it aside for later.

"You look surprised, Mrs. Hope. Didn't you know? We're all one big happy family, the Bulls and Knatchbulls. Well, maybe not always happy, but loyal." He frowned. "In the main. Keeley had been taken today to teach young George a lesson, but then I thought, afterwards, that it could be nicely fitting for you to be the recipient of that lesson, Mrs. Hope. And since George went to all the trouble of tracking down your address, I thought it would be a shame to waste his efforts. And it is quite fitting: it was Social Workers who took him from us, who ruined him. His punishment will be having you on his conscience. And he does have one, you know. He can be quite a moral person, he worries, which is peculiar, given his genes.

And so here I am. What do you think? You do-gooders are always going on about protecting children. Would you give your-self up for her, an eleven-year-old child?" He paused, sniffing and looked down at Keeley, mouth souring. "What is it with you girls, you always have to piss yourselves." He grabbed her arm, hauled her off the chair and nodded at Erin. "Take her to the toilet. Clean her up. And mind you're straight back down, no pathetic little escape attempts, or phone calls. I will know." He nodded towards the French doors. "My young assistant has got his beady eyes trained on this pretty little cottage. Just remember that I've got the knife. And your sister." He watched her and laughed. "Your face is very expressive. Why are you surprised? I know everything there is to know about what matters to me, woman. Go on, get her out before she pisses herself again and offends my nostrils some more."

Erin looked at Clarence, who nodded. "It's fine, take her."

"Those fucking felines are going to get their furry throats slit in a minute. Shut them up on the way." Erin grabbed Keeley's hand and rushed her from the room, closing the door behind them. Clarence heard the back door open and out of the corner of one eye saw her cats bound into the garden.

234

"Now then, it's just the two of us." He sat down on the dining-chair. "Trying to work me out, are you, Mrs. Psychotherapist? Am I mad, or bad or both, eh? See, I know the jargon. What's your conclusion? Go on, I'd like to hear what you make of me."

She looked at him steadily. "I think that you're someone who had poor primary caregivers when you were very young and that you subsequently developed a poor attachment, that you suffered a level of childhood trauma," she paused "and that you were probably once a victim, who because of that now feels the need to control everything. I think whatever happened to you when you were a child warped how your personality developed and that there's no going back from it. How's that?"

"Not bad, not bad. Do you think I'm mad?"

"Not in the conventional sense, you're not psychotic. I think you've got the potential to go that way, though, not before too long, I'd guess. What do you think?"

His eyes flickered rapidly. "I think I might be like Sherlock Holmes. He called himself a high-functioning sociopath."

"Possibly," said Clarence. "Do you think you might be over-stretching yourself there, though?"

He glared at her. "You cocky bitch. You don't know who you're dealing with. I'm not stupid, you know. I'm educated."

"Yes, I can tell. You style yourself well. You're also narcissis-tic." She watched a tic start a steady beat in the muscle next to his eye.

"So, I've got a narcissistic personality disorder, have I?"

"Quite possibly, probably an anti-social one as well. And do you want to know how I know that? How I knew it from the first time I heard your voice, before you knocked me unconscious?"

"Please do, I'm intrigued."

"The thing about criminally disordered people, Reggie, is that they leave their slime all over you. They make you feel their crap so that they don't have to acknowledge it, deal with it or take re-sponsibility for it. And when they've gone and you're alone, you go to the bathroom and you have a long, soapy, hot shower to wash off their dirt and the memory of them."

"You think that's what you're going to do, do you? Wash me off, send me circling down the plughole!" The tic was electrocuting his eye socket, a dirty-old-man winking fit. "Rinse me away, like I don't matter, like I was never here."

She smiled at him. "Oh, yeah. That's exactly what I intend to do."

His nostrils flared. "You fucking whore. I'll tell you how it's going to go. You don't get to choose." Outside, the sun was starting its diurnal march across the lawn; a blade of light bounced off the knife and spliced the wall in two. He took some deep breaths. The tic slowed down.

"Normally, Mrs. Hope, I hate blood, piss, any type of filth. Anyone who knows me would describe me as obsessive about cleanliness. I really, really hate dirt. But I'm going to make an exception for you. You owe me. You've a debt to pay: two debts, in fact. Firstly, for getting away from me the other day and, secondly, because you do-gooders took my little brother away all those years ago. And that's been very inconvenient for me. So, we're going to get very intimate, you and I, intimate in a way that you will never have known. I'm an old man, now, got prostate problems, sex is behind me."

He suddenly tutted and fidgeted, ran his free hand down the waist of sharply creased grey slacks and fiddled with his crotch. "But the interaction between us, well, it'll still be a giving and receiving. There are other ways. Different ways of getting inside someone." He ran his eyes over her body. "Physically and mentally, I'm going to penetrate you, Mrs. Hope. Cause you pain like you've never known." He ran a thick tongue around his upper gums and smacked his lips.

"It'll be a new experience for both of us. Jack the Ripper knew. Do you think that's why he did it? As a substitute for sex, or even intimacy?" He stroked his chin. "I think about it a lot. About what it must've felt like for him. Seeing inside a woman, right inside, getting slippery in her blood and splaying his hands and squeezing them through her slimy, fleshy, wet guts, feeling her innards snaking through his fingers, wondering at the length of them. I've never had the stomach for it myself. I tried once on cats." The flat of the blade was caressing his forearm, agitating dark, coarse hairs. "I liked the extinguishing of life, made me feel like God." He paused. "Thinking about it, I suppose everyone has the power to kill. The difference is that I use mine. And when I do that, I think I must become God." He nodded. "Yes, that's right. That's when I'm God." He frowned. "But the bloody squealing was too loud, and the mess is a fucker and cats are handy buggers with their claws. No, I've always had other people do my dirty work. I expect today will be the only exception." He had an afterthought. "Strangling them was ok, though."

He stood up. "But today, I have, as they say, girded my loins, readied myself for our little dance, prepared to learn this new type of intimacy." His thin lips stretched tight across unnaturally even, milk-white teeth. He took some steps across the room towards her and then stopped. He rubbed at the tic with his free hand, "Fucking thing, stops me seeing clearly." He faced her, raised the knife and screeched - a thin and reedy wailing, preternaturally high. "I'm ready to be God again."

He took two purposeful steps. Clarence's fists shot up in tandem and made violent contact with a groin that was at once bony and soft. He screamed. She stood up and rammed both her hands into his chest, pushing hard. Bull fell back against the dining-chair, catching his foot around one of the legs and crashing down onto the floor. The chair landed next to him. The knife clattered into a corner.

Clarence straightened the chair, bent and picked up the knife, walked over to him and looked down as he lay groaning, arms gripped around knobbly knees held tight against a thin chest. "You foolish, silly, old man. How did you think you'd get the better of me? You're what I do for a day job." She watched him glowering up at her, smiled. "We're all capable of narcissism, Reggie." She paused. "At least some of the time." Then she checked that the French doors to her garden were locked and removed the keys, putting them in her pocket. "Thank you for the security tip, though. I really didn't know that. You learn something new every day." She shut the dining-room door behind her. There was a small bolt at the top, put on, for whatever reason, by the previous owner. She pushed it home.

Erin was outside the door, phone clutched in one hand, large kitchen knife in another. She put it down and gripped Clarence in a tight embrace. "Keeley's locked in the bathroom with a can of deodorant, told her to spray it in his face, kick him hard and run if he came in. I was watching on the phone, from the camera. I could see from your face that you had something planned. You always get this really stubborn, determined look. I was about to rush in when you went for him. I would've stabbed him. You believe me, don't you?"

"Course I do but I'm glad you didn't, would just have made it more dangerous. I could see his plan, if you'd come in, it would have thrown him, made him even more volatile. I guessed that you'd be outside. But I always had it, Erin."

"Police are on their way. Mack's been watching on his phone, too. And he recorded it."

Clarence looked at her sister. "I thought I said that I didn't want him having access to that thing."

"Yeah, well, it's a good job he did, in the end, isn't it?"

There was a loud thumping on the front door and Mack's voice shouting through the letterbox. Erin let them in. Mack stumbled over the threshold, crunching over broken milk-bottle, followed by Dave Cooper and three uniformed constables. "Everyone ok? Where's Keeley?"

"Upstairs. I'll get her," said Erin.

Mack turned to Cooper and nodded towards the dining-room door. "Get him out of there. Arrest him and check he doesn't need medical attention: kidnap, false imprisonment, possession of a weapon and threats to kill." He looked at the knife that was still gripped in Clarence's hand. "I'll take that, shall I?" He gently prised open her fingers, let the knife drop into an evidence bag and passed it on a colleague.

Clarence's legs buckled. Mack caught her, gripped her arm and led her into the front room. "Come on, sit down. Do you need to see a doctor?" She shook her head. "No, it's just shock. He didn't touch me. He's an old man, Mack. I was always going to be able to beat him."

He shook his head at her. "You're a class act, Clarence, I have to say. Most people would've gone to pieces."

"Ah well, I have had training."

"Have you? When?"

She shrugged nonchalantly. "Various times. They do teach Social Workers self-defence, you know."

Keeley came into the room, ran up to Clarence and hugged her. "You see, Keeley. I told you it would be ok. We're all ok." She held her at arms' length and looked at her. "Are you all right? Did he hurt you anywhere?"

Keeley shook her head. "Only when he pulled my ponytail really hard."

"Ah yes," said Mack, he rummaged in his trouser pocket and found a latex glove, handed it to Clarence. "I need that ribbon, Keeley."

Clarence gently undid the ribbon and dropped it in Mack's evidence bag.

"I was really scared, though, Clarence. I wet myself."

"I was scared, too and nearly wet myself, so don't worry about that. You were very brave, Keeley. You did really well. I'm proud of you. Your mum and dad will be, too."

"But Clarence…"

"Hmm…"

"I told you someone was listening. I didn't know where, not exactly. But I knew someone bad was somewhere."

"You did. You were right. And I'm sorry that I didn't listen harder to you. I should have."

"Is Reggie arrested, now?" Keeley turned to Mack.

"He is. How did you know his name?"

"He told me when he made me get into the car."

"Ok, well, he'll be going to prison, for what he did to you today and for other things, too. And, there's something else to tell you. We've found Emma and she's fine. She's in hospital, but she'll be going home soon and you'll be able to go and see her."

A grin spread across Keeley's face, "Really?"

"Yes really. I'm going to put you in a police car with some police officers and they'll take you back to your mum and dad and Claire. We'll have to come back to talk to you a bit more about what's happened today, but you can go home now." He took her outside and saw her into a car, went back inside and watched through the window with Clarence and Erin as a hobbling Bull was led by Cooper and a PC through the front garden.

"Good grief, I didn't think I pushed him that hard," said Clarence.

A passing motorist slowed down to see what the drama was about.

She turned to Mack. "Do you think I hurt him badly?"

"He probably twisted his leg when he fell against the chair. Don't worry about that, Clarence. The man was threatening you with a knife. You were more than within your rights to act in self-defence."

"Oh, ok." She leant back into the sofa and closed her eyes, then opened them again. "Mack, Bull said that he had an assistant watching the cottage, a young assistant. That must be who climbed over the back gate, there's no way Bull could've done that himself."

"Yeah, I heard that bit from the camera. There's been a squad car driving around, seeing if there's anyone to find. But I reckon whoever it was scarpered when they saw police cars speeding down the road."

"How did you guess, Mack?" Erin tapped her phone and sidled a look at her sister. "Was it the camera?"

Mack shook his head. "Not initially. Bull made Keeley take a selfie in your dining-room to send to her parents. Some of that photo on the wall of your cats was caught in the picture. That's when I logged into the camera."

Clarence's mind was circling, still in survival mode. "Do we need to give a statement?"

"Clarence, can we talk about the rest of all this later?" said

Erin. "I really, really need a drink. I think you've more than fulfilled your civic duty. If we do need to give a statement, can we do it in a few hours, Mack? I think I just need a bit of time at the moment."

He nodded. "Yeah, the statement can wait a while. I've got all the facts down as you've given them. I'll send someone round this evening."

"Good, because right now, Mack, you're going to drive us into the village to the Fox and Pheasant, where Clarence and I are going to have a good lunch and an even better bottle of wine. We'll get a taxi back. I'll stay for another couple of nights."

"Hang on a minute, Erin. There's just something else I need to tell Mack now. When you were watching on the phone, did you hear what Reggie said about Keeley?"

He frowned. "Which bit? The sirens were going at a pace, Clarence, I couldn't quite catch everything."

"Bull said that Keeley was never meant to have been there. That she should've been at home for her tea. She was never a target. It was always only Samantha and Emma."

He blinked. "Yeah, I know that. Her mum had asked her to be home for tea much earlier. Looks like she just got caught up in it."

"No, Mack. Listen to the footage and what Bull says. I think Keeley's parents were in on the abduction."

Chapter 42

Back at Chelmsford station, Mack looked for Kennedy to give him an update. He was nowhere to be found. He eventually wandered into the Superintendent on the way back from the toilet. The man looked grave. "Ah, Mack, I was hoping you were back. Can you come to my office? I need a word." The Superintendent shut the door behind them. "We've had an incident, Mack. I'm surprised you haven't heard."

"I've not been back long, Sir. I was dealing with the Reginald Bull situation. You've heard we got him? He's in the cells."

"No, he's not. He's in hospital."

Mack stared at him, "Sorry?"

"He's got a broken forearm and a broken nose. And being elderly, he's having to have the arm pinned. They're operating later today."

"Well, I've got the footage of the incident on my phone, Sir. I can't believe that he sustained those injuries from that."

"Footage? What footage?"

"Mrs. Hope's sister left one of those indoor home monitoring cameras on Mrs. Hope's mantlepiece, originally to watch the cats while Mrs. Hope was in hospital. It all happened with Bull in the same room. She sent me the link, so when I realised there was a problem, I logged in and saw the whole thing. It was completely in self-defence. The man had a knife."

The Superintendent looked at him for a few seconds and then shook his head. "I think we're talking at cross-purposes, Mack. These injuries happened in the squad car. Dave Cooper attacked Mr. Bull."

"Cooper?" Mack closed his mouth. "No, I don't believe it."

"Apparently, yes, just completely lost the plot. Told the driver to stop the car, hauled Bull out and attacked him, had to be pulled off by the other constables. He's in custody now. The Inspector's with him."

Mack drew a deep breath. He thought back to the small

changes in Dave's behaviour recently, wished he'd done something: like Clarence had said to Keeley - should've listened harder. "Should I go down to custody, Sir?"

"They're trying to get to the bottom of it now. Yes, by all means go down. What's happening about little Keeley? She'll have to be interviewed."

"Yeah, actually Sir, there might be another consideration to bring to the case, but I need to review the footage from the camera before I know for sure."

"Ok, well, as ever, if the DI's tied up with Cooper, report directly to me, Mack. I really thought we were on the end strait here, looks like we're still only halfway through."

Kennedy was talking urgently on the phone, his brow furrowed. He hung up and looked at Mack. "Glad you're here. See if you can get anything out of him, will you? He hasn't said a word. I can't make head nor tail of it."

"Has he seen a medic?"

"Not yet, that's who I was just talking to, but he's with someone at Bellington station." He nodded at the cell door, "Go on, it's open."

Mack knocked gently. "Dave, mate, it's Mack. Can I come in?"

"Do what you like."

Mack closed the door gently behind him. Cooper was hunched up against the bunk, arms crossed, stony-faced. "Do you want a coffee, tea – anything?" Cooper shook his head. A vein throbbed in his right temple. Mack sat down on the bunk. "What's going on, Dave? S'not like you to do something like this. Have they charged you?"

"No. Still waiting for the duty brief so I can be interviewed."

"So what made you do it? Did Bull say anything, Dave, goad you? I've never even known you to get cross, let alone thump a prisoner. It must've been something pretty grim for you to have been pushed over the edge like that. Come on, mate. You can tell me."

Cooper ran a trembling hand across his face. "Did you know I spent some time in care when I was a kid, Mack?"

"No, no I didn't."

"Yeah, I was eight, my brother's quite a bit older than me, he was about thirteen. It wasn't for long. My mum got ill with cancer. She did recover, but the treatment wiped her out and she wasn't able to look after us properly. My dad had to commute for work, so my nan used to help out, but during the months that my mum was really ill, we used to go for respite with a foster carer once every fortnight, cos my nan was looking after my mum, too, she was really sick with the chemo. Anyway, we used to go for a weekend or for a week in school holidays. I didn't mind it, but my brother, Timmy, well, he hated it. I never did work out why and he couldn't seem to articulate it. I think, looking back, that he just hated being away from home and was scared shitless that our mum was gonna die." He wiped his mouth with the back of a hand. "The foster carer was nice, she fed us, had a nice dog, she was kind. But for whatever reason, Timmy never liked it. So, he used to hang around outside her flat most weekends we were there, went out early, only came in at tea-time. Guess where our foster home was?"

"Can't mate."

"Mead estate, where your friend, Knatchbull, lives. Anyway, one Saturday, Timmy just disappeared. Wasn't outside, couldn't be found. Kids didn't routinely have mobile phones then, so we had no way of contacting him."

"What happened?"

"I thought I recognised that Knatchbull name when it first came up on this case, but I couldn't remember why at first. But then it came to me. The foster mum knew them. Not well, just enough to say good morning, being neighbourly. She once took in a parcel for them and I saw the name, remembered it cos it was quite unusual and it had taken me a while to work out how to say it." He looked up at Mack. "Kids remember things like that, don't they?"

"Kids remember a lot of things, Dave. What happened to Timmy?"

"Turned up later that day, said some bloke had dragged him into his car earlier that morning. Timmy had been wandering along the arterial road, the A127, was planning to meet some other lads in one of the farmer's fields behind that big garden centre. I think they'd made a swing out of an old tyre, or something, just kids being kids. I'd wanted to go with him, but he said I was too young. Anyway, the man called him over, asked if he had the time, grabbed his wrist and that was it. Sped him up the 127, but Timmy managed to open the car door and rolled out when the car was slowing coming up to traffic lights. He bashed his head on the kerb. The car hadn't gone far and just drove off and Timmy walked back to the foster home. That's what gave him the brain injury, hitting the kerb. That's why Timmy is what he is today, that's why my parents spend their retirement looking after him. Because of that fucking, nasty, perverted bastard!"

Mack looked at his friend. He didn't know what to say, only that Bull had tentacles that seemed to spread everywhere. "You think it was Reggie Bull who took him, do you?"

"Given how this case has panned out, I think it's bloody certain that it at least has something to do with him."

"What did the police say at the time?"

Cooper's mouth twisted down. "Didn't even believe him. Said he was known for hanging around, being a trouble-maker, had probably tripped and done it himself, or got into a fight with another boy."

"There weren't any witnesses?"

"It was an early autumn morning, it was our half-term break, probably wasn't completely light at that point. No-one came forward, anyway. Not sure the police even asked, you know, put out a board on the road, or anything."

"But didn't he need to go to hospital?"

"There was hardly any visible damage at first, but he had a brain bleed. Luckily, the foster mum recognised how seriously ill he was later that evening and got him to hospital. That's what saved his life."

"Why're you in the police, Dave?"

"Fuck knows. You?"

"Same." Mack went to the germ-ridden bench behind the custody desk that counted as a kitchen, made a couple of strong coffees and found some melting chocolate biscuits in a ripped and grimy packet. When he went back into the cell, Dave had sat up straighter, the pulsing vein had calmed down. "Listen, Dave, you've got extenuating circumstances. You need to tell Kennedy all this. Do you think your brother would be able to identify Bull if he saw him?"

"Yeah, possibly, he has some cognition. But I'm still done for, aren't I? I just saw red, Mack. I lost it."

"Tell Kennedy and your brief. Then speak to your family and get your brother involved. You're gonna be suspended, and probably charged. But I think you might get off with a six month final warning."

"I won't, not if I get a criminal record. They'll sack me."

"You might get a caution."

"Give over, Mack. Bull needs to have his arm pinned."

Something occurred to Mack. "Has it been you watching Knatchbull?" Cooper nodded. "Why? He's been complaining, thinking it was me."

"Because I think Knatchbull had something to do with my brother. Don't know why, can't give you anything concrete. It's just instinct."

"Dave, see your brief. And the union. And you know I'll support you all the way."

Late in the afternoon, Mack showed Kennedy the footage from his phone. "Do you hear it, Guv? What Bull's said about Keeley."

Kennedy took off his glasses and rubbed his eyes. "I feel like this case is never going to end, Mack. Get Knatchbull down here, tomorrow. If what Bull has implied is true, I'd lay a bet George Bridge knew and that's the secret he kept referring to. And it means, Mack, that you've been on the right path all along with your suspicions about Knatchbull. If he won't come voluntarily, arrest him on suspicion of aiding and abetting."

Chapter 43

But Knatchbull agreed to present himself without quibble. He was quiet and meek on the phone, like all the fight had gone out of him. Mack and Kennedy saw him together late in the afternoon.

Knatchbull sat neat and contained in the hard plastic chair, slumped, smaller.

"So, Mr. Knatchbull, you know you're here of your own free will, you're not under arrest and you can leave at any point," said Mack.

Knatchbull nodded. "I know, but I'm tired. I can't go on dealing with this anymore. I'm tired of who I am, of the stress of holding everything in, of worrying about my daughters. And I'm tired of feeling constantly guilty. I've spoken to Janice. Reggie taking Keeley was the last straw for us. She agreed that I should tell you the truth."

"Ok, we're listening, Mr. Knatchbull."

He looked at Mack. "You were right. I was sent to live with Reggie once my mum died. The house in Poplar got handed back to the council and Reggie just took me to his. I had no choice, I wasn't asked. He came on the day of the funeral and took me back with him. And you were right about what he did to me. It started almost straight away."

Mack hadn't anticipated the need for tissues, particularly for Knatchbull. He took a new box from a cupboard in the corner of the room and put it on the table between them.

"I'd lost my dad, then my mum. It was the worst time. I cried for weeks. But in the end, I just accepted it. Kids do. It wasn't just Reggie who was abusive, in fact he's not that into boys, he just breaks you in. It was other men, they paid for it. Paid Reggie, not me, obviously. It stopped when I got to thirteen. I grew tall quite fast, got big. The men weren't interested then. Men like that want the kids to look like kids, so he let me go, but I was expected to work for him, help out when I was needed while I was still there."

"Did he send you to school?"

"Nah, don't think the education department knew I existed. But Reggie is clever and educated. He home-schooled me. Despite the abuse, he did make sure I could read and write, that I knew the basics – he even taught me about politics and economics. He was a good teacher. When I did go to school, I wasn't particularly behind."

"And where does your wife come in?"

"Janice's grandparents, on her dad's side, got out of Poplar after the war, moved to the Mead and kept their son and then Janice away from Reggie and the others. Janice's parents took me in after Reggie was done with me."

"Were there other children in Reggie's house when you were there?"

"I know there were. Sometimes I'd hear a child crying. But we were kept separate. I had my own bedroom. And it's a big house. You've seen his secret room?" Mack nodded. "That's for seeing clients, but I had my own room while I was there permanently. Had to keep it spotless, he hates mess."

"So you went to live with Janice's parents?"

"Yeah. Best thing that ever happened to me. I was worried, scared, terrified, when Reggie told me I was going, you know out of the frying pan… But her parents were kind, good. Really good. They helped me to learn how to deal with the medical stuff," he shifted in the chair, "if you get my drift and they showed me a normal family life. I started at the same school as Janice. We grew up together and then got married."

"So it is true that her parents changed their name?"

He nodded. "Yeah, it was her parents, not the grandparents, who changed the name. They really hated being part of the family. Changing their name was their way of trying to protect their kids. We realised a long time ago that Keeley had seen Janice's old passport, but we never thought it would matter, that she wouldn't even understand the significance of it." He smiled sadly, "But kids remember way more than we think, don't they?"

"How did Janice's parents manage to keep Bull away then, because they were clearly in contact with him, weren't they?"

"It's never free, Sergeant. If Reggie lets you off, there's always a payback, see. They were left alone, as long as they did their bit for the family, paid back the debt. And if you don't fall into line, don't do as he says, there's consequences."

"What's the payback, Mr. Knatchbull?" Mack shifted in his chair. His stomach was twitching, tightening. He was learning to trust his gut, to make friends with it.

Knatchbull moved out of his hunch, squared his shoulders and looked Kennedy straight in the eye. "Before I tell you, I need to know that you'll protect my girls. Cos I know that I'm gonna go to prison. When you find out, after you hear what I've got to say, you'll despise me. And I won't blame you. I deserve it. But you've got to promise to protect my daughters. Please. I'm trusting you with this."

"If your children are at risk, we will protect them. I promise."

Knatchbull drew a deep, ragged breath. He rested his hands on the table, laced his fingers together and looked down. "We have to identify kids for him to take."

"Reggie?" Mack's stomach moved into its spasm. Always trust your gut.

He nodded. "Every so often, Reggie makes contact with family members cos he needs fresh blood. Wants to know if there's any kids around who're a bit vulnerable, maybe unhappy at home, hanging around outside a bit too much. We give him the details and he arranges for them to be taken."

"So you identified Emma and Samantha did you?"

He nodded. "They were always out and about. We've never let Keeley do that, insisted on her being home at a set time, know exactly where she is. But their parents were a bit lax. And the council was planning to replace some of the kitchens on the estate in August; we got the dates, so we knew there'd be a couple of contractor vans around - another one waiting somewhere wouldn't look suspicious."

"You give their details to him and he puts in place people to take the kids? Or does he do it?"

"Either. I think lately he gets other people to do it, though. Sometimes he makes it look like the kids have run away, or sometimes he takes homeless kids, or kids who've really run away, especially from care - children's homes, usually. There's family all over the country. He spreads it out so that links aren't made. He'd have kids from up north one year and maybe just one from Devon the next. I'd bet that some of the homeless kids won't even have been reported as missing. It's been going on for years. A lot of missing kids on your books will be down to him."

"Was George Bridge part of this?"

"Of course, he's a teacher. Who has better access to children?"

"Was it Bridge who told Reggie that Keeley was seeing Mrs. Hope for counselling? Because that's why Reggie wanted rid of her, isn't it?"

Knatchbull nodded. "George told us that he'd told Reggie. I was livid. We didn't want Reggie to know, that's why I was so against it from the off. I knew that Reggie wouldn't like it, that he'd be suspicious of Keeley letting anything slip. But Janice could see that Keeley needed help. She arranged it without telling me at first, knew I'd be cross." He paused, "Not cross, I hated seeing Keeley feeling so guilty. I just knew it wouldn't be safe, I was scared and thought that Keeley's upset was the lesser of the two evils. But Janice was really worried about her."

"Why did Bridge tell Reggie, then? Bridge must've thought the same as you about it. And why did you tell Bridge in the first place?"

"Claire told him at school one day. He asked her how Keeley was and Claire just said that her sister was seeing a Social Worker with a funny name. Don't suppose it would've been difficult for George to track down who that Social Worker was. And he's terrified of Reggie, what he could do to George's kids. He probably just caved in, wouldn't take much. He was away from it for a long time, had a chance to get used to a more normal life, he copes with it worse than we do. I know he's tried to top himself. I'm not surprised. In the end, you can't hold onto the guilt and still protect your own kids, be a decent human being. Something has to give. I suppose, for George, it was himself."

"And what happens to the children when Reggie's done with them?"

"I don't know. Never wanted to. Maybe the same as what happened to me, maybe they get sent off to other family." He blinked several times. "If they survive, if they don't end up dead at the hands of one of Reggie's so-called clients, or do it themselves."

"You know that's happened do you, Mr. Knatchbull? Kids've died?"

"Come on, Inspector. You've been to the Poplar house, you must've found stuff. House was used for that for decades."

"Do you remember anything from when you lived there as a child?"

"I remember people coming and going; there's a park opposite, I used to get sent over there to play quite a lot."

"No-one ever tried to assault you, Mr. Knatchbull, while you lived there?"

"Not 'til Reggie got me. I think it was quite an organised operation, not random, so they could control it, I suppose. But from what Janice's parents said, Reggie was beginning to shut things down at the house towards the time my mum died. I've got no direct proof of any kids dying, no stories to tell, but there was always whisperings amongst Janice's parents and grandparents, as well. It all adds up to that – can't not. Some of these perverts aren't satisfied 'til they've caused a lot of damage." He paused, took another tissue and noisily blew his nose. "Suppose I'm lucky that I never had any like that – if you can call it luck. Some of them just want sex. They can't get turned on by an adult, not as much as they want, anyway, it's like they're stuck somewhere, not properly grown-up, might even talk to you like they're a kid. Some of the men used to try to give me presents, nice ones, expensive things. As I got older, I came to see it like they were passing on their guilt, making out, pretending like I was willing, doing, rather than being done to," his mouth twisted, "As if they thought presents could take away the hurt."

"What happened if you complained?"

"A vicious beating, that's what. In the end, I stopped saying anything, even stopped crying, soon learnt what happened when one of 'em complained to Reggie. But some men want more and more, need more and more, for the ones like that, murder would be the ultimate turn-on. I'm sure of it. The bastards convince themselves that it's just a different way of getting sex, but it's always about power, in the end. You're police. You know how it goes."

Mack waited for Knatchbull's breathing to slow down. "So, how did Keeley get caught up in all this?"

"She was never meant to, Sergeant. Should've been home for her tea. Her mum was calling and calling. I lied to you when you came round that evening. Janice had been out looking for Keeley, Janice wasn't there, in the bedroom like I said, when that woman brought Keeley home, she came running in a minute or so later, she'd heard the sirens."

"Did you know the planned date and time of the abduction?"

Knatchbull shook his head. "Don't know that level of detail. We gave him the dates of the kitchens being done, which was across a fortnight, but we didn't know the actual, specific day of Reggie's plans. Could've been any of those days. I suppose the blokes were watching, had to time it right."

"So how come you didn't keep Keeley at home?"

"We knew it was going to be a very late afternoon or evening snatch, after five thirty p.m., anyway – less people around. Normally, Keeley is really good about coming home on time. She's never even been five minutes late. And we couldn't have kept her in every day."

"You don't think Reggie was just going to take Keeley anyway? That he lied to you?"

"Nah, not his way, cos then he'd have no leverage. He would've stuck to the agreement. We weren't worried about that, we just didn't want Keeley seeing anything. I think the blokes he hired were just a bit thick and took a chance when they shouldn't have."

"So why did you used to keep all your windows locked, if you thought he'd always stick to agreements?"

"That's the point: he sticks to a specific agreement, but that doesn't mean you can trust him. It's all about the power and about him knowing he can do anything whenever he wants."

"How often does Reggie approach you?"

"Not often, hardly ever, to minimise the risk. This was only the second time. I think he's only asked George Bridge once. I'd heard that Reggie had as good as retired, was just running things at arms-length, so we were shocked when he called and said it was our turn. The first time was just after we'd got married, about nineteen years ago. There was a boy who was always alone, suppose he was about eleven or twelve, always hanging around outside on the estate. At first, we refused to do it. Point blank refused. But Reggie threatened Janice's mum and dad. They knew what he was like, what he could do. He's brutal, with people who are willing to do anything at his say-so. In the end, we gave him the information. Janice was physically sick for days with the guilt."

"Couldn't Reggie have done his own research? Found his own victims?"

"Yeah, but it's not just about that. Like I say, it's about him having control, power, making people do exactly as he says, when he says. You need to understand that about him."

"Why didn't you go to the police?"

He shook his head, "Couldn't see how to. We thought about it all the time. Sergeant, this is a huge network. We couldn't beat it. You think we didn't want to go to the police? We're not monsters, we don't wanna see kids abused and killed. But Reggie's clever. He makes you weak, complicit; he makes you take part in criminal activity when you're younger, so he's always got something over you, in case you get any funny ideas – as he would see it."

"Like what?"

"Receiving stolen goods, handling guns. He even takes

photographs of you doing it, so you're compromised and think if you go to the police about him, you're in the shit, too."

"Where are the photos? On a computer?"

"Nah, Reggie doesn't even like mobile phones. He uses a bloody ancient polaroid camera. Got a whole stash of film in his fridge, he planned when he knew they were going out of business."

"Do you know where he keeps those photos?"

"If they're not at his house, I honestly don't know. He's probably got somewhere else, some secret place that no-one knows about. He's like that, likes to have secrets."

"Ok, so you were saying about why you didn't go to the police..."

"We're raised to see officials as the enemy, it's drummed into you so as you don't snitch, so there's psychological barriers to get through before going to the police, as well as the risk you're taking if one of 'em finds out. You can't beat this lot, it's a massive criminal network. Janice's mum and dad are just a handful of them who tried to get away. There's been inbreeding for years, half of them are bloody thick and just fall in line. They marry amongst themselves."

"Like you and your wife?"

Knatchbull sniffed hard. "Yeah, ok. Like me and my wife. Except we are quite distantly related - we hope. Experiences like we've had, you want to be around your own, people who understand. I know it sounds contradictory, but that's the way it is. Can you imagine any other woman coping with marrying me, with what I've been through, what I am? Don't get me wrong, I'm not violent. I know that I sound aggressive a lot of the time, swear in front of the kids when I shouldn't, but it's just I get scared – a lot - and the stress of trying to manage it all gets to me. Didn't exactly have a good role model in Reggie, did I? It was Janice's dad who showed me what normal men are like and then I've only managed it part-way. He's a much better man than I am. And we do love each other, me and Janice. If it weren't for her, I don't know where I'd be." He smeared the back of his hand under his nose. "If we'd gone to the police back them, back when we were younger, all we would've done was put us and Janice's parents at risk."

"So what's changed Mr. Knatchbull? Why are you here now?"

"Everything changes when you're a parent. We went along with him about Emma and Samantha, cos we thought that we had no other way of protecting Keeley and Claire. When he took Keeley, well, it's like your heart's ripped out and trod underfoot. It hurt much worse than what he did to me when I was a kiddie, which I never thought was possible. We understood, then, what we'd done. But I know they'll have me for this. You'll never stop them."

"Well, we have now, haven't we? We've stopped it now."

He shook his head. "No, you haven't, not really. Think of it as being like the Mafia. Reggie's the head of the family, so if he's taken out of circulation, things will go quiet for a bit, but in the end, they'll get organised again, appoint someone new."

He wheezed a breath into shallow smoker's lungs. "You were right, Sergeant, to show me that Reggie isn't God. In my head, he always was, see, cos of what he did, the power he had. When you're a child, you've got no say: you just get done to. I needed you to point it out, make me realise. Me and Janice knew that we had to make it stop. And I'll always be grateful to you for saving my girl."

"Wasn't me, actually, Mr. Knatchbull. It was the Social Worker."

"Well, tell her I said thanks."

"So Reggie said something to the Social Worker, that seemed to imply that the Knatchbulls and Bulls are somehow related: one family. Is that the case? Was your dad related to the Bulls before he married your mum?"

"Yeah, distantly. Don't ask me how, cos I honestly don't know. This goes back generations. And it's not like they would've been diligent about registering all the births years ago, it would be impossible to trace. To be honest, I wouldn't want to."

"It's quite an unusual name, Knatchbull, I've never heard it anywhere else. Do you know what it means?"

"It's an old name. It's what they used to call the bloke who stunned bulls before they were slaughtered."

Chapter 44

Mack went home after Knatchbull's interview. It was his first early finish in days, but he could afford to sit up late - he'd caught up on his sleep. The weather in his head was calm. The effect of his mum's affirmation of his pain and acknowledgement of her guilt had soothed and astonished in equal measure and since then his nights were quiet, the dreams gone. His memories had become free-flowing, were weeping their pus, letting out the poison, but he knew that the cleansed wounds would scar over again and heal - properly, this time.

Mack thought about Clarence, Dave Cooper, Bridge, Knatchbull, even Kennedy, the pain they'd carried, sometimes in secret and how the confession of it took them to a crossroads: left or right, but never straight on. He thought about his mum. And Dad. He wondered about himself, about his integrity, his motivation for becoming a policeman, whether it had been to catch criminals, or to catch himself and whether there was really any difference, whether pain, hurt, was ever a justification.

He thought about his own secret. About how a memory had morphed into a fantasy and been kicked forward through time to become a memory again. And about how it, too, needed to face a light, although it would, for certain, only ever be the soft glow of his own conscience.

The night Mack became a murderer had been a dark one, violence kicking around the ether. Loud and savage gusts hammered across the North Sea mudflats and pitted boats against their anchors, before becoming trapped in the corridor of the Thames and whirling angrily upwards to break against London's monoliths. The tide was due. He could hear the galloping march in between blasts of wind, but when he looked out, the foreshore was lonely, unseeable and black, white horses still a good half mile away. It was an isolated spot, uninhabited and without a beach, on the mouth of the Estuary and dangerous to the uninitiated; a fierce spring tide could reach high and almost over the wall. It had been a coincidence, a quirk of fate that he was there. A gift from God. Maybe. It had needed a split-second decision.

His dad had been stumbling along in front of him, swaying back and forth from the waist, open palm periodically patting the seawall for balance. He had stopped, heaved, leant forward and retched booze and bile over and down onto the mud. His head dangled for some seconds, chest spasming, as he hacked and spat the aftertaste. Mack made the decision. Took his opportunity. The bomber-jacket was heavy with rain; it had hunched up around his dad's upper back, weighting him forwards. The synthetic fabric was clammy and slimy beneath Mack's open palms, the crack of bone against rock just another spike in the night's decibel count, the moaning swept up in the howling and then pummelled away into nothing.

After, when everything was different, had changed in a split-second, he huddled against the seawall, crouched low, holding onto himself tight to stop the shaking, tasting the sea, smelling the waves galloping closer and feeling the sting of salt on his cheeks. He'd heard the water crashing in on the back of the storm and felt its strength smashing against the wall behind him, driving ever higher, white foam leaping tall; it had been like his hair was briny for days. He had waited the hours past high tide - to be sure. And then he went home. Carried on. Got a life. A normal life, one free from violence and fear and hate. He waited for the guilt, waited for it to crush him, for his dad's ghost to swing its weight and floor him. It never did, not then and not since. Past was the past.

For all involved, it had been a case that brought the unveiling of secrets, a holding up of them to the light: a time when the veins and capillaries that fed dark corners of the mind and soul were ruptured open and glooped their viscosity towards the day. For some, it had been a time when their dead came calling, thrusting them forwards and into resolution.

He weighed up everything and reached his conclusion: his dad was gone, he and his mum were alive, friends he loved were safe. He was still taking Clarence's advice, acknowledging, knowing, accepting all of it and moving on. Working towards a future. Growing up. But unlike Clarence, he didn't need to grieve: not then, not ever.

Predictably, the Superintendents's budget was beyond redemption. Still, on the plus side, everything was progressing and yielding results quickly. Only two weeks after Emma had been found and one complete week into their searching and testing there were results: DNA on two of the ribbons were found to be matches on the national missing persons database. One of the Poplar basement skeletons was a match with another ribbon. There were going to be a lot of grieving relatives needing police liaison officers: more expense.

The Knatchbulls were charged with perverting the course of justice, aiding and abetting, and bailed. Despite their heinous actions, the Superintendent understood that they were the victims of a nasty, manipulative, powerful child abuser and, to boot, they had owned up. The police would be recommending leniency to the Court.

The white van found behind Bull's property was teeming with Emma and Samantha's DNA. The underground bunker was still being examined - the Superintendent wasn't sure that part of the case would ever be closed. Tony's body and clothing had been swimming in DNA and Samantha's had subsequently been released for burial. Emma had identified Reginald Bull as her kidnapper, digitally, from her hospital bed. A week after his arrest, the assault by Cooper and his subsequent operation, they were ready to go to interview with Bull on suspicion of Emma's kidnapping and all the charges relating to the incident at Mrs. Hope's house. The Superintendent knew that there would be further charges once all the evidence had been unravelled: all in all, the case was beginning to tie itself up nicely. And as much as he wanted to interview the bastard himself, he seceded to Kennedy and his sergeant; it had, after all, been their success.

The man who had been a monstrous, child-snatching Pied Piper in Mack's imagination was, in the end, as he remembered him from Clarence's house: a thin, slightly stooped man, who shuffled into the interview room, showing his late-seventies, wearing prison-issue clothes, forearm still plastered and in a sling. Tufts of grey hair had been slicked down with water across a chalky scalp stippled with liver-spots.

It was after he'd sat down in front of him and Kennedy, shifted in his chair, got comfortable, rested surprisingly well-manicured hands on the table, that he raised his head and looked at them. And then Mack understood. His imagination had only been part-wrong.

Hatred and spite were etched hard into Bull's eyes, glaring brightly under greying, unkempt brows. He stared at them both for several seconds, not flinching, while his solicitor got papers in order.

Kennedy started the interview by cautioning Bull and listing the grounds for which he had been arrested. "I'm now showing Mr. Bull photographs of Emma Downs and Samantha Evans. Do you recognise the girls in these photos, Mr. Bull?" Bull took a cursory look and leant back.

"What do you want me to say, Detective Inspector? Do you want me to deny it? Make you work for your money? Course I bleedin' recognise them." Bull's accent was educated received pronunciation, but in the confines of the interview room, the acoustics bounced back a hint of cockney waiting to edge in from the corners, straining to spit back.

"How do you know these girls, Mr. Bull?"

"Because, as you well know, I took them. Well, technically, wasn't me, but I arranged for them to be taken."

"You arranged for them to be taken? Could you tell us how you did that?"

Bull's elderly solicitor was already getting fidgety, his cheeks speedily moving through varying shades of red and towards a mottling purple. He put a hand on Bull's arm, "Er, Inspector, a word with my client, please."

Bull spoke straight over him, "Shut up, you old fag. And get your hand off me. What's the point in lying? I've been caught bang to rights, girl was found in my house, for fucks sake. I don't care. S'not like I haven't got influence, contacts, is it? It'll come good, you'll see." Bull looked into Mack's eyes. "You can look at me like I'm the scum, my spiv, but what do you know about anything? Young bluebottle like you, you don't know nothing."

"You say that you arranged for the girls to be taken, Mr. Bull. How did you decide that these particular girls would be your targets?"

"Ha! Now that's information that I'm not prepared to divulge, Detective Inspector. There are people I won't give up, not in my interest to do so."

"So, there are people who helped you to identify and then target these girls. Is that what you are saying, Mr. Bull?"

Bull didn't respond immediately. He leant back in his chair, crossed one leg over the other and slowly licked the tip of a taut tongue around pale, thin lips, looking at Kennedy.

"You people, police, Social Workers, the lot of you, what you forget, probably never even knew, was that for hundreds of years, kids have been prostituted out, specially poor kids, extraspecially orphans, to suck cock, wank, fuck – whatever. It was acceptable, what was done. The posh just turned away from it, never stopped it – and don't think, by the way, they weren't up for a bit of it. All this," he waved a dismissing hand towards them, mouth souring, "Spouting child protection, being indignant. How do you think the East End got by, before the welfare state, eh? All this is new, how long has this malarky about child protection been going on, twenty-five years, thirty? Seriously going on, I mean, you know, believing the kids when they say they've been raped, or whatever. You're trying to undo centuries of behaviour. People have always desired kids. It's in our DNA – humanity. It's what we are. You'll never stop it. You'll never stop me."

Kennedy interrupted him. "But you have been stopped, Mr.

Bull, haven't you? Look at where you are."

"True, but after a lifetime, Inspector, after a lifetime. A lifetime helped by some of your lot, I might add. I've had a bleedin' life of luxury on the back of this." The cockney was right out now. "True, it's all gone tits up and I'm gonna do bird, but that won't be for long, and I've lived like you could never dream: nice house, fine whisky, wine, every need met. I grew up in squalor, always hungry, filthy, scavenging on bomb-sites. This got me out of that. Me family's always done this to one degree or another, but I took it to a whole new level. I ran a fucking successful business. Didn't need no accountant or banker. Did it all meself. That crap salary that they pay you lot's never gonna get you what I've had."

He suddenly paused and looked at his left forefinger, examined it intently, rubbed it and then nibbled a flap of skin from the side of the nail and spat it out; Mack watched it land at the side of his chair. "I know about it from the inside."

"You say that you family's always done this, Mr. Bull. Could you give us some examples of what you mean?"

"It's in me blood. I grew up in that Poplar house. I know yous've been there, found out. Me family lived there for generations. We was poor, everyone was. It was squalor like no-one knows now: outside privy, no hot water, blitzed out buildings, bodies of war dead still being uncovered, hunger that could eat into your soul. But you know what I did?" He paused. Mack tried to keep a neutral expression, but Bull knew that he had them. "I got meself an education. Taught meself to read from books an' papers I found on the bomb-sites, trundled off to school with the other kids, got meself a place at grammar school, listened to 'ow they spoke posh, even got 'A' levels I did, could've gone on to Oxbridge."

Mack couldn't help himself. "So what happened? Where did it go wrong?"

"What do you think bleedin' happened? Use yer nut! They got me, didn't they? Truth be told, I was surprised I got away with it for as long as I did. Me grandad was a big, strong man and when 'e decided it was time, it was your time; there was no saying no to 'im. Grandad ruled the 'ole family. After that it was me job to keep the rich men happy."

"How old were you, Mr. Bull?" Kennedy was as hooked as Mack.

"Fourteen, as I say, I got away with it for longer, the little girls was initiated much younger and put out to work, from 'bout nine or ten." He raised his eyebrows. "No good looking shocked. You all know now it goes on: suddenly everyone believes the kids. Jimmy Saville an' all them. It's an irony, a'int it? Kids've been tryin' say for years – we all knew they was telling the truth. Politicians, bankers, actors, all the good and great; they're everywhere, the ones who like a bit of rough with a kid."

"So you were sent out to men, were you?"

"They liked me prettiness, me brains. Grandad said that I could keep going to school so long as I brought in the bacon. I got out of that malarkey, though, as soon as I could, moved into girls. The men liked that too – just watching."

"So did you finish school, Mr. Bull?"

"Yeah, I did. Got three 'A' levels, Maths, Physics and Economics – top grades." He tapped his temple with a forefinger. "Clever, see?"

"So what happened to university?"

"Biggest regret of me life, that is. But there was nothing for it. Grandad wasn't gonna let me get away. Family comes first, see. I 'ad to stay at home, 'elp out. Grandad liked me brains, needed me." He grinned. "Everyone liked Reggie's brains."

The interview was a lost cause, PACE in the same state as Bull's morals.

"Were all your relatives involved?"

"There's a lot of relatives, so I can't rightly say. But all the ones I knew was. An' when I took over, I made sure that everyone did their bit."

"What happened to your parents?"

"Mum died when I was 'bout five. She'd 'ad a baby girl, died afterwards. I never knew why, but looking back, I suppose it was blood loss."

"And your dad? Was he part of what was going on?"

" 'What was going on'? Say it by its name, bluebottle: rape, sex, buggery. They're just words, it's the meaning you give 'em that adds up. Yeah, 'e was part of it. Me mum weren't dead in the grave a few weeks before another one was moved in."

"Who looked after the baby?"

Bull's eyes widened. "Me, of course. All kids knew 'ow to look after babies back then, there was so many of 'em. There was always a couple of little 'uns lying about the house."

"What was she called, your little sister, Mr. Bull?"

Bull paused. His eyes fixed on a point on the wall behind Kennedy's head.

"Fay," he said eventually, "she was called Fay." He drew a deep breath. "Ain't thought 'bout 'er for years - decades, even. She was fey, too, pretty little thing. She 'ad fine blonde 'air and pale blue eyes. She 'ad a little crib, lovely it was, wood and wrought iron, been in the family years - generations. She used to love being rocked, would look up at me, like I was everything in the world to 'er." He exhaled. "And I suppose, in truth, I was. Weren't no-one else to look out for 'er. 'Er little eyes was round as buttons. I rocked 'er to sleep every night, slept next to 'er, to keep 'er safe."

"So you looked after her. Did everything?"

"Yeah, changed 'er nappy, potty-training, fed 'er. I found an old pink baby bath on a bombsite. My Fay was the cleanest baby in the street she was, smelt clean, powdery, like a proper baby. Not like all the other kids, dirty and smelly. She was my proper little Fay."

"What happened to Fay, Mr. Bull?" asked Kennedy gently. Mack wasn't sure that Bull even heard the question.

"One day, after she'd just learnt to walk, she toddled over to me. She 'ad a yellow ribbon in 'er little hand. Never did know where she got it. She loved that ribbon, carried it everywhere. I used to wash it when she was asleep, flap it out the window to dry it, curl it back into 'er squidgy little hand before she woke up. She'd cry if she didn't 'ave it."

Kennedy tried again. "And what happened to her?"

"Died when I was eight. I kept 'er ribbon to remember, still got it; s'all raggedy now. They buried 'er with the others, in the basement."

Mack knew that a look of horror had chased across his face. Bull caught it. He sneered and was back in the room. "What the fuck would you lot know anyway. That's what 'appened. Kids died easy back then. Can still die easily now, if you want. Yeah, I took 'em, I took the kids in the photos. I confess.

I wanna stop now. I'm tired, I'm an old man, 'n' I need a piss. Got prostate problems." He eased off his chair, wincing, using the table and his unbroken arm to support himself. He grinned again. "Tell you what, bluebottles, I'll give you a little present, some'ink to be thinking on. You wanna know 'ow I chose those girls. Think on this: me family's far and wide. In the main, I leave 'em alone, but when I call it in, I expect results. I expect loyalty an' if I don't get it, there's consequences. Me grandad was the same, I learnt from 'im." He shuffled towards the door, supported by a custody officer. As he left, he turned around and fired a parting shot. "'E's one an' all, you know, what you lot call a paedo – only boys, though," and nodded at his solicitor.

Chapter 45

For the first time since being remanded, Reggie was worried, confidence waning. He'd been certain that a lot of favours would come calling, begging for his salvation, but so far there'd been no requests for visiting orders for him. He watched as the other geriatrics shuffled off to see their nearest and fucking dearest, telling himself that his visitors would come the next day, or the one after, or the day after that.

And he needed to be out of prison: soon.

He knew that his mind was starting to splinter and before long might split open into a full-blown fracture. He could feel it. A curtain of madness was hanging heavy behind his carefully constructed walls of certainty, threatening seepage through the cracks, its strength capable of a tsunami of distortion. The Hope woman had known what was coming his way. She'd seen. Bitch.

It was at night that he was the most vulnerable. Locked in his cell alone, in the borderland of sleep, the past would come calling. Sometimes, pain tiptoed through the wall, disturbing the air, opening him up to a humming in the ether, to the bitterness of the generations of men who'd muttered their bile before him, the legacy of lives ruptured, torn, lost, distorted. At other times, tentacles of cruelty would slip under the door, seeking him out, beckoning, slithering, stealing the light and prodding his soul. And later, in his dreams, the walls and ceiling bled viscous blood that glooped downwards, banging hard onto his head, bashing into his mind, filling his cell so high he thought he might drown. He would wake up gasping and crying for something he couldn't name.

He'd put in a call to his barrister – different firm from the solicitor, who'd been suspended following Reggie's little revelation; he chuckled to himself when he remembered that – he'd thought the old git was going to have an apoplexy. He wanted to make a statement, was due to see the barrister the next day. Fuck those bastards, they obviously thought they were safe, that he wouldn't have the balls. He had news for them: if he going to spend the rest of his life in jail, so were they.

Mostly, his days were passed watching rubbish on the old-fashioned television, playing cards by himself, or watching fellow prisoners mooch around like the half-dead, but he spent the afternoon before the meeting writing down everything. There were two very prominent individuals whose details wouldn't have been fingered when the police went through his home. Name, address, sexual preferences all detailed and clipped to the back of each card, a condemning polaroid photo and used condom, all safely waterproofed behind a loose brick with some other of his treasures. Only he knew that secret place. He grinned to himself as he wrote, made sure it was all there, put it safely in an envelope, sealed it, stored it under his pillow. Insurance: it might yet pay off. The barrister knew who one of men was - he'd be even more shocked when he found out the name of the other.

Dinner that night was a miserable affair. Some sort of sloppy stew and mash, devoid of any nutrition. He washed it down with water that he fervently wished was whisky.

Afterwards, he sat on a worn armchair in the television room playing patience with dog-eared cards, watching the others, idly noting their weaknesses, their old-man stupidity, making mental notes, taking out more insurance – just in case.

The six o'clock news came on: usual dirge, politics, drone, drone. But after the headlines, the newscaster mentioned a name that caught his attention. He looked up and saw the photo on the screen. A prominent High Court Judge, Lord Justice Tanner, had been discovered that morning in his garage; he had committed suicide by carbon monoxide poisoning.

Reggie stood, the violence of his action throwing the chair backwards and bouncing it off the wall, the clanking rupturing the atmosphere. Roaring anger swelled from his lungs, crescendo'ing into a deep, wailing fury. He grabbed a nearby remote control and threw it at the television, cracking the screen.

It was then that searing pain gripped his chest. It sent him dropping to the floor.

Chapter 46

Mack was tidying up his final case reports, trying to work out how many rest days he was owed and looking forward to a surprising second date with Susie, when he got a call from the front desk saying that someone was there who wanted to see him. She had her back to him, but he would recognise the thick, blonde, hair anywhere. She turned. "Hi Mack, just popped in to say good-bye, I'm off on my sabbatical." The front desk officer was diligently writing nothing, pen poised, unashamed. Mack led Clarence into an interview room.

"So, you're really doing it, then."

"Of course, I'm flying out to Italy next week. All booked."

"Who's having your cats?"

"My sister. The kids love them. She's got a big garden and no main roads nearby. They'll be fine. To be honest, as long as they're fed and allowed to sleep on someone's bed all day, I don't think it'll make a jot of difference to them. If you want loyalty, you need to get a dog."

"Well, yeah, suppose..." he remembered waiting outside Scott's flat and watching the dog owners in the park opposite. It felt like a lifetime ago. "Make a lot of mess, though, dogs."

She laughed. "Mack, life makes mess, in all its various forms. People like you and I spend our careers mopping it up." She paused, raised her hand, pulled off the back of an earring and pushed it on again. "This has been a case and a half though, hasn't it? I think we've all changed a bit because of it."

"Kennedy certainly has; he's much happier, less stressed, nicer."

"Mmm, I've noticed." She watched him intently for a couple of seconds, grey eyes the endless draw of a stormy sea, irises flecked with white foam. "Maybe something's clicked into place for you, too, Mack; you've found yourself, resolved something, I think."

Her words drifted into his mind and found a home. He looked

at her: how did she always bloody well *know*?

She laughed and then her hand was warm and firm in his, the scent of her filled his nostrils and her soft lips momentarily brushed his cheek. "I'll be seeing you." He walked her out to the front doors, watched as she left the building.

His phone beeped. Kennedy wanted to see him; and, as it happened, Mack wanted to talk to Kennedy.

"Mack, sit down, please."

"Thanks, Sir."

"Heard about Reggie Bull?"

"Yeah, massive heart attack. Not expected to survive, is he?"

"That's what I understand." Kennedy drew in a deep breath and exhaled. "What a mess, for everyone, even him, he didn't ask to be born into that family." He paused, "Anyway, it is what it is; we can't save the world, but at least we found Emma. And then Keeley." He smiled at Mack. "But listen, I wanted to see you to tell you how pleased the Superintendent was with your action on this case. It's largely down to you and your tenacity that we found Emma alive. I'm sorry that I didn't listen to you sooner, you were always right about Knatchbull, weren't you? Your instincts about his home security, the links to Poplar." He tapped the side of his nose, "That's a copper's nose you've got there, Mack. Finally. When you're ready to apply for your inspector exams, let me know, I'll support you."

"Thank you, Sir, that means a lot to me." He was looking Kennedy in the eye, man to man, adult to adult: only weeks ago, he might have been looking down, hands tight in his lap or fiddling with something in a pocket, but the past was done and dusted. "As it happens, Sir, I was thinking of applying for a transfer when there's a vacancy. Broaden my skills and experience."

"Yes, well, I'll be sorry to lose you. Where do you want to go?"

"Special Branch."

"Ah, good, good, I think that would be an excellent choice for you, Mack. You've become a fine detective. I'm proud of you." Kennedy stood up and proffered his hand. Mack took it. "Take two weeks off, Mack, you're owed it and you need it. I've already told HR.

"Oh, great, thanks Sir, I will. So, I'll, um, see you in a fort-night."

Mack left Kennedy's office feeling lively and something else, an emotion that was unfamiliar. He searched around for the word: hopeful; yeah, he felt hopeful, about the rest of his life and every-thing in between. He walked to the building's entrance and the double doors swished open before him. The sky was louring and thunder rumbled around huge clouds. Suddenly, the heavens opened. A deluge dropped down, smashing into the heat and washing away summer's dry dust. A chill came in on a breeze. At last, thought Mack. He watched passers-by scurry for shelter, turned up his collar and stepped into the rain.

The End

Join Mack and Clarence in the quest to uncover the truth about her husband.

Redemption, due winter 2022.

That day started like any other cold, dark Saturday at the beginning of December. Its dawning was unremarkable, typical. Snow weighted grey clouds. A light hoar frost dusted roadside hedges and stippled bare fields and garden lawns. In the porch of a small, solitary, terracotta-brick cottage, two bottles of milk gradually froze and a broadsheet newspaper wedged open an old, brass letterbox, letting in cold air that snaked down the hall to collide with warmth emanating from the sitting-room. Two ginger cats sprawled on a cream hearth-rug, fat bellies turned to a stove still glowing with the previous nights's apple logs.

Clarence woke to pounding in her head and a mouth dry from over-indulgence. She winced and turned to rest her cheek on the coolness of a cotton pillow-slip. It was wet. On a bedside table, her phone beeped. She reached for it, fingers catching instead the stem of a wine glass. It tumbled to the floor, the fall cushioned by carpet, and rolled unevenly along sloping floorboards to come to rest against the wall beneath the window; when she looked, she saw that white wine trickled gently along skirting-board.

She pulled across a pillow from the other side of the mattress and cushioned her cheek against the dry fabric; her dream always ended in the same way, with her bedding wet with tears.

The noise had disturbed the cats. They pattered up the stairs and jumped heavily onto her chest, kneading and purring and mewing. She sat up slowly, stilled and waited for her head to quieten, ignor-

ing the repeated beeping of the phone. Eventually, she pulled off the covers, let her feet find slippers, wrapped a blanket around her shoulders and shuffled to the bedroom door.

Downstairs, she fed the cats, stoked the stove, retrieved her milk and paper, made a strong coffee and gulped it down with paracetamol.

And that was how it started, as a day that should have been like any other in the life that had become hers - unremarkable and typical.

Printed in Great Britain
by Amazon

14448908R00159